Northern Horizons

RETURN TO TELEGRAPH CREEK

AE LISTER

Return to Telegraph Creek
ISBN # 978-1-80250-545-0
©Copyright AE Lister 2023
Cover Art by Erin Dameron-Hill ©Copyright June 2023
Interior text design by Claire Siemaszkiewicz
Pride Publishing

Published in 2023 by Pride Publishing, United Kingdom.

Pride Publishing is an imprint of Totally Entwined Group Limited.

RETURN TO TELEGRAPH CREEK

Dedication

To souls lost and found.

Chapter One

A Desperate Request

I got you to look after me, and you got me to look after you, and that's why.
Of Mice and Men, John Steinbeck

By the middle of June, summer weather had come to Port Essington.

We'd folded and put away our woolen union suits and winter jackets in a cedar trunk that we kept at the foot of our bed. Now we went about in shirtsleeves — rolled up — and lighter trousers. I wore cotton underthings, but Oscar couldn't be bothered, liking to feel as naked as possible, I supposed. I could barely get him to wear shoes half the time. He'd say shoes were for chumps and laugh in that way he had that put all my sensible arguments to rest.

Our friend, Irene Trelawney, had shown us a swimming hole on the other side of their property, and t'was hard to keep Oscar away from it now that the weather was warmer. The kid wanted to strip every chance he got, and I can't say that bothered me, except that we had to be careful out here of someone coming upon us in a clinch. Though it seemed unlikely that would happen, considering how isolated we were, it made me nervous. Still, we'd indulged ourselves with a quick gamahouche or a hasty fuck out by that swimming hole more than once, and nothing had ever come of it. I don't think the folks in town knew about the place, and 'twas nothing to remark upon, although 'twas a pretty spot, and Oscar loved it so. He'd spent most of his life in a city, so it didn't take much to impress him when it came down to it.

Evenings out here were something special. After a winter stuck inside our small kitchen, we reveled in all the outdoor space, spending a lot of time on the porch, in the paddock with the horses or riding o'er the homestead and beyond.

Carson and I had walked the ten-acre property back when we'd first seen it, and now that we'd prettied up the space, it felt good to be landowners. The outlaws I'd run with had scoffed at folks owning land, being settled and staying in one spot all their lives. They'd glorified the nomadic lifestyle that was the only one they could possibly have and pretended to ignore its disadvantages. But I'd only ever wanted a place to call my own, where I could make an honest life for myself and, if I were lucky, for someone else.

I'd not expected a twenty-one-year-old man-child to be the bride of my dreams, but there 'twas. Oscar was my love, and I was his — and there weren't no turning back from that solid fact. And we didn't care a whit what other people might think, except we kept our deeper feelings to ourselves, since the laws in this beautiful land were harsh on things that weren't understood. I'd take our secret to the grave if it meant keeping Oscar with me.

I leaned back in one of the rocking chairs that our friend, Clarence, Irene's husband, had made for the porch of our brand-new house. The creak of the wood and the swoop of the runners going back and forth comforted me as much as the regular motion, and the peaceful sounds of crickets and birds soothed my mind. I gazed out o'er the grass to the barn, where our horses, Onyx and Dixie, and our sturdy mule, Poke, were put away for the night with a bit of grain and fresh hay. Sprite, the gray-and-white cat, perched on the railing to my left, one foot o'er the other as she napped, keeping alert for the rustle of field mice in the grass.

'Twas a fine thing to sit in a comfortable chair on your very own property after all the waiting and hard work of building and have all the time in the world to think. We'd survived our first winter in Port Essington in less-than-ideal circumstances, having had only one very small room to live in. We'd expected to be isolated from people, hunkered down together out here in the wilderness, and instead, we'd been fortunate to meet Irene and Clarence, who lived about a ten-minute ride from our place and had secrets of their own.

They'd guessed ours right away, but only because they were keeping a similar one.

Clarence and Irene were married, and that was a fact. But there were specifics about their relationship they wanted to keep from the general public, and I didn't blame them, because Oscar and I were the same. But 'twas a godsend that the four of us could be ourselves when we were together, and I hadn't expected to find such kindness and acceptance here. Even the folks in town, who believed that Oscar and I were bachelors and friends instead of lovers and soul mates, had been welcoming and friendly.

Carson Moore and Tim Jensen had aided us in planning and building this fine home, and they'd promised to help us find work in town for the summer and fall so's we could start making a proper living. The money we'd taken from the outlaws I'd killed back in September was dwindling, although it had made it possible for us to indulge in all kinds of luxuries that would serve us well in the future. We were gonna need at least one regular income, preferably two, in order to maintain the lifestyle we wanted. Not that 'twas fancy, but we'd gotten used to being able to buy the things we needed and not having to settle for second-best. We'd invested in the stove, the new pitcher pumps and in this beautiful two-story house that would stand for years and give us shelter and comfort. It seemed fitting that the money we'd looted from Spook and Whitlaw, after I'd got Oscar back from them, would go to making a fine life for us both.

Our future looked bright and, for the first time, comfortable.

The screen door creaked as Oscar came out to the porch in his bare feet with his trouser legs rolled up. He'd pushed his shirt sleeves up, too, since he'd been washing dishes and 'twas a warm day.

"What're you doin' out here, Jimmy?" he asked, coming o'er and giving the surroundings a quick scan before he bent to kiss me. We had to be careful out in the open, and 'twas a shame, but I'd take it. We had the inside of this big place now to do as we pleased without worry, and that was enough.

"Just thinkin'…and enjoying the evenin'."

"Hmm," he said, sitting in the other rocker. "What're you thinkin' about?"

I smiled at him. "Mainly, about how happy I am."

Our gazes held, and he gave me a slow, sultry smile then turned to gaze out at the barn and the paddock, peaceful now with the livestock put away.

"I'm glad."

I waited for him to say he was happy, too, and when he didn't, I cocked my head at him.

"Are you content, Oscar?" I asked. "Now we got this place built and a few weeks of leisure before we need to get jobs?"

He frowned and turned to me. "'Course I am. You really gotta ask that?"

I nodded. "I reckon 'tis important to ask it once in a while for any two people makin' a life together."

He raised an eyebrow. "You don't suppose I'd tell you if I *wasn't* happy?"

I laughed. "Oh, I'm pretty sure you would. That's true."

He leaned forward in his chair and put his hand to my knee. "You be sure to tell me if *you* ain't happy, won't you, Jimmy? And I promise to do anythin' I can to make things right."

"Oscar—"

"I will. I'll make sure you're happy every day, Jimmy Downing."

I covered his hand with mine and squeezed it.

"Oscar, I can't even imagine bein' unhappy with you by my side. You do make me feel wonderful every day, Oscar Yates. Every fuckin' day I wake up next to you and every day I go to sleep beside you, I'm content—more content than I have any right to be."

* * * *

"We goin' into town?" Oscar said a few days later. "We ain't got no more potatoes, and the sugar's gettin' awful low."

"You and your sweet tooth," I said, rolling my eyes.

"Don't you mean my sweet ass, Jimmy?"

"Sure."

I glanced o'er at the plain wood dining table we'd helped Tim make. Oscar was sitting in the chair with his bare heel up on the seat like a ten-year-old. I expected he was still stuck somewhere in his childhood in a lot of ways because his older years had been so rough. I didn't care, and, in some ways, I found it charming and sweet.

"How are those sentences coming along?"

"I'm almost done. I think I'm gettin' the hang of it."

He stood and brought the slate to me with a smile.

I looked o'er his work with some satisfaction. His penmanship was getting better. I'd buy him some paper and a proper lead pencil in town so he could practice on that instead of the slate.

"That's very good."

He nodded and gazed at me with a hopeful expression. "Can we get another book? Since we're finished t'other?"

"Sure. Or we can borrow one from Irene and Clarence. They've got lots."

He frowned. "Well, we *could* do that, but then how are we gonna build up our library here?"

"Our *library*? My goodness, I got you reading and now you want your very own *library*?"

He laughed. "Well, just a small one. I never knew books were so much fun, Jimmy. I'm glad you taught me to read, e'en though I was grumpy about it at first."

"Yeah, you were pretty grumpy...until I promised to reward you with a spankin' if you did good, rather than use it as a punishment."

Oscar winked. "What can I say? I like bein' over your knee."

"And I like havin' you there—and havin' you everywhere else in this house."

The house had been mostly complete for a month now, and we'd gotten up to mischief in almost every damn room. There still wasn't much furniture, but we made do, and we did have an old settee of Clarence and Irene's in the parlor and a chair that Carson had given us.

Seein' as we'd fucked o'er saddles and tree stumps on our journey, 'twas a far sight more comfortable in our own home, even though it might not be the coziest of setups just yet.

"Now I *don't* wanna go to town. I wanna stay here and have a tumble," Oscar said.

I gave him a stern look. "I reckon that's what you wanna do most of the time, and most of the time I indulge you. But we need to go to town, so you best get ready and go saddle that fine horse of yours."

He grinned and sighed. "Yes, sir. I will. But…if I'm a good boy in town, will you fuck me later?"

"For certain."

"And maybe spank me?"

"I'll definitely spank you."

"In the sitting room?"

I gave him a look. "Sure. Why the sitting room specifically?"

He shrugged and went redder.

"I don't know. It feels dirtier and more wrong, somehow, and I like that. Because it feels like… It feels like we're thumbin' our noses at polite society. Fuckin' in the parlor, my goodness, let alone that we're two men doin' it… And it reminds me a bit of Miss June's, where we could say whate'er we wanted in any room, and there was all kinds of mischief goin' on everywhere."

I walked o'er and took his chin, kissing him with softness before gazing into his brown eyes. "I like the way you think, Oscar Yates."

* * * *

The weather was warm and pleasant for our ride, and 'twas nice to breathe the air that smelled of new growth and blooming wildflowers. Oscar was almost as good a horseman as me now, and Onyx and he had developed a close partnership.

He loved that horse so much, and she loved him. Together, they made a good team—just as good as me and Dixie. Maybe better, because though Dixie and I cared for each other, she was a practical consideration and I reckoned she felt the same about me. I'd be sad when she died, but I reckoned Oscar would be devastated when the time came for him to say goodbye to Onyx, even more than he'd grieved for his first horse, Sprite, after which he'd named his kitten.

Oscar went out riding every day, now that the weather was better. Irene would often join him, since they seemed to enjoy talking to each other and their characters were similar. I loved that Oscar had such a good friend in Irene and that Clarence and I got on well. I tried to join them when I could, so Dixie would get some exercise.

In town, we hitched the horses outside the general store and went inside, the jingling of the door making our presence known to the gentleman working there— I believe his name was Samuel—behind the counter. He glanced up at us and smiled, then seemed to start.

"Oh, Jimmy Downing! You're the man I need to speak to."

I was caught off guard for a moment. "I beg your pardon?"

Samuel grabbed a small envelope from the counter behind him and came around, handing it to me. T'was battered, bent and a little roughed up, but t'was dry, at least.

"A fella came in here and gave me this here letter for you. Said it was real important and asked if I could make sure you got it. I figured you and Oscar would be in here this week, and if not, I'd have given it to Tim or Carson to bring out to you."

"A letter?" I glanced at Oscar, but he seemed as confused as I was.

"'Twas a fella wearin' soft bear-skin trousers and embroidered boots—one of the Tsimshian people. He spoke English pretty well, and he said 'twas a message from some folks you know in Telegraph Creek. They needed to get a word to you, and he said he'd take it. I reckon they probably paid him to do it...at least I hope they did. That's a long way to travel."

Oscar and I exchanged concerned glances. I opened the envelope, unfolded the letter and started to read it right there in the store, because I'd never expected anything like this, and I needed to know why Miss June might reach out to us, when she didn't even know for sure we were here.

Dear Jimmy,

I'm hoping this note finds you and Oscar, because I don't know what else to do or who else to turn to. You and Oscar were always so kind to Cal, and she's in a bit of trouble right now.

"It's Cal," I said.

"What's wrong?" Oscar replied, reaching for the note.

"Shh, I'm still reading."

He let his hand drop and stayed quiet so I could finish.

At least I think she must be. She hasn't been back to see us since she left three months ago. And she promised she'd let us know how she was getting on so we didn't worry. The man she left with, who said he was going to marry her, is someone I didn't entirely trust, although he claimed he was after the best for Cal, and she believed him. You know my girls don't have their pick of men except the ones who come to visit them here, and there's not often a man who really would do good by any of them.

But Cal was a little bit in love, and she was dreaming of a wonderful life and, well, I hope she got it. But, Jimmy, I don't think she did, and I'm scared to death of what might have happened.

If you get this letter, please think of us and consider coming back to The Angel if you can, to help me find her. I don't know what to do.

Sincerely,
Your Good Friend,
Miss June Blaise
The Angel,
Telegraph Creek, British Columbia, Canada.

I stared at the paper in a daze while Oscar tugged on my sleeve.

"What does she say, Jimmy. What about Cal?"

I looked up at him.

"She says Cal went off with a man to be married."

"Oh!"

"But…but she don't think things have worked out well because Cal hasn't been back, and she promised she'd come to let Miss June know she was happy in her new life."

Oscar frowned. "If she said she'd come, she would. Cal would do what she promised, Jimmy."

"I know it…and so does Miss June." I licked my lips and scratched at my chin with the hand that wasn't holding the letter. "She wants us to come to Telegraph Creek."

Oscar stared at me. "She does?"

I nodded. "She doesn't know what to do, and she needs our help — to find Cal and do what we can."

Oscar was silent, which meant he was thinking about what I'd said and didn't know what to say. I couldn't blame him.

"'Tis a long way," he said.

"'Tis."

"And we're settled here, in our brand-new, beautiful house."

I didn't reply. I'd already decided we had to go — or I had to. But I wanted to let Oscar come to that conclusion himself.

His forehead wrinkled. "Can I see it?"

I handed him the letter. "It's in cursive, but see if you can read it."

Oscar's gaze tracked Miss June's neat writing. It took him a while, and I could see his mouth moving as he made out the words. I doubt he read every one, but he'd be able to get the gist of it.

Finally, he looked up.

"Jimmy, I'm worried about Cal."

"Me too."

"Do you…do you want to go?"

"I reckon I have to. But you can stay here if you want."

Oscar gazed at the door we'd come in only moments ago, when things had been much less complicated. Then he looked back at me.

"You ain't goin' anywhere without me, Jimmy Downing," Oscar said in a firm tone that brooked no argument. "Don't even try."

I smiled, relieved. T'would be safer for Oscar to stay here with Clarence and Irene, but I wanted him near me. I couldn't bear the thought of leaving him, even for a month or two. Anything could happen in this wilderness, and if we met up with trouble, at least we'd be together. And as dangerous as it might be to travel again, we knew we had a safe place in Telegraph Creek with Miss June.

"I wouldn't think of it."

I took the letter from him and folded it up, placing it in my pocket for safekeeping.

"I suppose we should buy supplies for our journey since we're here, rather than things to stock our cellar."

I sighed as Oscar's gaze met mine with a look of regret. I supposed the days of relaxing on the porch and fucking in the sitting room were over, at least for now.

Chapter Two

Questions

We got the supplies we needed from the store, including various items for the journey, and rode home in the afternoon. We dropped everything off at our place and rode out to Clarence and Irene's.

Clarence was cleaning his gun in the front yard when we arrived. He waved as we approached.

"Heya! Jimmy, you wanna go hunting? Irene could use a rabbit or a goose to make somethin' tasty for supper, and you're welcome to stay."

"Well, normally I'd take you up on that offer, Clarence. But we got some news to share."

He straightened. "What's that then?"

"I'm afraid we have to travel back to Telegraph Creek. We'll be gone for a spell, but we'll be back. Don't worry."

"Well now," Clarence said, his face a picture of disappointment. "That's a shame. Irene won't be happy."

"No, I suppose she won't be."

"I don't wanna go, really," Oscar said. "But Jimmy feels we have to, and I'm goin' where he's goin'."

The front door creaked, and Irene came out with a smile.

"Hello, neighbors! What a fine day it's turned out to be."

Clarence turned to her. "Irene, Oscar and Jimmy gotta leave us for a bit."

Irene's face fell as she looked between Oscar and me.

"Oh no! Truly?"

"I'm afraid so," I said. "We got a message from a friend of ours in Telegraph Creek. She's asked for our help."

"Oh dear," Irene said, holding her hand out for Oscar's. He took it and she drew him to her for a hug. "But I'll miss you so! And your brand-new house..."

She and Oscar exchanged a sorry look.

"Yeah. I ain't really lookin' forward to being out in the wilderness again," he said.

"Well, it's something we gotta do," I said.

"I know it. Miss June and her girls saved my life, no doubt."

"Oh! Miss June who runs the cathouse?"

"Yes," I said. "One of her girls has gone missing."

Irene raised a hand to her mouth. "Oh, goodness."

I exchanged a look with Oscar. "Cal left to get married to some fellow, and they ain't heard back from her since."

Irene frowned. "Oh no."

"When are you headin' out?" Clarence asked.

"Tomorrow, most likely," I said. "As soon as we can."

Irene's face relaxed and she smiled, not with as much unfiltered joy as before, but with a renewed commitment to making the best of things.

"Then you've got time to come inside for something to eat."

We did owe Irene and Clarence some kind of an explanation. So, despite my sense of urgency that we needed to get ready for our unexpected trip, we went inside, and over a cup of tea and some leftover fruit cake, we told Irene and Clarence more about our stay at The Angel and how we'd become friends with the people there.

"Well," Clarence said, "you have led an interesting life."

Oscar snorted, glancing at me. "Well, I ain't no outlaw."

"Stop it. 'Twasn't interesting at all. 'Twas monotonous when 'twasn't terrifyin'. I'd not wish that life on anyone."

"I know it," Oscar said.

"And, as to that," I said to Clarence, "we've been enjoying our plain life here in Port Essington with our friends and our domestic cares. It's been a blessing, and if it weren't for caring so much for Cal and Miss June and the others and feeling obliged because they were there for us when we needed them, we wouldn't go."

Oscar had suffered an awful fall from his horse on our journey from Whitehorse, and if not for the care of Miss June and her girls at The Angel — a reputable and well-run cathouse in Telegraph Creek — he might not be here with me now.

"I understand," Irene said. "We're blessed to have the two of you as friends, and that's a hard fact. Aren't we, Clarence?"

"We are." He scratched at his chin. "That fella, Cal—I'm sorry, I mean, that girl you met there…Cal—she seems like a fascinatin' person."

Irene had a kindly smile on her face as she looked at Clarence, and I realized what it must mean to him to know there were others who felt pulled to be different to their born sex in the way that he did.

"She surely is. Sweet as punch and smart—and always up to something."

"Like helpin' me dress as a lady for you," Oscar said in a quiet voice.

I laughed, remembering how surprised I'd been. I hadn't even recognized Oscar in the clothes and the paint.

"Oh my," Irene said, glancing between us. "Now that's a scintillating piece of information."

Clarence rolled his eyes, but he smiled.

"I'm sure you looked lovely, Oscar," Irene said.

Oscar preened. "You bet I did. Jimmy didn't even recognize me."

"Not till you bent o'er."

They burst into raucous laughter as Oscar blushed.

"Anyway," he said, "we're awful worried about Cal. And if Miss June sent for us, she needs us pretty bad."

"Well, then," Irene said, "you must go help her. As hard as it will be for Clarence and me, since we've got used to your companionship, we'll look after your place for you while you're gone."

"Thank you," I said. I looked at my hands. "Oscar and me, we didn't have anybody before we found those folks, and we left them to come here." I looked at Irene then at Clarence. "We're mighty—"

My voice choked up on my emotion and I coughed.

"What Jimmy is trying to say" —Oscar took over, putting a hand on my back and gazing earnestly at them — "is that we're mighty glad to have met you, and we're truly lucky to count you as friends. We're sorry to leave you, to be sure."

I nodded. "That's right. That's all."

"Will you pop over now and then to feed Sprite, Irene?" Oscar said. "She'll have water at the creek, and she can get into the barn in the bad weather, and she'll probably catch and eat some mice, but—"

"Of course, I will. I'd tell you to bring her over here, but I reckon she'd only end up back at your place. Cats like to stay where they're used to."

"True enough. Thank you, kindly," I said.

Clarence smiled. "And that way we can check on your place and make sure everything's all right while you're gone, so it'll be standing right where you left it when you get back."

Irene stood and came o'er to hug me, then Oscar, while Clarence offered his hand to us to shake.

"You two are a wonderful addition to this town. And we hope you come back as soon as you're able," Clarence said.

"We surely will," Oscar said. "Won't we, Jimmy?"

"Port Essington is our home now, and 'twill always be our home, I reckon. So, you can count on us returning."

* * * *

Back home that night, we sorted out what we needed to take with us. We'd pack up the mule in the morning and head out by noon. I was glad I'd taught Oscar to shoot. He had his revolver, and I had the rifle.

I didn't want to think about the wolf attack outside of Port Essington last fall — or what had happened with Spook and Whitlaw on our way to Whitehorse. Well, we didn't have to worry about them outlaws since they were dead and gone, and nobody else from my gang possessed the motivation or the skill to track us down. 'Twas true that traveling through the wilderness was dangerous, and unexpected things could happen. We'd have to keep our wits about us. But Oscar was a better rider now, he had a horse that understood him and he could protect himself, so we were in a better position than we'd been on our way here.

I only had to keep telling myself that.

* * * *

We had our packs and the animals ready when we'd planned to. One of the great things about Oscar was that, if he had specific instructions and a defined goal, he worked hard to get there.

Of course, now he was saying his goodbyes to his cat, and we might be delayed.

"She'll be fine, Oscar. Let's go."

"Hold on," he said, giving me an irritated look. He scooped the gray-and-white cat up from the porch and cuddled her to his chest, like he had when she had been a tiny kitten. She flicked her ear as he whispered something to her. She made a little mewl, and Oscar threw me another look.

"Oh, I know it," he said out loud. "But he has other, better qualities."

I rolled my eyes. "Come on, now. We gotta go."

"Fine," he said, and put the cat down gently. She ran toward the barn, and I reckoned she'd be hunting for her supper now. There were lots of mice and birds around for her to get.

Oscar grabbed the reins and the pommel of Onyx's fancy, tooled saddle, and swung himself up.

"All right. I'm ready."

"Hold on a second," I said, taking a look at our brand-new house where it rose up in front of us.

"Really? Now *you* wanna wait?" He followed my gaze and saw where I was focused. "It truly is a beautiful house, Jimmy. I'm sorry to leave it."

"I reckon I feel the same. But she'll be here when we return." I gave him a smile. "Now, let's go."

The smell of the fish canneries hit us hard when we got close to town. As soon as the ice on the Skeena had broken up, business had gone back to normal, and the docks had become chaotic and congested. There were already more people here than there'd been all winter, and more would come all summer long.

We stopped to say goodbye to Carson and Tim, and they expressed their dismay at how we had to leave right after our house went up.

Tim said he had some goods in the back we could have for the trip, and Oscar went with him, while Carson touched my elbow and gestured to a spot out of the way of customers.

"I need to ask you something, Jimmy," he said, in a hushed voice, and a chill crept up my spine.

"Sure."

Carson's gaze followed Oscar and Tim, then returned to me, with eyes that sparked with intelligence. His cheeks flushed and he stumbled o'er his words. "I'm sorry, but I noticed how...close you are to Oscar, and he to you, and I wondered..."

He seemed to be searching for something, and I wasn't giving it to him. Not yet.

I swallowed. "You're gonna have to speak a bit plainer to me if you want an answer. I need to know what exactly you're askin'?"

He cleared his throat and grabbed his hat off the bar, putting it in front of our faces to hide us from anyone that wanted to look.

"You don't have to tell me if my supposition is correct, but please don't be mad that I'm asking. I don't care a whit, and I know it ain't my business, except I want you to know it don't matter to me. And I don't reckon it would matter to Tim, either, except I haven't said anything to him, because I wasn't sure."

I kept my breathing steady, even though my heart was going a mile a minute. "Said anything about what?"

He held my gaze with an intensity that rattled me.

I stared at him for a long time, until Oscar and Tim came back, and I turned to greet them. But I hadn't denied it, and I figured Carson knew the truth. He'd sussed it out. And what that meant for me and Oscar, I didn't yet understand.

I shook Tim's hand and hoped my arm was steady.

"Thank you kindly for your help with the house and everything, and for welcoming us to Port Essington. We truly are grateful."

Tim bobbed his chin and smiled, as he gave it a hearty shake. "You're very welcome, Jimmy Downing. I hope you're not gone for long."

"I hope so, too."

"Goodbye, Jimmy," Carson said, smiling at me with an earnestness I couldn't hide from. It seemed he didn't care what our relationship was, and he had to know why we hadn't been up front about it. "Oscar. I'll miss you both."

"Bye, Carson. Thanks for everythin'," Oscar said, grinning and tipping his hat.

We rode out and along the street. Clouds were coming in, but I hoped we wouldn't get rain on our first day of travel. When we were well out of town, I pulled Dixie up to wait for Oscar and Onyx to come up beside us.

"What is it?"

I tilted my head back toward the town.

"He knows."

Oscar stared at me, eyebrows knitting in confusion. Then his expression changed to one of comprehension and unease.

"Who? *Carson?*"

"Yeah."

"Fuck," Oscar said, glancing behind us. "What did he say?"

I shrugged. "Somethin' 'bout how close we seemed…"

"Goddamn it."

"But he said he didn't care, and he figured Tim wouldn't either, though he hadn't told him of his suspicions — which I'm glad of. I hope he doesn't."

Oscar nodded, chewing on his lip. "Did you say anything?"

"I didn't — but I didn't deny what he was suggesting, either."

"So maybe it's good we're leaving," Oscar said.

"Maybe. Except, we're gonna come back. And I don't know what we're gonna come back to, if Carson tells anyone else what we are to each other."

Oscar frowned. Then he said, "Hmph."

"That all you got to say?"

"No, Jimmy, that ain't all I got to say. I'm glad Carson figured it out, and I'm glad he knows. I believe him when he says it don't matter to him, 'cause why should it? Who the hell cares but us?"

I stared at him, taken aback by the vehemence of his righteousness, though why I was surprised, I don't know. Oscar had always defended our love this way.

"This is our life, and if we want to spend it together, as friends, or sweethearts, or anythin' else, that's our right, as long as we ain't hurtin' nobody."

"Of course," I said. "I know."

"Then let's not worry about it. We won't be back for at least a few weeks, and probably it'll be longer. And I ain't gonna think about anythin' except our cozy house, Irene and Clarence and the friends we're goin' to help in Telegraph Creek—and how much I love you and want to always be where you are."

"All right," I said. "Then I'll do the same."

Chapter Three

Mischief

After a long day's riding, we came upon a promising spot at the edge of a mountain stream, in the thick of some brush. We watered and fed the horses, took a quick dip ourselves and sat down to eat some of the beef jerky, bread and cheese that we'd brought with us. Tomorrow I'd see if I could hunt us a rabbit or a fox for some fresh meat, but this was good enough for our first night.

I brought out the whiskey.

This time we had two tin cups — one for each of us — and after I poured us each a dram, I proposed a toast.

"To what, Jimmy? To having to leave our nice home and worry about a friend in trouble?"

"Oscar, I know things ain't perfect right now, and we're heading away from a place of safety and friendship, but" — I settled a hand on his knee and gazed into his dark eyes, where the reflection of the campfire's flames leapt and twisted, while owls hooted and frogs chirped, and the comforting smell of wood smoke surrounded us — "we're together, and that's what counts. When I met you in Dawson, I expected to spend a day or two with you, then see you off with a full belly and a good sight cleaner, but I never expected what happened."

Oscar gave me a leer as he was reminded of that fateful morning.

"You never expected to wake up with your cock in my mouth."

I blushed, still conflicted about it. I'd not known Oscar's age at the time, and I'd suspected he might be awful young. Yet, I'd not protested when he'd thanked me the only way he knew how, and that had led to other questionable but thrillin' things. He'd told me later he was twenty-one, a fact I'd accepted at face value with relief, e'en thought he didn't look it. And not too long ago he'd admitted that he didn't exactly know the year he was born, so how could he even know how old he was?

Oscar was a man, sure enough, but he was a young one, and eight months ago when I'd hauled him o'er my lap and spanked him for kicks, he'd been even younger.

"No, I didn't. Not at all."

Oscar chuckled. "Didn't take you long to adjust, though."

I raised my eyebrows at him and sipped my whiskey, enjoying the burn as the amber liquid slid down my throat.

"That's a fact, though it ate at me for a few days. I didn't rightly know what had happened."

"Well, I did. I'd woke you up to what you wanted...and needed. And I'd only hoped 'twas me and not simply the fun of bein' with any other man."

I smiled and cupped his chin. "Oh, 'twas you all right. I suppose I might have figured it out eventually with someone else, but I'm glad 'twas you who did the deed. I thank God every day for sending you to me and giving me a chance to do the right thing."

We sat gazing into the fire and remembering those early days of insatiable passion.

Oscar cleared his throat. "You, uh, you…remember how you laid me o'er your saddle that time, when we'd barely started out?"

At those words, my cock, which was already half-hard, went to a full stand in about three seconds, and I nodded.

"I think so."

Oscar gaped. "You *think* so?"

I grinned wide at his outrage, but I had a plan.

"You tell me what I did, if you remember it so good."

An expression of understanding dawned on his features, and he grinned.

"Oh, well, I-I remember eating that roasted fox, what tasted so good. And I might have made more of a mess with it than I needed to, because I wanted —"

Oscar licked his lips, eyeing me up and down.

" — because I wanted you to start thinkin' of other places I'd put my mouth and slobbered."

I gaped at him. "Why, you little devil. I thought you were just real hungry and messy."

His grin widened. "Well, I was hungry — but not only for the meat on *that* bone."

My breaths sounded loud now, and I shook my head in disbelief.

"You had me all figured out, I guess."

"I thought I did. I didn't think about the *saddle*."

I grunted. "Hmm. Good thing I got a practical side and a healthy imagination." I tapped my finger against my forehead.

Oscar's face went sober, and his eyes lit up with the fire I knew so well.

"You got the best imagination, Jimmy. I loved that so much."

"I know," I said, smiling. "Me, too."

We sat there, caught up in remembering, both of us aroused and wanting.

"Jimmy, I wanna do that again."

I almost choked on the whiskey I'd sipped. "You do?"

"Yeah. Only, which saddle would be more comfortable? Dixie's or Onyx's?"

I stared at him, holding my tin cup in trembling fingers, but amused all o'er again. "Which saddle would be more *comfortable*?"

Oscar frowned and rubbed his chin. "I figure maybe we should use Dixie's saddle, since that was the one from before."

I stood, and Oscar followed me with his eyes.

"Or is it because you don't want to mess Onyx's fine saddle with three loads of sorry spunk?"

Oscar's eyes went wide, and a shudder went through his whole body.

"*Three?*" he whispered with a reverential air.

"Isn't that what I said, son?" I used my sternest voice to give him what he wanted.

"Yes, *sir*."

I nodded. "Now you go get Dixie's saddle and lay it out here by the fire. Not too close, 'cause I reckon we'll be providin' our own heat."

Oscar scrambled up and strode to where I had laid Dixie's saddle. He picked it up, along with the saddle blanket, and brought it o'er to a spot I indicated, where we'd be close enough to the fire to be warm but far enough not to worry about getting scorched. At least, not by the campfire.

"Now what?" he asked, breathing hard from exertion and a different kind of hunger.

I gestured in an offhand way. "Take your trousers down. I won't make you go buck naked, 'cause it's a mite chilly still, and I reckon it's more scandalous if you're half dressed, anyhow."

Oscar's mouth quirked into a grin.

"Oh, it is, Jimmy. It is," he said, pushing his suspenders off his shoulders and shoving his trousers down to his calves, then unbuttoning his drawers and pushing them down, too. I'd persuaded him to wear underthings on our journey, to protect against chafing and keep him warm enough at night.

I let my gaze run o'er him, feeling the desire surge in my gut. "Look at that silly little thing, tryin' to stand tall but lookin' small still. It ain't nothin' but a nubby."

Oscar closed his eyes and made a sound like he was in Heaven itself. "Oh, God."

"Now you turn around, go down on your knees and bend yourself o'er that saddle."

Oscar's forehead creased like he couldn't handle the way he was feeling, but he turned around and did as I'd told him, like the very good boy he always was for me—at least when it came to personal handling. This was about the only time he didn't give me cheek, and I was thankful for it.

And there he was, laid out for me on the smooth, hard leather, with his elbows in the dirt and his shoulders tense under his shirt.

I nudged between his knees with the toe of my boot, none too gently.

"Spread 'em. You know how."

"Yes, sir," he panted, moving his knees wider, the dark cleft between his cheeks beckoning me with promised pleasure.

"Now, you've been a good boy, Oscar, but I reckon you need to be shown your place still, don't you?"

His breath caught and he jerked. "Yes, sir. I reckon so."

"Oh, I know so," I said, kneeling down behind him and running a palm o'er his fleshy bottom — a good deal plumper than it had been when I'd done this the first time. I'd succeeded in putting more meat on his skinny bones and now he was perfect — not fat in the least, but filled out and muscled properly, like a grown man should be. He'd blossomed and bloomed in my care, and I couldn't help feeling a bit puffed up about it. If I'd done one thing to make up for my sorry life as an outlaw, it was this.

But 'twasn't the time for maudlin emotion, so I tamped those feelings down and got to business.

"You ready?"

"Yes, sir," he said, with a hiccupped breath of anticipation.

"All right. You say your word if you need to."

"I won't."

"You might."

He gave a small laugh and nodded in obedience.

But when I brought my hand down on his right buttock, he gasped. "Oh...Jimmy!"

"You like that?"

"Yes," he hissed. "Oh, yes."

I slapped the other cheek, causing a similar reaction. I went back and forth, taking my time and being casual about it, so he didn't know when another was coming. And in between, I'd tickle the inside of his thigh or run a finger down his crack, until he could barely contain himself.

"Oh my God. Oh fuck! Oh *fuck*."

"You're a good boy, Oscar Yates."

"Yes, sir!"

"And I'm gonna reward you for bein' so good."

"Please, oh, please. Sir!" His breaths were ragged in his throat, he widened his stance, and I couldn't hold off anymore.

I fucked him o'er my saddle then, using the grease I'd set beside us, easing into him like 'twas my mission in life, which it felt like 'twas, to be honest. A deep, intense groan tore outta him and echoed in the darkness like the cry of a wild animal.

And he *was* wild, my Oscar—wild and free and beautiful.

After I spent inside him, I turned him o'er and sucked his cock like 'twas all I'd ever wanted, as he splayed out with his arms on either side and his face turned up to the stars. His head and shoulders rested on the saddle as he lay there, his chest rising and falling with his slowing breaths—a willing sacrifice to my hunger and my worship.

When we'd recovered, I crawled forward so I hovered o'er my precious boy, and I leaned down and kissed his forehead, what was slicked with a sheen of sweat and sparkling in the moonlight.

"I love you so much. You're mine and I'm yours, and nobody's ever gonna part us."

His eyes opened and he gazed at me, lying there all wrecked and well-fucked. He quirked his lips into a lazy smile.

"Yes, sir, I am. And you're mine. And I ain't never leaving you."

Chapter Four

A Slippery Slope

'Twas rough getting used to travel again, after spending so much time in one spot, but we managed. 'Twas reminiscent of our previous journey, except we were leaving friends behind and moving toward people and a place we knew, rather than trying to reach a dot on a map. And we only needed to go about two hundred sixty miles instead of more than seven hundred. After that journey, this one seemed like a hop, skip and a jump once we got going. 'Twould likely take less than a week, except for all the difficult terrain and having to skirt rougher, dangerous areas. If we could have gone in a straight line, we would have been there in three days. But we had to go around a couple of mountains, and that added time.

We were blessed with mild weather, except for one day of solid rain at the midpoint. Now that the skies had cleared, I hoped we'd get to the relative comfort of The Angel before they broke again, since 'twasn't much fun wearing wet clothes. At least the days were warm.

The nights were chilly and would get colder as we moved north.

We were on day five when I recognized some of the landmarks I'd used on the journey out from Telegraph Creek to Port Essington the past fall.

"Oscar, look! There's the bent pine and the rock wall. Remember?"

His gaze followed to where I was pointing.

"Well, I don't rightly, but I believe you do."

"It's where we had to turn that first time. It means we're gettin' close."

"Good!"

Oscar had become progressively grumpier the farther we got from Port Essington and the comforts of home. No doubt he'd been so desperate on that first journey and simply happy to be with me and under my protection that he'd been a mite more thankful and able to tolerate being out in the wilderness. But now, he had good friends and a warm bed to recall when he was lying on the ground in our tent. I reckoned he was excited to see Miss June and the girls again, but we were both worried about Cal, and that didn't help — only made us more anxious to get there.

"We'll be there soon. Don't worry."

"I ain't worried. I only wanna stop itchin'."

The mosquitoes had been worse on this trip, since it was only the middle of June. I'd thought to bring some tonic from the general store, but we were getting low, and it didn't solve the problem. So we were both covered in bites and using mud to stop the itch as much as possible. But we weren't used to being so travel-dusty and dirty. The strain was starting to show.

"I know it. Me, too."

"Do you think Miss June will have something we can put on our bites?"

"I bet she will."

"Good!" he said, scratching at his neck. "I sure hope she can give us our own room and a cozy bed again. Honestly, Jimmy, 'tis the only thing keeping me goin'."

I felt the same. I hoped that we'd find as much of a welcome and the same level of comfort at The Angel as we had when we'd arrived from the other direction. We had no reason to think we wouldn't, but it had been a long time since we'd been there. And 'twouldn't be the same without Cal.

We were heading down the low side of the last mountain we had to skirt around, and the terrain was rocky and strewn with gravel. I must have misjudged the steepness of the slope and thought Dixie could handle it. As soon as we started down and her hooves lost their purchase, I realized my mistake and let go of Poke's lead so he wouldn't be dragged down with us. I shouted at Oscar, hoping it wasn't too late for him and Onyx.

Then we were sliding, Dixie and I, down a gravel slope and into the trees below. At least 'twasn't a long enough fall to kill us, but even as I thought that, I slid off my saddle and landed hard, a sharp pain slicing through my side. But all I could think about was Dixie and Oscar and Onyx.

I shouted Dixie's name, heard Oscar yelling mine and glanced back to see him and Onyx still on the ridge, thank God. Poke stood right on the ledge of broken dirt and gravel, his hooves braced firmly against the path, with his lead rope dangling.

I looked in the other direction and saw Dixie lying in the dirt, and my heart just about stopped. But then she made an angry grunting noise and hefted herself to her feet, shaking her head like she was humiliated, embarrassed and pissed the fuck off. She didn't seem to be hurt otherwise. She wandered o'er to a patch of grass and started eating.

Thank fuck.

I laid my head back on the ground and gazed upward at the blue sky, thanking God as well, as a softer slide of gravel announced Oscar's presence beside me.

"Jimmy! Oh, my God, Jimmy!" His voice held the same note of terror I remembered from the wolf attack, when Sprite had gone down and Oscar had prepared to go to his defense with nothing but his fists, before I'd hauled him up onto Dixie's back with me.

I gazed into his frantic face and smiled. "I'm all right."

"No, you ain't! You're bleedin'!"

I shifted my gaze to where he was pointing. Sure enough, my shirt was torn, and a red stain was spreading.

"Well, will you look at that?" I said, only then feeling the sharp, burning pain of an injury. I was sore in other places, but that one spot was on fire. I'd taken off my jacket as the sun had heated everything up so much, and so I'd had no protection as I'd slid through the gravel and larger rocks.

Oscar knelt beside me and moved the torn fabric aside.

"Aw, fuck," he said.

"That bad?" I commented, grimacing at the pain now.

"Well, it ain't pretty, and it's bleedin' bad. You got a decent gash there."

"Yeah, I can feel it."

He gazed at me with barely restrained panic that I had to put an end to or he wouldn't be able to help with anything.

"How deep is it? It hurts, but it don't feel like it got anything important."

Oscar pulled back the cloth of my shirt and prodded the spot a bit. When he spoke, his voice was calmer.

"There's a lot of blood, but it don't look like it's all that deep. It's long and jagged, and I reckon you'll need stitches."

"Hmm. All right."

Problem was, I couldn't stitch myself up at that angle, and I wouldn't want to do it out here anyhow, because the risk of an infection was the big worry.

"What do I do?" Oscar asked.

"Take off your shirt and press the inside of it—the cleaner part—against the gash for a good ten minutes. Hold it and press it, hard. That should slow the bleeding."

"Okay." He did as I'd instructed.

Even injured like I was, the sight of Oscar's lean muscles and bare chest and shoulders gave me a thrill, and he must have noticed.

"Well, I guess you can't be too badly hurt, if you're still ogling my nakedness," he said.

I started to laugh but that made the pain worse, then Oscar pressed his inside-out, wadded-up shirt to the gash.

"Shit," I cursed, gritting my teeth.

"Sorry. You said to press hard."

"Yeah, I know. You got to…to stop the bleeding." I took a deep breath. "It's fine." I nudged my hand under his to take over, keeping the cloth of Oscar's shirt tight against the wound.

"Get the first-aid kit. It's in the satchel near Poke's left shoulder."

He scrambled up, looking to the horse and the mule on the ridge. I followed his gaze. The slope was steep where we'd tried, and failed, to descend safely. But ten meters on from that was a safer spot for him to try.

"Look there. You should be able to climb up, and you can lead Onyx and Poke to that spot and bring them down." I cursed. "If I'd only waited another minute to get to that spot, none of this would have happened."

Oscar frowned. "You couldn't have known. 'Twas a misjudgement, that's all."

I gave a bitter laugh at his naiveté. "Oscar, a misjudgement out here can get you killed."

He narrowed his eyes and looked like he wanted to slap me. "Well, you *ain't* killed. You only gotta slice outta your side. I'll go, but don't you move."

"I won't. I'll stay here."

I was trying to joke, but he didn't seem to think 'twas funny. He got up and moved in the direction I'd indicated.

I was certain that he and the animals would be fine if he went that way, so I lay back and returned my gaze to the sky. Fluffy clouds drifted across the blue expanse, and I focused on how pretty 'twas, praying that this injury wouldn't delay us. We needed to get to Telegraph Creek more'n ever now. I didn't want to look at the wound again, because the sight of the blood would only make me fret more, and I was already feeling queasy and lightheaded.

I sent another prayer up to a God I didn't even know if I believed in and waited for Oscar.

He was back in no time and seemed a mite calmer, so I figured the animals had got down from the ledge okay.

"I've got the kit. Now what do I do?"

"How's the bleeding? Has it slowed at all?" I lifted the wadded-up shirt away from the wound.

Oscar bent his head to have a look. "Maybe? It don't seem to be gushing no more."

"That's good."

"Are you in a lotta pain?"

"I've had worse. Now, get some of them long bandages from the kit. You'll have to help me to sit up, then you gotta—" I gasped as a twinge hit me. "I'm okay. You gotta wind it around me a few times, then tie it so it keeps the pressure on the wound. Is there another bandage in that kit?"

"Yeah, I think so."

"You'll have to wad that clean bandage up and put it in place of this shirt, underneath the bandage. You think you can do that?"

"I reckon."

Oscar helped me into a sitting position. 'Twas painful, but I kept his shirt pressed firmly on the gash. It hadn't completely soaked with blood yet, so I took that as a good omen.

I tried to take deep breaths, but every movement of my torso hurt. Oscar's forehead wrinkled with concentration as he did as I'd instructed. I held the clean, folded up bandage to the gash while he wrapped the other one around me a couple of times, then tied it off with a good knot.

"How long do you reckon we have to travel still?" he asked.

"I'm thinkin' 'tis about five or so hours. We can make it before dark if we ride hard," I said. "But we'll rest here for a bit longer."

"How the hell you gonna ride hard with a slice outta you, Jimmy?"

"I'll manage. Dixie'll do most of the work."

"I know, but you gotta stay on her."

"I will," I said.

Chapter Five

The Angel

Oscar looked doubtful.

"Oscar, I been riding since I was five. I can do it. I could probably ride that horse with one hand tied behind my back *and* a gash in my side."

That made him laugh but he rolled his eyes. "All right, all right."

"Help me into the shade o'er there where the horses are grazing. I need to sit against one of them trees for a bit. And cover the blood that's on the ground here with some dirt. The last thing we need is to attract the local wildlife."

Oscar went a bit pale. He helped me into the shade then went back to cover the evidence of my injury. He went o'er to his horse and spoke to her in quiet whispers, scratching her behind her ear. Then he came and sat down beside me.

"How long we gonna rest?"

"Maybe a half hour, to make sure the bleedin's really stopped. Then we best get goin'."

We sat there, in the middle of the day, swatting away the mosquitoes that somehow found us wherever we were. They didn't bother me as much as they did Oscar. I supposed he tasted better.

In a moment, he stood and started to do a little dance, swatting at the annoying insects and cussing like a sailor. 'Twas too amusing for words, and I couldn't help laughing. But the sharp pain in my side took my breath away.

"Stop it, Oscar. Stop." I raised my hand in protest, and to block the image of him waving around like a windmill. "I need to be still."

"Are you laughing? Are you laughing at me, Jimmy Downing? You fucker." He stopped his frantic dance and stared hard at me. "I saved you from bleedin' to death and you're laughin' at me."

"I'm sorry. You just— You looked—" I grimaced with the pain of laughing and tried to calm myself down.

He strode o'er and stood in front of me, his arms across his chest. The mosquitoes buzzed around him like devoted acolytes, but he ignored them, except to twitch his head and blow at them when they came near.

"How do I look, Jimmy? Like a fella who's plumb tired of traveling and only wants to get to where we're goin'?"

"You look like you're showin' me…some kind of new dance."

"New dance? I'll show you a new dance," Oscar said, falling to his knees in the dirt. He came close and put his mouth to mine so's I'd stop making pained noises, and I did, opening under his kiss and trying to catch my breath. When he pulled away, he glanced down at the bulge in my pants that I couldn't hide and the pain didn't hinder.

"Well, I guess you really are okay, then, if you can laugh and get hard. Can we get going? Now?"

I sighed, cupping his chin and kissing him sweetly before I nodded.

"I reckon. You need to help me up onto my horse."

Oscar rolled his eyes. "Come on, Old Man."

* * * *

Turned out riding with a jagged gash in the side of your vulnerable underbelly was a tricky and tortuous business. I had to keep my elbow pressed down against the bandages else 'twould seem like my insides were at risk of comin' out, and the movement of riding would be too much.

Thank goodness Dixie was a steady horse and didn't give me any trouble. As long as I could keep my seat, we'd be okay. But as we went along, hiding the pain I was in from Oscar got to be more of a challenge.

I saw him eyeing me from time to time, as Dixie went o'er some difficult terrain, and I winced or grimaced. 'Twasn't until we had to wade through a mountain stream that I let go a whimper so pitiful it made me blush with shame.

When we got to the other side of the water, Oscar grabbed Dixie's bridle and led us up onto the bank.

"Jimmy, I can tell you're strugglin' with it."

I nodded. "I'll be okay."

My voice sounded rough and far away, and I hoped I wasn't about to pass out.

"How about I lead Dixie, then you only have to hold on and not fall off."

I frowned. "Oscar, that's gonna add time onto this journey that we ain't got."

He narrowed his eyes. "Jimmy Downing, you listen here. It won't be much good to go fast and have you fall or faint before we get there, will it?"

We stared at each other—a battle of wills that I generally lost when Oscar was this determined. And I didn't have much fight left in me.

"Sure. Okay."

Oscar gave a curt nod and moved Onyx closer. I passed him Dixie's other rein.

"Thank you. Now concentrate on keeping your seat, and I'll get us there. I promise." Oscar looked about him, then back at me. "I know the way, now. I'm sure of it."

I hoped he did know the way, because I was barely able to keep my wits about me with the throbbing agony of my injury. I wondered if he'd been honest that it didn't look like a deep gash, because right now it felt like it went through all my inner organs and up into my chest. 'Twas probably the pain making an echo of itself, as it tended to do in situations like this. At least, I hoped that was it. I wondered what Miss June would do if the bandage came off and my kidney tumbled out.

I worried about Oscar having to manage leading both Poke and Dixie and also guide his own horse, but there wasn't much I could do but keep from falling, like I'd promised.

The rest of the journey seemed to take forever, but I managed to stay conscious, though the pain was brutal. We rode into the town of Telegraph Creek as the sun was setting. There were only a handful of streets in the small village, and it didn't take us long to find The Angel. In a world where most of the big cities had electricity, folks in towns like Port Essington and

Telegraph Creek still lived the old way, without the new-fangled conveniences that still seemed like magic. The gas lamps shining in the building's windows, and the shadows of people moving about inside were a salve to my fretting, and I knew we were finally safe.

We rode the horses directly to the stables behind the building. I caught a glimpse of William and tried to speak, but a jab of pain prevented it.

"William! Thank Christ!" Oscar said. "Can you grab these horses? I gotta help Jimmy."

"Oscar! Where did you two come from? 'Course I can. What happened to him?"

Strong hands grabbed my arm as I swayed and slid toward the ground.

"Easy, easy," Oscar murmured as he helped me down as carefully as he could. I hissed as he put pressure on my injury, but there was no way he could avoid it. "Fell down a mountain, the git," Oscar said with some irritation, and I was glad to hear it. If he could be mad at me, it probably meant I wasn't dying. I tried to laugh but ended up groaning at the sudden increase of pain in my side. I couldn't get to a soft bed soon enough.

"Sorry. It's all right. We're here now," Oscar murmured in my ear as he held me.

I sank against him, clutching his narrow shoulders, glad he was stronger than he looked. At least the movement of the horse was gone, but I'd have to try to walk in a minute, and I wasn't too sure I could do that.

"I'll go get Miss June," William said. "'Tis so good to see you!"

The thump of William's boots up the wooden steps and the creak of the door as it opened, then the slam as it shut behind him sounded in the evening stillness.

"Oscar, I-I'm so sorry to be a burden."

Oscar huffed and held me tighter. "Quiet now. You ain't a burden to me, Jimmy," he said. "I reckon I'm glad to have a chance to make up for all the times you've had to help me out. Can you walk, if I help?"

"Maybe? We can try."

Oscar moved us forward, one slow step at a time, while I grimaced and hissed.

"How's the bleedin'? The bandage feels wet."

"It ain't too bad. Anyway, Miss June will fix you up." There was a vulnerable quiver to Oscar's voice, and I wondered if he was being honest. The bandage felt cold and clammy against me under my jacket, and maybe he couldn't see it all that well in the darkness.

The door banged open, and I heard a familiar voice, but 'twasn't Miss June's.

"Jimmy? Oscar! Oh fuck, it *is* you!"

"Trick!" Oscar said, with so much relief I could feel it.

"What happened?" Trick said, concern in her voice.

In a moment, soft, strong hands grabbed my arm on the other side of where Oscar was holding me.

"Hello, darlin'," I managed to grunt.

"He was in a rush and slid down the side of a mountain," Oscar explained.

"Oh hell," Trick said. "Miss June's comin'. Don't worry, Jimmy. We got you."

With Trick's help, I made it up the steps and inside the back door, where I heard a familiar voice through the haze of pain.

"Jimmy! Oscar! Good gracious, what on earth?"

"He's got an awful gash in his side, Miss June," Oscar said. "I reckon he'll need stitches, and it seems to have started bleedin' again."

"All right. Trick, go get Gus. He can carry Jimmy upstairs."

I tried to protest but Miss June and Trick shushed me. "Never mind. You let Gus carry you. You won't be able to climb the stairs."

Chapter Six

In Good Hands

She was right, so I shut my trap. A sudden dizziness o'ercame me, and I reckoned I must have passed out, because the next thing I knew I was lying in bed and Oscar was frowning o'er me.

"Jimmy! Jimmy, it's all right, now." He looked so worried, and I hated to cause him such stress.

Then Miss June's face came into view, and I don't think I was ever so glad to see a person other than Oscar.

"Well, there you are," she said with a smile. "I've had a quick look at that gash and we're going to need to stitch you up, but you should be just fine."

I was relieved to hear it. I tried to push myself into a sitting position, but the sharp stab of pain and Oscar's hands holding me down prevented it.

"Jimmy, I swear—" Oscar said, with more anger than I'd expected.

"Be still," Miss June advised me. "You're going to have to rest for a few days as well, and you'd better not fight me on that."

I relaxed and lay back into the comfortable mattress, as helpless as a newborn.

"I reckon I ain't up to a fight right now."

"No, you ain't. You gotta do as Miss June says, because I want you—" Oscar made a noise that sounded suspiciously like a stifled sob. "I want you to get well and strong again. I need you well and strong, Jimmy. You know I do."

My gaze flashed to the love of my life, and it hurt to see him so upset. He was more used to me taking care of him than the other way around.

"I know you do," I said, reaching out to clasp his hand. "I'm sorry."

He rolled his eyes, and it soothed me to make him tetchy and irritated.

"Don't be sorry," he grumbled, smoothing his thumb o'er my knuckles and holding my hand tight in his. "Just do as Miss June says."

"I will."

"And the next time you feel like takin' the quick way down, you think twice, all right?" He sounded stern and fed up, and I forced a smile.

"I will, for certain. Maybe you better go in front next time."

He rolled his eyes again. "Yeah, maybe I better."

He leaned down and kissed me on my forehead, the press of his sweet, soft lips like a balm to my soul.

Trick came in then with a steaming basin of a milky liquid that she placed with care onto the bedside table.

"Hey, Jimmy," she said, flashing me a smile. "Good to see ya."

"Trick," I said, grinning. "I'm glad to see you, too."

"Trick, will you and Oscar help Jimmy roll onto his good side, so I can see what I'm doing?" Miss June asked.

"Yes, ma'am," Trick said, and Oscar said, "Sure."

With their gentle assistance I moved into the position Miss June wanted me in, with more than a little discomfort.

"All right, let's have a better look at this wound. This is going to sting. I'm going to use carbolic acid to clean it, but I've diluted it quite a bit."

"What's that smell?" Oscar murmured, wrinkling his nose.

"It's the phenol."

That must be the carbolic acid she was talking about. 'Twas a sweet, acrid scent that made me a bit sick to my stomach. Or maybe that was due to the thought of Miss June touching me where it already hurt so much.

Miss June cut away the bloodied bandages then began to disinfect the injury.

I tried not to make any noise, but it hurt like hell. I reckoned I was on my last legs when it came to withstanding all this pain, and a few helpless whimpers escaped.

"I'm sure Oscar won't think less of you if you make a sound, Jimmy. It has to be painful."

I grimaced. "Sure." But it was hard to go from stifling everything to being plain about my suffering. Seemed second-nature to be stoic.

"He only makes those sounds when he's caught up in a tumble. And even then, only right before he spends."

I glared at Oscar while Miss June grinned. "Is that so?" she asked.

"'Tis." Oscar looked smug as he perched on the corner of the bed with his arms crossed.

"You should" —I grimaced at the pain but gestured at Oscar—"hear the noises Oscar makes. You'd think I was killin' a goat," I panted out, feeling like I needed to defend myself.

Oscar made a shocked face, but then he started laughing.

"A goat? Jimmy, that's not fair."

"Oh, yeah, 'tis," I grunted. "But I like it, so don't change."

"Okay, I won't."

He moved closer and took my hand again as Miss June prodded and poked and wiped up the fresh blood.

"Well, it's not too bad. I've seen worse."

"You have?"

Miss June nodded curtly, pressing her lips together.

"I have. One night a bastard client sliced one of my girls through the thigh and almost killed her. She bled so much we didn't think there was much hope. But she made it."

"I'm glad to hear it."

"That was Trick."

Oscar and I exchanged a glance.

"God," he said.

"That's awful," I concurred.

"Yes, it is. I do my best to protect my girls, but sometimes..." Miss June looked tired.

"You do a good job here, Miss June. It ain't gonna be perfect," I said.

"I know," she said. She looked me in the eye. "This needs stitching."

"I know it."

"I have laudanum if you want it?"

I thought about it. "No, not that. But I'll take some willow bark tea before you start, if you have some. And probably another cup soon after."

"Of course. Oscar, can you go ask cook to make it? Let her know I sent you."

"Sure."

Oscar let go of my hand and stood up. "I only wanna say that—Jimmy and I are very lucky to have friends like you, Miss June."

"Thank you. I feel the same. It's not many men would journey across country at the request of a woman of ill-repute."

Oscar nodded and left, shooting a concerned glance my way before he did.

Miss June gazed at me as she held a fresh cloth soaked in the disinfectant to the gash in my side.

"Jimmy, I'm glad you're here, I truly am, but I'm not sure you're gonna be able to ride out to look for Cal anytime soon."

"Oh," I said, forcing a smile, though the thought of having my wound stitched, and the pain that would cause, made me a bit faint. "I'll be fine after a day and with a good night's rest."

She narrowed her eyes. "Now, Jimmy. I'm not going to stitch you up and care for you, only to have you ignore my advice and not heal well."

"Fine. What then?"

Miss June looked at the door, and I knew what she was thinking.

"No," I said. "No, way. Oscar's not going out to look for Cal by himself."

Miss June fixed her gaze on me with an arched brow. "Do you honestly think I'd send him out by himself?"

"No, but—"

She held up a finger. "Let me speak, please."

"Yes, ma'am."

"Now, I need Mr. Hanover here to keep me and my girls safe. But I was thinking of sending Trick with him."

"*Trick?*"

Miss June nodded. "She can ride better than many men, Jimmy. She's a good horsewoman and doesn't have any shame in sitting astride, which is safer — and I don't have any side-saddles. And she can shoot."

"She can?"

Miss June gave a curt nod. "Yes, sir. She made Gus teach her after she recovered from her injury. She keeps a pistol hidden in her room. I taught all of them to shoot after that. And most of them are good, too. It's amazing what a woman can do when she's taught."

I didn't doubt that that was true.

"Yeah, I taught Oscar to shoot. He was such a city boy that he hadn't ever used a gun before. Me and Clarence — that's my friend in Port Essington — we taught him to shoot a rifle, too, and he's a pretty decent shot. He carries a revolver, but I reckon I can let him have the rifle if they go out."

"Are you okay with that?" Miss June asked, knowing how protective I was of Oscar.

I huffed a laugh then winced. "I reckon I'd better be. 'Cause Oscar's gonna want to."

Miss June smiled. "I have a feeling it will make a nice change for Trick, too. She gets mighty bored around here sometimes."

"Hmm. Even with all the —" I made a gesture.

Miss June shrugged.

"That's her job, Jimmy. She may get some pleasure and fun out of it—I hope she does—but any job gets monotonous after a while."

"I suppose."

I'd never really thought about it. I knew that women were as capable of enjoying a tumble as men were, but I hadn't considered if that was your means of making a living, that it might get to be not so much fun after a while—which was a sobering thought, for certain. Not to mention that having to do it for money meant you might not always be feeling an attraction. Maybe most of the time you weren't.

Oscar came back with a cup of the willow bark tea, cooled a bit so I could drink it down quickly, which I did. Then Miss June set up and got to stitching.

Oscar looked a tad queasy as he sat on the bed holding my hand like a good husband. But when I glanced at him, he'd gone a mite pale and his gaze was fixed on Miss June's delicate and skilled hands.

"You okay?" I asked him.

He scowled. "I'm fine."

"You don't have to look."

"I ain't lookin'," he said, averting his eyes. "Don't it hurt?" he whispered in a quiet voice full of suffering.

I gasped every time Miss June poked the needle in, but I squeezed Oscar's hand.

"Sure, but I've suffered worse. This ain't nothin' compared to the pain I felt when you got taken on our journey—or when you were lost in the storm and Clarence brought you back." I squeezed his hand. "I can handle this kind of pain better than that kind."

I could see he was torn between watching that Miss June was careful with the needle and avoiding the sight of my skin getting punctured so matter-of-factly. Miss June seemed to notice that, too.

"Oscar," she said, not looking up from her careful work.

"Yes, Ma'am?"

"Could you please ask Trick to come up here? I need to speak to both of you."

Oscar's hold loosened on my hand.

"Sure. You gonna be all right?" he asked me.

"I'm fine. Go on."

I relaxed my fingers so's he could slip his hand from mine. He walked to the door, glancing back to check on me. I gave him a smile, which he returned before walking out and closing the door quietly behind him.

Miss June met my gaze and smiled. "That boy is so in love with you."

"I know it." I hesitated, but I wanted to talk about something with the only person who might understand. "Speaking of which... I found out he don't...he don't really know when his birthday is. And he can't be sure of the age he told me when we met."

I felt some shame curl up inside my chest. My old friend had come back. Though compared to the sorts of things I'd been involved with in the outlaw gang, this was maybe not as brutal or careless, but the thought of it made me uneasy.

Miss June nodded. "You think he might not be twenty-one, you mean. Or even twenty," she said wryly.

"That's the crux of it."

Miss June continued her work and thought about what I'd said.

"Well, Jimmy, I don't know. I had my doubts when you said Oscar was twenty-one, but you seemed so certain he wasn't lying, so I didn't want to say anything more."

"He wasn't *lyin'*. I know he wasn't. It's only that…there ain't no way for him to be certain. And I…I would never have preyed upon a child."

Miss June paused her stitching and stared at me with curiosity. "You think that's what you were doing?"

I shook my head. "No, I-I don't feel 'twas. In fact, Oscar was the one who — the one who…started everything," I said weakly.

Miss June's smile widened.

"That doesn't surprise me one bit. That young man is fearless."

I rolled my eyes. "Don't I fuckin' know it."

She laughed. "He's old enough to know what he wants and how to go about getting it."

"I suppose."

"Oscar is smarter and more sensible about a lot of things than most folks twice his age. He understands the world and his place in it. He knows it's not a fair place, and he's not afraid to do things outside of what might be expected of him."

I nodded. "He ain't had much of a life up to now."

"Mm-hmm," Miss June said. "I have a funny feeling neither have you, Jimmy Downing."

Chapter Seven

An Honest Conversation

"No, ma'am, I haven't. Oscar is the best thing ever happened to me."

She nodded. "You're lucky to have his love, Jimmy. And he's lucky to have yours. How are things in Port Essington? Did you find Oscar's uncle?"

She was trying to distract me from the pain of the procedure. I knew that, but any help was much appreciated.

"In a manner of speaking. We found out he'd passed away."

"Oh, I'm sorry. Did Oscar take it hard?"

"Yeah, he did — only because he'd been so focused on finding him. He didn't know him at all."

"I see."

"But it turned out all right, because the gentleman that was friends with Oscar's uncle, he told us we could take the run-down land and homestead that belonged to him."

Miss June made a happy noise. "You don't say! Well, I'll be damned. Isn't that a lucky thing?"

I hissed as she poked me again.

"Sorry. I'm almost done."

"Well, it wasn't much of a place when we first saw it. But we'd made friends in town, and they helped us get the kitchen built up enough that we could stay warm in that room all winter. We used the money I told you about to get a nice new stove to heat it and the materials to build up that room and the stables before the snow came. And that's where we wintered, all squished together in the kitchen with a bed in it." I shook my head.

"Did you mind being in such close quarters with Oscar?" Miss June asked with a coy look.

"No, ma'am. We had a good time."

She nodded.

"I'm teachin' Oscar to read and write."

Her gaze flashed to mine. "That's wonderful! He's smart enough."

I returned her smile. "That he is. He can read simple sentences now, and he's starting to write them."

"Good for Oscar. And good for you for teaching him." She used her scissors to cut the suture and sat back. "I'm done now. Let me tie this off and we'll let it air out a bit. It's bleeding, but that's normal after stitches go in."

Miss June finished her work and washed her hands, then came around to sit on the side of the bed I was facing. She tucked her skirts under her knee and sat there smiling at me while a wave of gratitude surged through me.

"Miss June, I want to tell you something else — something amazing."

"Of course!"

"Well, I'm not supposed to share this secret, but I reckon you'll never be anywhere near to Port

Essington, and I know you wouldn't tell anyone there about it, so I reckon Clarence wouldn't mind."

"You mentioned a Clarence. Is he a friend of yours?"

"Our neighbor. He and his wife, Irene, live a short ride from our place. Clarence brought Oscar back when he got lost in a snowstorm, and we've become good friends with both of them. We spent a lot of time at their homestead this winter."

"That's wonderful."

I traced a seam in the blanket with my finger, thinking about Irene and Clarence and the home we'd left behind.

"And Clarence, why he's a man through and through. When I first met him, he was gruff and not very friendly. I thought he didn't like us. But 'twas a form of self-protection, I reckon. Anyway, we went o'er for a visit and when we got there, Clarence was bein' attacked by a bear right in his yard beside the house!"

"No! Oh my, Jimmy!" Miss June looked truly horrified.

"Yes, ma'am. Lucky for him and us, Irene is a crack shot. But Clarence had a deep gash in his thigh and Irene didn't want to go for the doctor. I couldn't understand it!"

Miss June gazed at me, and I figured she knew all about secrets needing to be kept.

"But I do know a little bit about healing wounds and looking after people. And anyway, while I was examining Clarence's wound, I saw that he had what — what I would expect to find on a woman..."

Miss June blinked but she didn't seem all that shocked. "You mean, a cunt instead of a cock?"

"Yes, ma'am, that's what I mean." My cheeks were aflame. 'Twas hard getting used to folks like Miss June and Oscar who said words like that out loud with no problem.

"Well, I'll be damned. And he's married to a woman?"

"Yes, ma'am."

"Well, my goodness." Miss June seemed as pleased as I'd been to discover that. "What a coincidence that you ended up with them as neighbors!"

"I know it. I almost feel like — like maybe God put them there for us to meet and befriend, because maybe...maybe God thinks I'm not entirely a bad person."

Miss June gazed at me with tenderness and concern. "Do you think you're a bad person, Jimmy?"

I averted my eyes all of a sudden, because I couldn't take the disappointment in hers when I told her what I'd done.

"Sometimes. Sometimes, I do think that." My voice was barely there.

Miss June put a gentle hand on my knee where it rested under the bedclothes.

"Jimmy, look at me."

I forced myself to.

"Now, I know we never spoke much about your life before you showed up here with Oscar, but if there's things in your past that you're — "

"There is," I said, louder. "I mean, there are things that I...I don't even want to think about." I swallowed thickly. "I dream about 'em sometimes."

"Oh?"

"Yeah. I got..." I licked my lips, suddenly thirsty. "I got caught up with some nasty folk when I was young, who went about robbin' and murderin' people with no remorse — or at least, very little. I regret every moment of it now. Except — " A thought had suddenly occurred to me, and I licked my lips, my brain going a mile a minute. "Except, I suppose if I hadn't, I might never have met Oscar. I don't know."

I'd never really had that thought before, and it brought me right up all of a sudden.

Miss June nodded. "That's true."

"But—I can't be glad about it. 'Cause they found us and took Oscar and almost…almost did fearful things to him, and I wish that had never happened…"

"Jimmy," Miss June said, looking very serious. "Jimmy, you can't change the past."

"I know, but—"

"Uh-uh. You can't. No matter how much you may want to. All you can do is lead a good enough life going forward and hope for forgiveness."

I kept my gaze on hers, feeding off her wisdom and her tenderness like it was a cup of hot tea.

"A good enough life?"

"I don't believe that anyone in this world is truly good. We all have wicked thoughts and feelings inside us, and sometimes they do escape and become reality. But it sounds like you got caught up in that outlaw life through no fault of your own, maybe?"

I sighed. "I suppose. My parents died when me and Robert were pretty young. We were sent to live with some elderly relatives, but that weren't much good for us, although Robert took to it better at first. I ran and was found by a fella who seemed like the most fascinatin' and impressive person I'd ever met for the first little while, and he took me under his wing. I got involved more in the gang, and by the time I realized what kind of a life it truly was, 'twas too late to get out. I was pretty young and had nothing else. And I did try to go back one time, but that ended in disaster. Because Robert decided he wanted to come with me when I went back to them, and I couldn't bear to leave him behind." I made a face. "My grandpa was not a kind man, and I don't think he wanted to raise us anyway."

We were silent for a little while. Miss June got up to adjust the brightness of the lamp so that the room was bathed in a soft light instead of the intensity she'd needed for her stitching. She peered o'er at me while she turned the little brass key and the lamp dimmed.

"Did Robert join the gang, too?"

"Yes, ma'am. I think... I think that's the thing I regret most of all."

She returned to the bed and sat down, taking my hand in one of hers and laying her other hand o'er the top of it. Her skin was so soft, and her touch was a soothing comfort after a rough day.

"What happened to Robert?"

I frowned and shifted my gaze to the bed covering as the memories returned to me. My voice was rough when I continued speaking.

"He died. Got shot in the back and left in the dirt by a rival gang. And the hardest part was... The worst of it was that the men I'd had a bit of respect for in the gang, they didn't even want to look for him. I found him, and I can still see him lyin' there."

"Oh, Jimmy, I'm so sorry."

The tears slid o'er my cheeks, and I was too exhausted to fight them. Probably all the stress and the pain had caught up to me. My face didn't even have the will to crumple, and I didn't make a sound.

Miss June slipped closer and clasped my hand to her warm bosom, stroking it and saying soothing words to settle me. I didn't protest, because it felt real good and like 'twas something I needed.

Once my tears had dried and I wasn't sniffling anymore, she patted the back of my hand and glanced at the door. "Whatever is keeping Oscar? Maybe he couldn't find Trick, or —"

Our gazes met and we both grinned. Then Miss June laughed.

"Or maybe he decided 'twas a good idea to wait while she finished up with something," she said.

"I reckon that's probably what 'twas."

"Well," she said, patting my hand again then letting it go and standing, "'twas good to talk with you, Jimmy. I think you need to stop agonizing over your rough past and accept it. It made you who you are today, and I think you're a good man. In fact, I know it."

"How can you?"

She grinned. "Didn't I mention? I've got a second sense when it comes to people. Works for me well around here — most of the time, anyway."

I tried to smile.

"And I can see it in Oscar. He loves you, and he knows you're a good man. And you've got to start seeing yourself through our eyes, Jimmy, because you are a very special person *now*, no matter what happened before."

"Maybe," I said.

"Surely," she replied as the door opened and Oscar came in with Trick, whose lips were red and swollen, cheeks were flushed and hair was rather disorderly.

"I got her when I could. She was" — Oscar glanced at Trick, who shrugged, then he looked back at us — "busy."

Trick sucked a finger into her mouth, then used it to smooth back some hair at her temple. "Girl's gotta make a living."

Miss June put a hand on Trick's shoulder and kissed her rosy cheek, then stepped back and gave her a steady look.

"I have a proposition for you, my dear."

"Oh, bloody hell. Now what?" she said, but the fondness she held for Miss June was in Trick's good-humored countenance.

"I'll tell you in a minute. First, I need you two to help Jimmy to sit up so I can wrap up this wound."

Trick and Oscar did as Miss June asked them, and I managed to have a glimpse of my injury before she covered it up. The jagged edges had been neatly stitched together with proper medical sutures and, though it looked angry and red at the moment, I had no doubt I had the best chances at a full recovery under Miss June's care.

She wrapped a clean cotton bandage around my middle and tied it off, then Trick and Oscar lowered me back down to the bed. For the first time in a while, I felt comfortable and able to relax.

Miss June glanced at Oscar. "Now, I've disinfected and stitched Jimmy's wound and he's going to be fine, but he'll need to rest for a few days so the stitches hold and it starts to heal well."

I bit my tongue when I wanted to protest that I'd be fine to ride out before that, since we'd already had that conversation. Oscar's stern gaze flashed to mine, as if he expected me to give Miss June trouble about it, so I only frowned and kept quiet as Miss June continued. Oscar looked at her as Miss June shifted her gaze to Trick.

"But I was hoping that we could get started on looking for Cal. So, I was thinking that you and Oscar could go out and scout around the nearby spots where we might find her."

Oscar returned his gaze to me. I shrugged, since it was blatantly obvious 'twas out of my hands. Then he looked at Trick.

"Can you ride?" he asked, in such a surprised voice I reckoned I understood when her hackles went up.

"Better'n you, probly." She gave him such a scornful look I thought he'd get mad. "I can ride—and I can shoot." She put her hands on her hips and looked Oscar up and down. "Can you?"

Oscar looked ticked off for a second, but then he collected himself.

"Better'n you, probly," he said, with exactly the same tone Trick had used on him.

She grinned, then, and Oscar relaxed as well. "Hmm, I don't know. I can shoot pretty well."

"So can I," Oscar said, crossing his arms o'er his chest.

"Well, then," Miss June said, "that's settled."

Oscar glanced at me. "Should we put Trick on Dixie, or give her Onyx and I'll ride Dixie?"

I glanced at Trick. "You know how to handle a horse that gets grumpy and stubborn from time to time?"

"Sure," Trick said. "I can handle men like that, too. I got all kinds of skills."

I grinned. I'd missed Trick and her cheeky ways. "I bet you do."

She raised her eyebrows. "I offered to show you that once, Jimmy Downing, but you turned me down."

That seemed to try the last of Oscar's patience.

"You *what*? You offered to bed my man?" The outrage and offense in Oscar's voice made my heart warm in my chest. I liked it when he got possessive of me.

Trick raised her hand. "Now, that was before I knew how much in love the two of you were. I do beg your pardon." She grinned. "You'll be happy to know that Jimmy refused me right quick, e'en though you were upstairs unconscious and wouldn't have known a thing about it."

Oscar blinked. "Oh." He turned to me. "That true?"

"I suppose 'tis. I can't remember. I was outta my mind with worry about you back then."

"Anyway, I grew up with horses," Trick said, "and Gus taught me to shoot. I'm a good shot, ain't I, miss?"

"Yes, you are."

"Oscar's a good shot, too," I said, fixing him with a stern look. "But you need to be goddamn careful, all right?" I said. "You never know what you might run into."

"We'll stick together, Jimmy. Don't worry," Oscar said, and I could see the excitement in his face. He turned to Miss June. "But can I get a bath and a solid night's sleep first? And some of that tincture for our mosquito bites?"

"Of course. The two of you can set out tomorrow."

Chapter Eight

A Soft Bed and a Kind Hand

Oscar got himself a bath in the room down the hall, and Miss June had one of the girls give me a sponge bath because she said 'twouldn't be a good idea to submerge my wound in water right now, and she'd cleaned my middle with soap and water before she'd bandaged me up.

I was filthy from the travel, and the girl she sent in was awful sweet and pretty in a plump way. My cock didn't behave very well.

"I'm sorry. I can't help that," I said, my face on fire as she cleaned me with a warm cloth.

She gazed at me out of deep brown eyes. "Oh, that's all right. I'm plenty used to men's privates, Mr. Downing."

I nodded. "Sure. Of course."

She giggled, and 'twas a lovely, musical sound. "You want me to get you off? Wouldn't take but a moment."

I coughed with embarrassment and said 'no thanks'. She was a lovely girl, with skin that was almost black, bright white teeth and dark hair that fell in curls to her shoulders.

"All right. Suit yourself."

She finished cleaning me, then brought out a small bottle of something.

"Miss June asked me to dab some of this on your bites. 'Twill help with the itching."

The mosquito bites were the least of my plagues, but I supposed anything to help me get a good night's sleep would be welcome.

"Thank you kindly."

When she'd finished, she helped me get into a clean cotton shirt to sleep in. "It's one of Gus's, so it's big on you, e'en though you got some bulk. Kinda like a nightshirt."

"Thank you so much. I feel much better bein' clean."

'Twas true. It hadn't been a priority, and I was so tired I only wanted to rest, but it did make a difference.

"You're welcome, Jimmy. Miss June's told us all about you and Oscar, and I think its sweet of the both of you to come and help look for Cal."

"Well, we got to know Cal when we were here before. I hate to think of her bein' treated badly or bein' prevented from coming to see her friends here."

"I like Cal very much, too. My name's Sally, by the way. And if you need anythin'," she glanced at my crotch. "Anythin' at all, you ask for me. All right?"

"Yes, Miss, I will." I weren't gonna ask for that, though. I could guarantee it.

My cock was still at a stand, e'en after everything I'd been through on this trying day. I lifted the blankets to frown at it right stern and told it to behave until Oscar came back, and maybe he could do something about it. I hoped he could, because I missed his touch, his dirty words and his laugh. And now that I'd fought some much-needed sleep for so long and was feeling better, my body buzzed with energy and my brain spun, worrying about Cal and now about Oscar going out with Trick to try to find him. I reckoned I might need something to settle me down.

When Oscar came back, he was wearing a shirt like mine. I hoped Gus still had some of his own left to wear.

"You look sweet in that," I told him, a blush returning to my cheeks as I watched him walk into the room. "Reminds me of that first night at the hotel in Dawson City, when I gave you my shirt that was way too big on you. Remember?"

Oscar smiled. "I remember that."

His skin had a fresh rosy tint from the hot water and his hair was damp and starting to dry, looking fluffy from the toweling, with strands going every which way. It had grown long again after the trim Irene had given him. I wasn't sure if I preferred it this way, or short, like it had been. His lovely eyes stood out more when 'twas real short like last time, but now soft waves of it fell o'er his ears and around his neck, and he seemed like a delicate, fairy-like creature. I reckoned I liked that a lot.

"You were so kind to me. And I didn't deserve any of it. I was nasty to you."

I grinned, remembering Oscar snapping at me like a wounded animal when I'd first offered a friendly hand.

"You were starvin', and you'd been mistreated. I don't blame you a'tall, and I didn't then," I said. "And you did deserve it. You deserve all the kindness in the world, Oscar Yates, and I aim to give it to you."

Oscar blushed and came o'er to sit beside me. "Look," he said, showing me his bare face. "I shaved an' everythin'."

I reached up and ran my thumb along his smooth chin.

"My, my, my. Don't you look fetchin'." I stroked his cheek with my finger, and Oscar closed his eyes and leaned into my touch. He opened them after a moment and his gaze scanned me where I lay beneath the soft sheets.

"Did, uh, Sally treat you well?" he asked.

I narrowed my eyes. "Well, she gave me a good seein' to with the sponge."

"A seein' to?"

"She cleaned me up, if that's what you're askin'. Didn't do anythin' else," I assured him.

"Hmm. Did she offer?"

I couldn't keep the smile off my face at his proprietary interest in my activities. "She may have."

Oscar's head snapped up, and his eyes shot invisible bullets at me.

"I declined, of course."

"Oh." He gave a curt nod. "Well, good."

"What the hell difference would it have made? I'm still in love with you." For some reason I felt like riling him up. He was so cute when he got mad.

"I reckon it wouldn't have meant anythin', and maybe you're right. But…I feel like I got some ownership rights…or somethin' — after all the trouble you put me to."

I raised my eyebrows, my dick standing up again like Oscar was its rightful owner and only had to beckon. "Ownership rights!"

We gazed at each other, both of us feeling possessive, I reckoned, now that we were in a house filled with others who had relaxed attitudes about physical affection.

"I don't want you bein' so friendly with anyone else, Jimmy."

"I know it. I don't mind that, as long as it goes both ways."

"A'course, it does. I ain't even interested in girls." He turned up his nose at the thought of them. "But..."

"But, what?"

He shrugged again, and slipped his hand under the covers to find my cock. I gasped as his fingertips made contact.

"I know you were, at one time."

Uh-huh. That was the crux of the matter, I suppose.

"That's true, I suppose, back when I didn't have any inkling of the kind of pleasure a man could give me. Sure."

He gazed at the ticking on the bedcover, pretending to be casual as he played his fingers along my erection.

"Would you ever...? Do you think you could ever bed a woman again?"

I chose my words carefully. "I suppose I could do it...maybe."

Oscar frowned.

"If my life depended upon it," I said.

Oscar's touch disappeared, and his gaze flashed to mine. "If your *life* depended upon it?"

I tried not to smile, but 'twas so much fun to get him worked up.

"Well, I don't know. What if I got captured by some wild, sex-addled woman, and she said she'd kill me if I didn't fuck her?"

Oscar stared at me, then he quirked the corners of his mouth. "You think that might happen?"

"You never know."

Then he did laugh. "Well, I suppose I'm glad you'd be able to survive somethin' like that, Jimmy."

I found his hand and clasped it. "Look, Oscar. I ain't got any interest in bedding anyone but you, no matter how many offers I get. You ain't gotta worry about that...at all."

He blushed and gave me a sweet smile. "All right. Nor you."

"I'm mighty thankful for that," I said. "I'd hate to have to put a bullet in someone."

Oscar grinned.

"I'm jokin'. I ain't killin' anyone ever again if I can avoid it. But I would have to do something."

"Like what, then?"

"Well, I don't know. Beat 'em to a pulp? So, if you don't want anyone to get hurt, you best stick to me."

If Oscar did take up with another man, I don't know what I'd do. But I didn't think I had to worry about it, and neither did he. Although I was glad Miss June didn't have a stable of molly boys working here, to be honest. Seems she mostly catered to the men that liked girls, and that was fine with me. I did wonder, though, now that Cal was gone, whether Miss June would think to take in a young man with those tastes, if one came to ask. I reckoned she would, because men liked all sorts of things when it came to debauchery, and I was an example of that—thanks to Oscar, who'd introduced me to all kinds of fun.

"Are you still in a lot of pain?" Oscar asked. He'd come to sit on the bed beside me and slipped his hand under the covers again.

"Not too much, no. I had some more of the tea, and it seems to be helping," My voice sounded a mite strained, what with Oscar's fingers finding my dick again.

"That's good."

I gazed at Oscar and beckoned him closer with a finger, so's I could kiss him. He tasted of something sweet, like peppermint.

I grinned against his lips. "Someone's feedin' you treats."

He laughed. "You make it sound like I'm a pony," he said, pulling back.

"You're my pretty pony, and that's a fact."

I didn't know where that had come from, but it seemed right.

"My pet," I murmured, stroking his cheek and sliding my fingers into his hair.

Oscar smiled, seeming pleased as punch at the endearments. "If you must know, 'twas Trick. She gave me some peppermints, and I had one after my bath."

"Oh, I see," I said, kissing him again.

Oscar responded then pulled away again so he could speak.

"I had a feelin' I'd want to kiss you, and I wanted my breath to smell nice."

"That's awful kind."

"I'm always thinkin' of you, Jimmy."

"Sure," I said, caught up in the scent of him, with his freshly washed hair and skin. "Oscar, you smell like flowers."

Oscar sighed and traced the tip of his tongue along my lip. At the same time, he slipped the palm of his hand o'er the head of my cock, where 'twas wet with my need for him.

"I know."

I gasped. "Does your...taint smell like flowers, too?"

"I reckon."

"I'd sure love to taste it."

Oscar pulled back and gave me a stern look.

"Now, Jimmy..."

"Or maybe you could climb up onto this stand I got here and" — I inhaled an unsteady breath, desperate all of a sudden — "fuck yourself on't?"

Chapter Nine

A Frustrated Patient

The expression on Oscar's face transformed into shock then amusement, before returning to severe.

"Stop it, now," he said, but his breath hitched. "Miss June asked me not to make you exert yourself in any capacity, and I reckon I know what she meant."

"Oscar, I feel fine. It barely hurts 'tall." I protested, which was a falsehood, but the need to bury myself in Oscar was overriding any of the pain I still felt, which had diminished quite a bit—or else I'd got used to it.

"Jimmy," he said, speaking to me like I was a child, which was an amusing turnaround for us. "I am more than willin' to bring you off with my hand, but that's all I can give you right now. You want it or not?"

I swallowed.

"Sure I do."

"Well then, I'm gonna latch the door so nobody disturbs us."

"All right."

Oscar walked to the door and slid the latch shut as I gazed at where the long shirt sloped along his buttocks and ended at the midst of his slim thighs, wishing I could fuck him like that. I'd have to do it someday, when I was in tiptop shape and not a shadow of myself.

When he turned back, he must have seen the raw need in my gaze.

"Christ, you're gettin' me hard with the way you're lookin' at me."

"Good. If not for this damn injury and Miss June's interferin', I'd be tuppin' you by now."

"Oh!" he said. "My, my, my… Pretty sure of yourself, ain't you, mister?"

At Oscar's use of that particular honorific, I was transported back to the first night in the hotel, when he'd been so argumentative and ornery, and I hadn't even realized how much I'd wanted him. I'd had no reference point for those feelings, and I'd figured I was horny for anything since I'd lost my chance to rent a nice whore for an hour. But, looking back on it now, I know 'twas simply Oscar and the way he affected me, the way he'd done so from the moment I'd met him.

He sat beside me on the bed, with one leg crossed o'er the other, and kissed me sweetly before pushing the bedclothes down, exposing my randy cock in all its ruddy glory, rising out of the thatch of dark curls at my groin. Then he took something out of his shirt pocket and showed it to me.

"I got this from Trick."

He took the top off the little bottle of oil and poured some into his hand, then replaced the cap and put it on the bedside table. He rubbed his hands together to warm them up then reached for me.

I watched with hooded eyes as he wrapped his long and delicate fingers, shiny with oil, around my cock and stroked me up and down, slowly at first, making me shudder and groan with the exquisite torture of it.

"Oscar," I moaned.

"Now, Jimmy, you be a good boy for me and don't come till I say."

I gave him a narrow-eyed glare. "Now, hold on. I ain't your good boy. You're *my* good boy."

He raised his eyebrows and gave my cock a long stroke in a corkscrew motion that made my lips part and a sound escape me.

"Oh, really? Why? Are you gonna be my *naughty* boy, then?"

"Fuck," I said, suddenly understanding why Oscar liked me to talk like that. "Maybe," I grunted. "I don't know. I can't think right now."

He grinned. "Well, you don't gotta think. You just gotta pay attention — because I want to show you how hard it is to hold off when you're told you can't spend."

"But I... Oscar, I been *injured*," I whined, and gasped as he teased me with his fingers.

"Not in your cock or your balls. I don't know what a slice in your side's got to do with obeyin' me."

He switched hands and worked me harder, making me groan and causing sparks to light up in my balls and my gut. I didn't know if I was gonna be able to hold off or not.

"Oh, fuck," I groaned, spellbound by the sight of Oscar's talented hands on my cock, all shiny with oil, and the sheer poetic beauty of it all about sent me o'er. I wrapped a hand around his wrist and stilled him.

"Now that's cheatin'," he pouted.

I made a face and held myself together by a force of sheer will. When I opened my eyes, I fixed him with my gaze.

"Now look. You're a pro at this game, and I ain't. Please make me spend? Please?"

Oscar rolled his eyes, but he shrugged. "Fine. Let it be noted that you ain't very good at doing what you're told—not as good as me, anyway."

"I'll never be as good as you," I said, with a sheer sincerity that brought a blush to Oscar's cheeks.

"No," he said, shaking my hand off his wrist and resuming his work. "You won't. You wanna spend, then spend. I wanna see your fine cock shoot spunk up to the ceiling, though, when you do it."

Oscar's words sent a bolt of lightning through my dick, and he hadn't given me three strokes before I spurted in his hands with a cry, like a hose shooting water when you weren't expecting it.

"Aww, hell," Oscar breathed as he watched my cock overflow in his fist, globs of white spend spattering his knuckles and landing on my hip, as I panted and groaned and whimpered. Oscar had aimed my dick so I didn't ruin Miss June's clean bandages, and I was grateful for that.

Oscar released my cock and gathered Gus's shirt up in his clean hand as he kneeled up. He used his spunk-covered fingers to point his cock at my bare thigh and hip, and he brought himself off in a matter of moments, his own spend mixing with mine.

He was so beautiful to watch, his drying hair falling o'er his forehead, his mouth open and eyes closed as he made staccato cries of "Ah, ah, ah" and spent on me in desperate bursts.

"Oh," he said, milking the last few drops as he watched me with an apologetic smile. "Sorry. I couldn't help myself."

"Oscar, don't apologize. That was the loveliest thing to watch."

"'Twas? Truly?" he said, grabbing a cloth and drying his hand.

"Oh yeah. Trust me. Anytime you wanna do that, you go right ahead." I frowned and scratched my chin. "Well, unless I've forbidden you to spend, of course."

"Of course. I wouldn't even dream of disobeyin' you, Jimmy."

I grinned. "Oh no, I know it. You're such a good boy when I'm dominatin' you, ain't you?" I said, reaching out to swipe some spunk off my skin and holding my finger in front of Oscar's lips.

Oscar sighed, opened his mouth and took my finger inside the wet warmth of it, sucking the juice off and closing his eyes.

"Goddammit," I whispered. "You're gonna get me all randy again."

But just then, there was a knock at the door, interrupting us.

"I'm sorry to disturb you fellas, but I need my oil back."

'Twas Trick's voice, and Oscar rolled his eyes.

"Figures," he said.

He made his way off the bed, let the shirt fall so it covered his bits and picked up the little bottle from the side table. He walked to the door and opened it a crack, passing the oil to Trick.

"Here... I don't need it no more," he said with some smugness.

Trick laughed and said, "Fine," so Oscar shut the door, latched it and came back to me.

"Why, you look a right mess," Oscar said as he eyed the puddles of drying spunk on my thigh and hip.

I raised my brows. "You gonna clean me up, since you had more'n a hand in it?"

Oscar sighed. "I suppose I should. Then we best try to get some sleep. If I'm to ride out with Trick and look for Cal tomorrow, I'll need my rest. And you need to let your body heal by lookin' after it."

* * * *

'Twas pleasant to sleep together in a warm bed and wake up snuggled under the blankets to sunshine streaming in the room. The sounds of the town outside reminded us that we weren't in the middle of the wilderness or at our homestead. It brought me back to our earlier stay at The Angel, when it had been Oscar needing rest and recuperation.

'Twas probably about nine in the morning, taking into account where the sun was in the sky, and I was startled to hear a knock on the door this early. If my recollections were accurate, nobody except the cook and the scullery maid had been conscious before eleven during our previous stay.

"Jimmy? Oscar? May I come in?"

'Twas Miss June's voice.

"Sure," I answered as the knob turned, and Miss June tried the door.

"Jimmy, get Oscar to unlatch the door, please. Don't you dare get out of bed yet."

"Yes, ma'am," I said. I shook Oscar awake. "You need to let Miss June in."

"What?" he said, yawning and blinking like a kitten.

"Miss June's here, but she can't get in."

"Oh. Hold on." He slid from under the sheets, made sure the shirt was covering him, then padded across the wood floor to lift the latch and open the door.

"Good morning," Miss June said, moving into the room and giving Oscar a glance. "Did you have a nice evening?" she asked.

She was carrying a basin of steaming water and a bundle of cloths, which she placed on the bedside table.

Oscar yawned and shut the door behind her. "Yep. And Jimmy didn't move a muscle."

Miss June raised an eyebrow at him, and Oscar snorted a laugh.

"Well, I moved it for him."

I rolled my eyes as Miss June nodded. "I'm sure it helped him to get a good night's sleep."

Oscar nodded. "Oh, it surely did. He ain't moved all night. I reckon he slept like a newborn babe, didn't you, Jimmy?"

I blushed and muttered something while Miss June lifted the bedclothes and met my gaze.

"May I have a look?"

"Of course," I said, though I was a mite embarrassed in the light of morning to be so vulnerable.

She rolled the blankets down to my where the bushy hair around my cock began but no further, which I appreciated, especially since I'd just awoke and my cock was swole of it's own accord, as tended to happen most mornings. Strange to think of modesty in a place like this, but I supposed I was more conventional in some ways than one would expect. I didn't have Oscar's blithe way with nakedness and talking about physical acts so plainly, though I was getting there, at least when 'twas only the two of us.

"Oscar, can you help me sit him up and get his shirt off?"

"I can do it," I said, using my elbow to push myself up and feeling a sharp tug of pain at the site of the injury.

"Let me help you, you silly git. You're gonna rip them stitches if you don't," Oscar said, sliding his arm under my shoulders and helping me to get into a sitting position. Then he had me lift my arms, and he slid Gus's shirt o'er my head and laid it aside.

"Thank you," Miss June said. "Jimmy, you're going to need to rest today and not get out of bed."

I opened my mouth to protest, but she continued.

"If you do that, I promise you'll feel much better tomorrow, and you can start walking around the place. If you rip these stitches, we'll have to start all over, and you'll be laid up even longer."

She had a point.

"You want that?" Oscar said.

"No. Course not."

"Then you listen to Miss June and do what she says. If she can keep a house full of working girls healthy and strong, I reckon she knows what she's about."

My gaze flicked to Miss June's, and her calm dignity reminded me that I was under her care and that I needed to listen and do what she said.

"All right."

Miss June and Oscar unwrapped me like I was some kind of strange Christmas gift, while I held on to Oscar's arm for support. His gaze flitted from the wall to the window and to my face and back again—anywhere but the wound that Miss June was examining.

"These bandages aren't all that bloody, so that's a good sign. The bleeding didn't last long after the stitching was done."

"That's good," I said, craning my neck to see. Miss June had stitched it nice and straight, with delicate sutures that you could barely see. It looked better than

I'd expected. 'Twas still a bit red and angry at the edges, but I reckoned that would reduce with time.

"Well, that doesn't look too bad," Miss June agreed. "I'll put a fresh dressing on it now, and another one this evening. We'll change it twice a day for the next few days, and when it's healed enough for you to go out riding, you should keep it covered so it doesn't get dirt and dust in it. I figure after a week you won't need a bandage at all, *if* you do everything I say, and it doesn't get any worse. Infection is the thing we need to watch out for now."

"Yes, ma'am."

I knew that was true. We'd lost an outlaw or two as the result of an injury that wasn't properly cared for.

Miss June sponged the wound with a clean cloth soaked in the warm water she'd brought, then had Oscar help to wrap me up again in the clean bandages.

"How does that feel, now?"

"Good. I ain't got hardly any pain, 'cept when I move."

She smiled, and Oscar looked relieved.

"Wonderful. I'll have cook send up some breakfast for both of you, and some willow bark tea for you, Jimmy. She'll put something in it for the swelling, too, so drink every last drop of it, all right?"

"All right. Thank you."

Miss June placed a tender hand on my shoulder.

"You're very welcome, Jimmy. We'll have you in ship shape in no time."

She turned to Oscar.

"Now, I'm hoping you and Trick can set off by noon, Oscar. I made sure she got rid of her last client by one this morning, and I'll wake her at ten. In the meantime, keep Jimmy company and don't let him distract you by asking for favors, you understand?" She gave a pointed look at where my cock lay under the blankets, then looked to Oscar. "He needs to rest. In a little while, he'll be well enough for any mischief you want to get into, as long as it's gentle and slow."

Oscar snorted. "Gentle and slow? Jimmy ain't ever —"

I cleared my throat and covered his mouth with my hand, enjoying the startled look in his gaze and the quick flick of his wet tongue against my palm.

I cleared my throat and lowered it, begging Oscar with my gaze to be quiet. "Yes, ma'am. Thank you kindly."

Miss June gave me a lovely smile, and I reckoned I saw a hint of her youthful beauty from long ago. "You didn't have to come all this way to help me and Cal, but you did, and I'm very thankful. The least I can do is make you comfortable while you're here."

Chapter Ten

Fretting

"Now, look... You be careful, Oscar," I said, when he was getting ready to ride out.

Miss June had allowed Oscar to prop me up with pillows so I could at least look at something besides the rafters. I'd had some porridge, a boiled egg and a cup of willow bark tea. I was feeling good, but I wasn't looking forward to spending the day apart from Oscar.

Oscar was getting dressed to go out. I'd watched him pull on his underthings and his trousers, then a fresh shirt from his pack, then socks and boots, and now he lifted his suspenders o'er his slim shoulders and drew on his light jacket. He noticed me then.

"What?"

"I just... I like the look of you. That's all."

Oscar grinned and walked to the bed. "Oh, I know it. Maybe when I get back you can watch me take it all off again."

I matched his smile. "I reckon I'd like that." I sobered and gave him a stern look. "Now I need you to take care today."

"I will, Jimmy."

"You got lots of cartridges for your revolver?"

"Yes."

"And for the rifle?"

"Yep."

I sighed and made a fist in the bedclothes. "I don't like bein' laid up and you goin' off with Trick to look for Cal. I wish I could go with you."

Before we'd left Port Essington, I'd bought Oscar a proper leather belt with a holster for his gun. He buckled it on now and bent to lace the holster to his thigh but glanced up at me. His hair, so clean from his bath that it looked like delicate feathers, flopped o'er his forehead. He still had swollen bites from the mosquitoes in a few places, as did I, but Miss June had given him some of the same salve she'd applied to mine to stop the itching, much to Oscar's relief. I'd make sure we had some of that good salve before we rode back to Port Essington. And he and Trick had put on some of the tincture of marigold that would keep them at bay.

I wanted to run my fingers through his hair and kiss his soft lips, but there wasn't time for that. Oscar finished with his holster, tossed the hair off his face and walked o'er to me.

"I know. But Trick is as tough as any man, Jimmy, and I'm fierce, e'en though I'm small."

I took Oscar's hands in mine, gazing into his eyes with a strength that matched his. "You are, Oscar. You're fierce and quick, and I want you to use your head and not get into a crazy mess out there."

"Yes, sir. You know, I wouldn't dare."

"That's right. You keep yourself safe, else I might have to come lookin' for you and ruin this fine stitching Miss June put in my side."

Oscar grinned and lifted one of my hands to his lips, kissing the skin on the back of it with the utmost tenderness. Then he lowered it and did the same to the other.

"I'll be fine. We'll be back well before dark. You'll see." He pulled something from his pocket and held it up. "I got this pretty pocket watch, see? The one that you gave me for Christmas, with my name on the back." I smiled as he dropped it back in his trouser pocket. "I only hope we find something encouragin', even if we don't find Cal herself today. Miss June gave us some places to look."

"You just do the best you can and get back here safely."

"I will. I love you."

"I love you, too. Now git, before I change my mind and come with you."

* * * *

The rest of the day dragged. I ate some soup and bread that Sally brought to my room—seemed she was my dedicated nursemaid, and perhaps Miss June had given her some time off her regular duties. She seemed happy to wait on me and not in a rush to get anywhere else.

I heard the sounds of strange men about all afternoon, the footfalls from the hall, the shrieks of laughter and ribald comments, the music from the piano downstairs and some sounds of congress from the room next to mine. I knew from experience 'twas worth a pretty penny to spend a few hours among women when your life was all about men, even if I was in love with Oscar now. The women I still had in my life—Irene and Miss June and even Trick—were precious to me. And something about the girls here, whom other men paid for favors and took their pleasure with, made me happy—the way they were in control of their lives as much as they could be, since Miss June kept such a reputable establishment, and able to be more themselves than perhaps a wealthy married woman who was constrained by the expectations of polite society. If I hadn't dedicated myself to Oscar, I might have been sorely tempted to pass the time in a more interesting way.

But I was a married man now, and I took the vow that I'd made very seriously, even if it hadn't been at all legal.

I drifted in and out of sleep, and when I woke again to see the light of the room dimming and no sign of Oscar having returned, I felt a spike of fear. They should be back by now. 'Twas getting dark, and the thought of Oscar out there in a place he didn't know, riding around with only one other person to help him, made me sick to my stomach.

My pocket watch was on the nightstand, beside a glass of water and the soiled cup from my last bit of willow bark tea. I reached o'er to check it. 'Twas nigh ten o'clock, which was late, to be sure, but up here this far north, the sun stayed out a long time at this time of year. Maybe they had come back but Oscar hadn't wanted to disturb me, but I needed to know.

I decided that in this particular circumstance, I was justified in disobeying Miss June's instructions to stay in bed. I sat up and pushed the covers back, being very careful not to strain my stitches too much. I was comforted by the fact that moving seemed to hurt less than it had the day before, but when I pushed myself to my feet, I swayed a bit and had to sit right back down.

Which was when the door opened.

"Oscar!" I said as relief flooded me.

"Jimmy Downing, what on earth are you doin' out of bed?"

"Lookin' for you. I didn't know you were back."

Oscar shut the door behind him and came to help me get back under the covers.

"Back to bed now. I'm fine. Trick's downstairs. We were talking to Miss June. I had a peek in on you, but you were sound asleep." He pulled the covers back o'er me like a proper nursemaid and sat down on the coverlet.

He was dirty and dusty, but I'd never seen anyone so beautiful.

"Did you have any luck?"

Oscar sighed and shook his head. "Not yet. But we'll try again tomorrow."

I was not looking forward to another day without him. I was sure hoping Miss June would give me leave to get out of bed, at least.

"You want me to sing you *All the Pretty Little Horses* so you can go back to sleep?" Oscar asked, smoothing the hair back from my brow.

"Well, I—" In fact, that sounded like the best thing in the world right about now. "I would, in fact."

Oscar took off his boots and got up on the bed, leaning back against the pillows and soothing me with soft touches and loving glances, as he sang the familiar words that lulled me right back into the land of Nod, safe in the assurance of his proximity and care.

* * * *

I was fortunate that once Oscar and Trick had left again the next morning, Miss June came to change my bandages, and she gave me leave to move around a little, as long as I promised to sit when I could and go slow and easy.

I puttered around in the room for the morning and early afternoon, and it was enjoyable to sit in the chair and look out of the window onto the backyard. I felt a good deal recovered, except for the occasional stabs of pain from the healing wound. When I couldn't bear it anymore and the fretting of waiting for Oscar to return was too much, I left the safety of my room and walked gingerly down the stairs, 'holding the railing and moving like molasses.

The parlor was full of scantily clad girls, lying about on the furniture and getting ready to receive any men who might come in. This was the way of cathouses, and 'twasn't anything I was unfamiliar with. Although now that I'd had the luxury of seeing Oscar dressed in some of them frilly underthings, I found my eyes wandering and my cheeks heating. Seems I still found some things fetching, even if I was more interested in Oscar's parts and the heart attached to them.

"Hi, Jimmy," one of the girls said, waving at me and smiling with a coy flirtatiousness that made me a mite uncomfortable. I recognized her as the girl who'd given me the sponge bath—Sally.

"Hello," I said, with a polite smile, and tried not to remember how she'd seen me.

"You worried about your beau?"

My husband.

"Yes. A little."

A lot.

"Aww, I'm sure he'll be back soon," one of the other girls assured me, pulling her peignoir open on purpose so I could see the flesh plumping out of her corset.

I tore my eyes away, but then found myself gazing into the pretty green eyes of another girl, who smiled and giggled.

"You're awfully sweet to worry about him, Mr. Downing."

Perhaps coming down here hadn't been the best idea, but I wanted to know when Oscar got back.

An older whore named Bertha, who had hair as dark as coal, bright blue eyes and seemed more experienced than the others, leaned o'er to slide her finger along my chin, gazing into my eyes with a smile.

"You know, Jimmy, we can distract you until Oscar and Trick come back. Wouldn't that be nice?"

"Oh, no thank you—" I protested, shaking her off as politely as I could. I felt a might trapped because I didn't want to be rude to these girls, who were only trying to help me.

The thump of boots on the porch interrupted my protests, and a moment later the door opened.

Chapter Eleven

An Impromptu Celebration

I craned my neck to look past Bertha and saw Oscar come inside, the soles of his boots thumping on the floorboards.

"Oscar!" I said, placing my hands on Bertha's waist to try to nudge her aside, and realizing how I must have looked and what Oscar might be thinking.

Fuck.

"Hmph. I see you're entertainin' yourself in my absence," he said in cool tones, staring at me and the girls with narrowed eyes.

"No, I— I only came downstairs to wait for you," I said, gazing about me at the girls, who seemed to be highly amused at my situation.

"Oh, really?" Oscar frowned and stepped forward. "You seem to be mighty comfortable in the middle of all these pretty girls. I know for a fact they've been wantin' to get their hands on you."

Bertha laughed, standing up and putting her hands on her hips as she regarded Oscar and me with amusement.

"Well, you're right about that, Mr. Yates," she said.

Oscar gazed pointedly at the women gathered around me.

"Git. All of you. Off my man, if you don't mind."

'Twas exciting in a way to be claimed, though I still thought I might be in some trouble, until I noticed a quirk in the corner of Oscar's mouth as the girls sighed and retreated to spots a bit farther away.

"I swear, Oscar, I—"

"Quiet," he said, as he took off his boots and gloves and laid them on the table beside the door. He took off his hat and placed it on a hook. Then he stalked forward and climbed into my lap real careful, so he didn't put pressure on my stitches, snuggling against my chest like an affectionate cat, then kissing me on the mouth in a calculated show of possession.

I kissed him back, putting my arms around him to hold him against me, so relieved to have him back and to show that he didn't care a whit about the girls. He knew I'd never do anything to take advantage of his absence like that.

The kiss softened and sweetened, and when he pulled away, he held my lower lip between his teeth to stretch it out before he released me with a smile.

"I'm back."

"I see that."

"So, you don't gotta be worried no more."

I was a little breathless from that kiss, and I raised my brows. "Until next time."

Oscar shrugged, playing with the stubble that had grown in on my chin and seemingly quite content to show off how close we were. He turned to the girls.

"Thanks for keepin' Jimmy busy. I know you'd never think of getting too friendly with my husband."

Gasps and exclamations of surprise filled the room.

"Your *husband*?" Sally said. "How on earth did the two of you get married? I ain't never heard of such a thing!"

She gazed at the others. Some of them shrugged, and some of them smiled. Bertha gazed between us with a calculating expression.

"You ain't got rings. And I reckon 'twasn't a legal ceremony."

Oscar nodded.

"True. But, uh…" Oscar smirked and moved closer, snugging into my neck to run his tongue along my throat. I gazed at the ceiling as shocks of desire shot through me. Who ever knew I'd love to be possessed so boldly by anyone. But I did love it. "Jimmy and I are husbands in every sense of the word, if you know what I mean. And I would ask you to respect that."

Bertha gave Oscar a wink. "Of course, we will, sweetie. Your husband is safe with us, I promise."

Oscar looked doubtful, but he got off my lap as the door opened. Trick came in, looking flushed and the better for having been out in the wider world.

"Hey, Jimmy. I kept him safe for you. See?"

I smiled at her, cupping my hand o'er Oscar's shoulder where he sat in my lap.

"I do see. Thank you."

Oscar laid his cheek against my chest. "How's your injury?" he asked, glancing at my other side, which he'd been careful to avoid in all his petting. "We oughta get you back into bed."

The girls hooted and hollered and laughed until Oscar held up his hand.

"Not for that," he said. "Jimmy needs to rest."

"Uh-huh," Bertha purred. "Sure. *That's* why he needs to get to bed."

"Oscar, I don't want to go back to the room. I'm losin' my mind 'tis so borin' up there. Let's stay down here for a spell.

Oscar opened his mouth, probably to tell me to get my tail upstairs, when Miss June came into the room carrying two bottles of wine and a little cloth bag full of something.

She placed the wine bottles on the table and tossed the bag to Bertha, who caught it with a cackle. "The girls and I are taking a night off to properly celebrate your return."

"Woohoo!" Bertha exclaimed, taking what looked like a little notebook out of a drawer and sitting down near the table with the bag, which she opened and bent to sniff. "Oh! Is this the good stuff you got from River?"

"It is. I've been saving it for a special occasion. Can you roll us a few, please?"

"Of course, I can. Mmm." She frowned and gave Miss June a questioning gaze. "We got any peanuts or dried fruit to bring out? You know this is gonna make everyone want a nosh."

"I'll ask cook. I'm sure we've got something." Miss June nodded, as if 'twas the only thing missing with her plan and could be remedied with ease. "You girls work hard for me and The Angel. It's only fair to give you time off for a party."

"Is that what we're doin'?" Sally said as Gus came into the room carrying a big bottle of whiskey and some glasses.

Gus was a giant man from some faraway island in Polynesia, Miss June had said, where'er that was. His English wasn't too good, but he understood enough, and he took real good care of the folks livin' and workin' at the Angel. I knew for a fact Miss June paid him a good wage to do so, but he was also a caring, friendly fella, and I reckoned he felt a part of the family.

Someone shrieked and Bertha came and hugged Miss June, burying her face in the older woman's plump neck.

"Put the *Closed* sign on the outside of the door, Gus," Miss June said. "And latch it shut. We're havin' a party."

"A party?" Oscar said from his spot on my lap. "Truly?"

"Yes, Oscar Yates. Now why don't you stop hogging Jimmy all to yourself and come get him a glass of something?"

Oscar got off my lap and went to grab a glass that Gus had half-filled with whiskey. He brought it to me.

"Why, thank you kindly," I said. "You get one for yourself, too. You been workin' hard."

"But we ain't found Cal yet—or gotten a lead or anythin'," Oscar said, a little morosely.

"Never mind," Miss June replied. "Something will turn up. I'm sure of it."

"You feel better, Jim?" Gus asked from where he was pouring drinks.

"Yes, thank you. Much better," I said, raising my glass.

"Good. Miss June, she know how to heal. She a healer."

I nodded, smiling at Gus. "You sure don't need to tell me that. Probably neither of us would be here if she weren't."

There were a couple of girls upstairs with clients, and when the men came down, they were let outside. Then the girls showed up, surprised at the state of the parlor, with all the whores, and me, Oscar, Gus and Miss June, drinking and laughing and talking.

Trick was happy to stay in the clothes she'd worn out, which were a pair of brown trousers, suspenders and a gray-and-white striped shirt. She'd hung up her cloth jacket and she had her shirt sleeves rolled to the elbow. I'd say the look suited her pretty well. She caught me staring and raised her eyebrows, lifting her glass of whiskey to her lips and taking a sip and a swallow before speaking.

"Yes, Jimmy?"

I grinned. "Nothing. Only" — I gestured at her — "you look very comfortable *and* fetching in them things, if you don't mind my saying so."

"Well, Jimmy, turns out I ain't workin' this evenin', else I'd take you upstairs and show you what's inside these trousers and under this shirt."

Oscar, who'd gone to sit in one of the armchairs and was nursing a glass of wine with a drunk girl at his feet with her head on his knee, blinked and opened his mouth in shock.

"Trick! What did I tell you while we was ridin' and you told me you *'liked the look of my man*?' Hmm?"

Trick snorted and rolled her eyes, before dragging them from my feet to my face in a deliberate way. "You said I'd better not try anythin' or you'd talk to Miss June about having my hourly rate reduced."

"Now stop it," I told them. "You look comfortable and cool, is all. Must be nice to not wear corsets for a spell."

"Yes, that is refreshing."

"Jimmy, you should have seen her. She handled Dixie as good as you."

I raised my eyebrows and folded my arms o'er my chest.

"Is that so?"

"Well, Dixie's a mighty fine horse, and I reckon she knew I wouldn't put up with any nonsense," Trick said.

Oscar laughed. "Is that how you deal with clients, Trick? Let 'em know who's boss?"

"As a matter of fact, sometimes I do. Other times I let them think they're in charge, but really, 'tis still me guidin' things."

Oscar grinned and raised his glass to Trick, who did the same.

"I do not doubt that one bit," I said.

We drank, joked and made merry that whole entire evening, and 'twas a welcome respite and a good way to mark a return to this special place. The girls were glad to relax and not have to worry about turning tricks for one night, and Miss June seemed content to let them. Oscar enjoyed being among people again, and so did I.

We even took turns smoking paper rolls of quality hashish that Miss June had brought out in her little bag, and it gave me a cozy, floaty feeling that I did enjoy. Some of the girls started singing bawdy ditties that had me blushing and Oscar about dying with laughter. Miss June had Cook bring out platters of meat and cheese and bread and fruit for everyone, and you'd have thought we'd never eaten anything so tasty before.

But along about ten-thirty I was struggling to keep my eyes open, and I pushed myself up to standing, wincing at the pain in my side that seemed a bit worse for all the sitting and standing I'd done.

"What's wrong? You need to use the privy?" Oscar asked.

"Yep. Then I should go to bed. I'm beat," I said, and shrugged. "Even though I didn't do anythin' today."

'Twas embarrassing, but I knew 'twas because my body was using its resources to heal the sewn-up gash in my side — and because of the lingering fatigue of our journey and the shock of being injured.

"It's okay. I'll help you," Oscar said, getting up out of his chair and weaving a little.

I narrowed my eyes. "You can barely stand. I'll manage fine on my own."

"I go wit' you," Gus said, standing up from his chair and not looking like he'd had too much to drink. "I need to piss."

Gus made sure I was all right. He waited for me to finish before using the facilities himself. We walked back inside, and I found Oscar waiting for me by the stairs.

"I'll take you up."

"Oscar, I can move around on my own."

He frowned. "Excuse me? Maybe I wanna go with you? You gotta problem with that?"

"No, of course not. Come on, then."

We made our way upstairs, and I let Oscar put me to bed, since it seemed to make him happy to do it. I enjoyed the care that he took with me, and I figured 'twas good for him to be looking after me for once, since it was generally the other way around — or had been.

Oscar was a man as capable and as strong as me, and 'twould be good to remember that.

Chapter Twelve

A Trying Day

The next morning, Oscar and Trick headed out again.

My injury hardly pained me at all while moving around in bed by then, and when Miss June changed the dressing, she said I should start walking around more. So, after a small breakfast in the room, I went downstairs with a book Sally had lent me and sat in the parlor. 'Twas nice to enjoy the morning in peace and quiet, while the girls slept in upstairs.

A cathouse didn't normally come alive until after eleven or twelve, since most of the business was done in the evenings and at night. I'd woken when Oscar had gotten up, which had been early, and 'twas a good thing we'd left the party and gone to bed when we had. I reckoned the others had stayed up until the wee hours to make the most of a rare night off.

The book I was reading was *The Call of the Wild* by Jack London. 'Twas set in the Yukon and 'twas about a dog that was half St. Bernard and half wolf, and about the life he went through as a sled dog then a fighting dog. Seemed like he was gonna constantly change owners until he died or broke free of human hands.

I was enjoying it, so far. I knew the land up there, so the descriptions of the area resonated with my memories. I kind of felt like that wolf dog, Buck, in the sense that I hadn't felt I belonged in the outlaw life I was leading, but I hadn't seen a way out of it. I had felt trapped by circumstance and pitted against my fellow man, like Buck had found himself alert to the threats of the sled dogs he was forced to associate with by circumstance.

"The dominant primordial beast was strong in Buck, and under the fierce conditions of trail life it grew and grew. Yet it was a secret growth. His newborn cunning gave him poise and control. He was too busy adjusting himself to the new life to feel at ease, and not only did he not pick fights, but he avoided them whenever possible. A certain deliberateness characterized his attitude. He was not prone to rashness and precipitate action; and in the bitter hatred between him and Spitz he betrayed no impatience, shunned all offensive acts.

"On the other hand, possibly because he divined in Buck a dangerous rival, Spitz never lost an opportunity of showing his teeth. He even went out of his way to bully Buck, striving constantly to start the fight which could end only in the death of one or the other."

I disappeared into my head while reading and, before I knew it, 'twas on about noon and the girls began to come down the stairs, yawning and pulling their peignoirs about them as they came.

"Good morning," I said to young Sally, who had lent me the book I was reading.

She smiled and glanced at it.

"You enjoyin' it?"

"Yes, I am. Thank you for letting me borrow it."

"When you finish it, you're welcome to come to my room and pick out another one, Jimmy. I got a lotta books."

I wondered how a woman who could read and presumably write had ended up in a cathouse. The Angel was the most fancy and well-run establishment I had seen, but 'twas still not an ideal place of employment, unless you had nowhere else to go. Of course, simply because Sally could read and write didn't mean she hadn't fallen afoul of the random rules of an unjust society and ended up an outcast. Perhaps she'd had a child out of wedlock or had been assaulted and her reputation ruined by a man's hand. I was blessed to have been born a white man, because it seemed the world was made around our whims, and though my life hadn't been ideal and had been difficult, I reckoned that if I'd been female 'twould have been ten times worse, and I'd have likely ended up in disgrace myself and without another means of survival except what Miss June's girls had. At least she took care of them as best she could and gave them a safe place to do their business.

For 'twas a business. They provided a valuable service to men who had no other outlet, and they should be paid handsomely for that. They should be able to screen their clients, as they did here, and demand to be treated with respect.

Sally sat down in one of the armchairs and gazed out of the gauzy curtains at the street, her expression hard to figure out. She seemed sad.

"You all right?" I asked.

"Sure," she said, turning to flash me a wide smile. "Nothin' much to complain about, I guess."

I held my tongue. 'Twas true that The Angel was a far sight more comfortable than a lot of other cathouses. But 'twas still a cathouse, where Sally had to sell her body and her smile for enough money to live on.

"Where are you from, Sally? Did you grow up here in Telegraph Creek?"

She shook her head. "No, I was born in New York City," she said, and I about fell off the settee.

"New York City?" I said, amazed. "Why, that's miles and miles from here."

"Yeah," she said, leaning back in her chair and regarding me with caution, perhaps deciding whether she trusted me enough to be honest about her past. "My momma died, and my daddy brought me west, through Ohio, Indiana, Illinois, Wisconsin, Minnesota then up to Canada. I reckon he was hoping to get to Alaska, for the gold. But we only made it this far."

I shook my head. "Must have been a rough life for a girl. 'Specially a—a—"

"A colored girl?" She gave me a little smile that held all the sadness of the world. "Most of life is hard for any girl, I reckon. Harder than 'tis for any man." She blinked and looked at the floor. "Even a white woman who grows up in wealth and comfort can die in a second from birthing a child. And if you're colored, like me? Well, things is even harder. But I don't wanna think about that." She looked around her at the fine furnishings of Miss June's parlor. "Here, in this place, I'm treated the same as any of the others—and that suits me fine."

"That's good," I said.

"My momma died birthing me. And I swore I weren't never gonna have children, e'en though that's what they say all women are made for."

I thought about that for a while.

"My friend, Irene, in Port Essington? She's married, and she don't want children. I reckon 'tis a woman's choice, whether to have little ones or not—or it should be."

Sally shrugged. "Sometimes it happens, and nobody can help it."

"True enough," I said. "Where did you get your learnin', Sally? If you can read novels, you must have had some."

"Oh, my daddy was smart and educated. He made sure I learned my letters and my numbers and sent me to school when he could." She gave me a look that spoke volumes. "He was a good person, my daddy, and I loved him very much. I reckon...I reckon he wanted more for me than the life I'm leadin'. But it can't be helped."

"I'm sorry."

Sally nodded. "Well. I'm fed and I'm clothed." She gazed at her peignoir then gave me a wry smile. "In a manner of speakin'... And I'm surrounded by good people. That's gotta count for somethin'."

I thought back to my life with them outlaws.

"I reckon that counts for a whole lot, Sally."

We sat in silence for a bit, listening to the sounds of the town out of the window as people moved about. Miss June kept the doors locked until about three or four in the afternoon, so we didn't have to worry about men coming in to look for comfort as yet. 'Twas nice to sit in the quiet and talk with Sally. From the sounds of more movement and noise upstairs, I figured more of the girls would come down soon, looking for breakfast and easy conversation.

"What's it like in Port Essington, Jimmy? You and Oscar got a good setup there?"

I hadn't thought about home in a while. I'd been so anxious to get here, then concerned about my leg and now worry about Oscar. All of a sudden, the memory of our beautiful new home and the people we'd left behind made my throat ache.

"Yeah. Real good."

She smiled and raised her brows, urging me to continue.

"We got some good friends there," I said, suddenly remembering my conversation with Carson before we'd left. I hoped Carson was enough of a friend to us that he'd keep our secret. He'd said he would, and I had no reason to doubt him, except for an eerie sense that things had gone well for us and that was bound to end at some point. 'Twas the same sort of feeling I had with Oscar out in the world without me, that my life was too blessed, and I didn't deserve this happiness.

"We built a house," I said.

She raised her brows in surprise.

"You did? You and Oscar?"

I laughed. "Not only us. We had a lot of help, since we didn't know how. 'Twas a huge undertaking, but we got it done, and our house is standin' and" —I blinked, remembering how it had looked and how it had felt to be living in it—"'tis such a lovely house, Sally. I never thought I'd ever live in a house like that."

"Oh! Is it real grand?"

I laughed and shook my head. "Nah, 'tis a plain two-story house made of regular lumber. 'Tis plain, I reckon, but 'tis real cozy and has lots of space for the two of us. More'n we need, probably, but I'm plenty grateful."

Sally nodded. "I'm glad you and your beau — excuse me, your husband — are happy and able to be together. You're lucky to have found each other, I reckon. 'Specially because of the way the world is."

"I know it," I said, emotion rising in me, and unease because my young husband was out riding with Trick — and who knew where he was right now.

Just then, a couple of the other girls came down the stairs and convinced Sally to go to the kitchen with them for some breakfast.

"You want somethin', Jimmy?" Sally asked. "Cook makes cinnamon rolls sometimes for breakfast, and they're mighty tasty. I can bring you one, if you'd like?"

"Sure. That would be awful kind of you."

My appetite was coming back, and I hoped I'd be well enough to ride out with Oscar and Trick tomorrow. I'd had some willow bark tea when I'd woke this morning, and the residual pain was still manageable hours later.

The girls and I ate cinnamon rolls, and they told me stories about their business and how funny it could be at times. They said a lot of the men that came to them didn't know anything about giving a woman pleasure. Some of them didn't even know a woman could get pleasure from sex. Miss June's girls figured 'twas in the public interest for them to teach these men a thing or two, if the men wanted to learn. They said most of them did catch on, even though the main reason for their visit was their own enjoyment. The usual technique was to get them off quick one time, then show them how they could pleasure their wives, get them all randy again, convince them to practice their skills and *voila*! That girl could get her own as well. 'Twas clever and no doubt ended up delaying the departure of the man in question and earned the girl more money, as well as providing some much-needed education.

I didn't know too much about women, but I did know they could get as much pleasure from sex as a man. And I supposed, now that I thought back on it, 'twas a whore who'd taught me that. I hadn't told Miss June or her girls that I'd been in the habit of paying for these kinds of services back when I'd run with them outlaws, but I doubt they would have been surprised if I had told them. Things got to a point for most men who weren't married or involved with someone, who got tired of bringing themselves off with their own hand and were driven to search out a proper tumbling — and pay for it, if necessary.

Of course, knowing I was firmly with Oscar and not looking for anything else must have seemed like a challenge to some of them girls. I couldn't count the number of times a peignoir fell open or a girl's tits got close to my face, all through innocent means, of course. But I did catch a few sly looks, and I figured these girls didn't get to have much fun. Why shouldn't they try to tempt me?

But all I could think about was Oscar, and the way he'd looked in the peignoir and frilly panties when Cal and Trick had dressed him up for me. Cal was such a nice person — funny and sweet and witty. I only hoped we could find her and help her if she needed it. When I'd first met her, I'd thought she was a young man only dressed in women's things. But after talking to her, I learned that Cal thought of herself as a woman and dressed accordingly when she could. And the folks that knew her accepted this without argument, for they could see the truth of it, and it made sense to them.

If Cal was in some kind of trouble, we needed to find her. I only hoped that, if Oscar and Trick didn't find her today, I could help them search tomorrow.

I spent the morning reading, but after lunch I couldn't stop fretting about all three of them. 'Twas frustrating lounging about like I was. I was a man of action, and even when things were quiet, I liked to keep busy — only I knew Miss June wanted me to rest.

Along about three o'clock or so, I tracked her down.

"How are you managing, Jimmy?" she asked, when I found her sewing a skirt in the kitchen, while Cook chopped vegetables and added them to a simmering pot on the iron stovetop.

"I'm feeling much better," I said with hope and cheerfulness. "My side hardly hurts at all now. I think it's healin' up pretty good."

"I do appreciate you following my instructions."

When Miss June had examined the stitches this morning, she'd said the wound looked real good and was healing well, with no sign of infection. She'd left it open to the air and made me promise to be careful not to rub it or bang against anything. I still had to be careful, but she reckoned I was on the path to a good recovery.

"I imagine you're wanting to go riding out with Oscar and Trick tomorrow."

I blinked. This woman had a sixth sense.

"Well, yes, that is what I wanted to talk to you about."

She rested the skirt in her lap and gazed at me with some concern. "I suppose you can, but I want you to be careful. Don't get into any scrapes or over-extend yourself."

"Yes, ma'am."

"Maybe the three of you can go out for a few hours tomorrow, rather than the whole day."

"Sure. But we need to find Cal. I reckon I can manage for a bit longer than that."

She narrowed her eyes at me. "Jimmy, you want to heal and avoid an infection, or else you'll be in worse trouble and so will Cal. She needs you in fine form."

I nodded. "All right. That's true."

Miss June gave me a kind smile. "I am so grateful to you for coming. It makes me feel less anxious to have Oscar and Trick out looking for Cal, and if you're with them, why, she's sure to be found."

"I hope so."

I didn't remind Miss June that Cal could be anywhere — that she could have left the region entirely. But I reckoned Miss June was well aware of that possibility and was trying to be optimistic.

"Was it hard to leave Port Essington?" she asked.

"Yes, ma'am. We'd barely finished building our house."

"Oh, Jimmy! I'm so sorry."

"It's not your fault. We needed to be here for you and Cal. There weren't no way around that. If you hadn't sent that letter and we'd found out later that something terrible had happened, 'twould have been hard...real hard. At least, this way we can do somethin'. E'en if it comes to nought, we'll know we tried." We gazed at each other, considering all the possibilities. "Oscar might not be alive if not for you and your girls. I can never repay you for the help you gave us."

Miss June's breath hitched. "You repay me every day that you do right by Oscar and make a loving and safe home to call your own."

Emotion rose in me, and I couldn't speak, so I only nodded, blinking my eyes to hold it back. Miss June must have noticed, because she stood, put aside the skirt she was sewing and stepped forward, opening her arms to me.

In that moment, I missed both my momma and Irene so bad it hurt, and I moved easily into Miss June's embrace. She held me close and firm, and rubbed my back like I was four years old and had lost my pet dog.

I clutched her to me, squeezed my eyes shut and tried to breathe. I wasn't gonna cry. Even though I knew 'twould be all right, that I was safe here and that she wouldn't think less of me, I knew if I let the first sobs out, I'd be wailing like a babe in less than five seconds. So I held on to my dignity and control, and focused on the comfort she was giving. When I got a better grasp on myself, I pulled back, and she relaxed her grip.

"I keep thinkin' God's gonna take Oscar from me," I said, before I even knew I was gonna speak.

Miss June took hold of my arms, and she gripped them with some ferocity.

"Why on Earth would you think that?"

"Because... Because of all the terrible things I did when I was helping them outlaws." The words came out mumbled and thick, like I wasn't aiming for her to make them out.

Miss June's mouth pursed. "Did you do those things because you wanted to do them or because you were trapped into it?"

I took a deep, shuddering breath. "I did feel trapped, and like there was no other option. But maybe that ain't true, and I just didn't try hard enough to find one."

"Here, sit down," Miss June said, guiding me to the bench beside the dining table. "Now, you told me you were pretty young when you got involved in that life."

"Yes, ma'am. I was around about fourteen."

She gave me a kind look. "That's pretty young. I'm sure the men in that gang knew how desperate you must have been, and they took advantage of that trust and yearning for adventure you might have had. Right?"

I nodded. "They did. But—"

"Jimmy, you were a child. Those men had no right to involve you in their evil-doing."

"I was young enough to know right from wrong. Maybe I shouldn't have gone with them. But…they fed me, and they talked me up, said I was big for my age, and I would make a valuable addition to their 'company'. They were real nice at first."

Miss June's face showed sympathy and regret for what had happened to me. "I'm sure they were."

I huffed out a laugh. "Once they had a hold on me, they stopped bein' so nice."

"That's usually how it goes. I'm so sorry."

Some tears squeezed out of the corners of my eyes, and I brushed them away with anger and frustration.

"I wanna do right by Oscar. I hope God knows that. I want to…make up for all the awful stuff by doin' good things from now on."

Miss June smiled. "That seems like a wonderful idea."

"But every time Oscar's outta my sight for longer than I like, I worry I ain't ever gonna see him again. I can't seem to help it."

"I think that kind of worry comes with loving someone so much, and there isn't a way to avoid it. But

I don't believe for a second that God would take that man from you as a punishment for your past deeds — not for a second. Not the God I believe in, anyway."

Her words gave me comfort, and her steady hands on my arms gave me an anchor that I badly needed.

"Thank you."

"I think that what happened to you with those men might be happening to Cal right now, except only with one man. But I have this awful feeling that his intentions are less than honorable."

I looked at her with some curiosity because I wanted to hear more about this man that had stolen Cal's delicate heart and might be doing terrible things to her right now — or making *her* do terrible things.

For the first time, I saw plain on Miss June's face how truly worried she was. "Oh, Jimmy. He seemed sincere at first, and he only ever had eyes for Cal. He knew what she was, and it didn't seem to bother him at all. He seemed to like her for who she was, in fact. He treated her real well. He treated her…like she wasn't any different to the other girls, which was the only thing Cal had ever wanted from anyone."

"I see."

"He brought her flowers — and sometimes jewelry. They struck up a friendship, then he seemed to be wooing her. Cal ate that up, as you can imagine. She was in heaven. I had my doubts by that time, but I didn't let on because I didn't want to ruin it. You know?"

"I know."

"I wish I'd said something. I wish I'd cast some doubt on his intentions. But I didn't know for sure that he was going to be wrong for her. And…and maybe my gut intuition is leading me astray even now. I don't know." She put a hand to her forehead, her face a picture of concern.

"I reckon you know the world well enough to have a pretty good sense of the truth of things."

She huffed. "Sometimes I wish I didn't."

"I feel like…like Cal would have been back to check in by now, if things were goin' well. E'en if it ain't her husband's fault, maybe they're in some kind of trouble. Maybe they both need our help."

"Maybe."

"We'll find her. Oscar and me, and Trick, we'll find Cal. Don't you worry."

I didn't have a clue if we would, to be honest, but I knew she needed to hear it. And we would do our very best to find Cal and make sure she was all right.

Chapter Thirteen

A Hot Bath

'Twasn't until after nine that Oscar and Trick turned up, and I was about gone outta my mind with worry. Luckily, this time of year, the sun this far north stayed up later than it did down south, so the light was only beginning to fade when they returned.

The Angel had been busy with men needing comfort, and there were still folks going in and out, so I sat in a corner of the front parlor and tried to be inconspicuous while I waited for my man and his friend. 'Twas exhausting to work up hope every time the door opened, when it ended up being someone else. The girls kept me company and tried to distract me while they showed themselves off to the men who turned up and, one by one, they disappeared upstairs. 'Twould go on like this most of the evening and night until Miss June shooed everyone out at three o'clock in the morning and locked the doors.

I'd said she ran a tight ship, and I meant it. She knew her girls needed food and rest as much as they needed their pay, and it kept them healthy and looking fetching, so 'twas a business investment, really, as much as 'twas a kindness. She kept those doors locked to folks coming in until three in the afternoon, so she and the girls had twelve hours of uninterrupted relaxing time. The other thing that made The Angel stand out among most of the cathouses I'd frequented up in Dawson City was that she didn't sell booze or cheap dope as part of her business. She didn't e'en let people in that were too far gone with the whiskey. The men knew that they had to be sober and respectful if they wanted to partake of what was on offer here, and I reckoned not too many of them complained, because the state of the place was so clean and welcoming and Miss June's rules were fair, though they were strict.

Despite my worry, I had almost nodded off when the front door burst open and gales of drunken laughter regaled me. The last person I expected to see was Oscar, with his arm around Trick as she helped him inside and pushed him toward me with a wicked, sober smile.

"I brought your man home, Jimmy."

"Jimmy!" Oscar slurred as he almost tripped o'er his big feet on his way to me.

I blinked in surprise and stood to catch him in my arms before he brained himself on the floor.

"What the hell? Why're you drunk?"

He gave me a silly smile and smooched his lips as if he expected a kiss. Even as drunk as a skunk, he felt good and solid in my arms, and I was glad to have him with me. I looked at Trick for an explanation.

"Oh, he's all right. I reckon he's overactin' to get your sympathy."

Oscar shot her a deadly look. "You be quiet."

Trick rolled her eyes.

"Weren't you two supposed to be lookin' for Cal? I suppose you might find her in a saloon, but that don't seem so likely."

Trick took off her hat and loosed her long honey-blond hair. It fell in charming golden waves past her shoulders. She shook it out and ran her fingers through it, then put her hat back on top of her head and winked at me. I found her almost as fetching as Oscar, to be honest, in the way that she looked rough and sweet at the same time.

"Oh, well, we *were* lookin' for Cal, then some mad dog went to attack a woman and her young uns, and Oscar took one look and fired his revolver and shot it dead. He's a goddamn hero, Jimmy," she said. "Seemed the whole town wanted to buy him a drink."

Of all the things I might have expected Trick to say, that was not any of them. I swiveled to gape at Oscar, who had the biggest smile on his face as he gazed up at me.

"You taught me good, Jimmy. I got him in one shot," he said, pushing out of my hold so's he could pretend to aim an invisible revolver at the window and shoot it. He made the sound of a gunshot then blew pretend smoke from his pretend gun.

I stared at him for a long moment, hardly believing what Trick had said. Only I *could* believe it, and when I pictured it, I felt nothing but pride for my sweet boy.

My man.

My *husband*.

"You did?"

"Yep."

I crossed my arms and looked him up and down.

"And now you're drunk off your tree—or are you only pretendin'?"

He grinned. "Well, I only wanted you to catch me, you see," Oscar said, sidling up to me and leaning in.

"I see."

Then his eyes went wide, and he jerked back, gripping my arms with excitement.

"Oh, but Jimmy, Jimmy, Jimmy!"

I tried not to laugh at his sudden urgency.

"Somebody saw Cal!"

All tendency toward laughter fled as my chin dropped, and I glanced at Trick for confirmation of this.

"'Tis true. We got a lead, finally," she said.

She walked o'er to us, pointedly ignoring some interest from a few of the men in the parlor, and sat down, crossing one trousered leg atop the other.

"If we hadn't been at the saloon, we might not have heard about it. We was talkin' about Cal and how we needed to find her, and some rough-lookin' fella said he'd been in Agnes Hill the week before and met a woman named Cal, who was buyin' some bread and milk."

"How far away is that?" I asked.

"Not far," Trick said. "But 'tis in the other direction from where we were lookin', so 'tis a good thing we heard of it."

"If it *is* Cal and not somebody else," I said, ever the steady observer.

Oscar gave me a look. "It is. I know 'tis."

"How do you know?"

"Just a feelin' in my heart."

We gazed at each other, and I knew he felt it and mayhap he was right. I sure hoped so.

I gave a quick nod.

"Miss June says I can ride out with you and Trick tomorrow, if I'm careful of my injury."

Oscar's face lit up. "Truly? Then you can come with us to Agnes Hill, and we'll see if we can find her!"

I gazed at my beautiful boy, considering. "Did you really kill a mad dog with one shot?"

Oscar shifted his shoulders back and straightened up, like a soldier. "I did. You taught me real well."

Trick uncrossed her legs and leaned forward, placing her elbows on her knees like a regular cowpoke. "You shoulda seen it, Jimmy. He was like some kinda sharpshooter or somethin'. I had my gun at the ready, fully expectin' him to miss. But he didn't." She smiled. "The townsfolk were pure amazed."

"I reckon," I said, smiling at Oscar and imagining the scene.

I often had to remind myself that Oscar was a full-grown man and could take care of himself, e'en though I liked to take care of him, and he liked me to, at least in some ways.

"I'm sure glad you're back. I worry when I'm not with you."

"I know you do. I ain't never had someone like that. My parents never cared much when I'd go out on my own, then they weren't there to care at all."

We gazed at each other with intense emotion until Trick let out a snort.

"Jimmy, you'd better get that kid upstairs. He looks like he's about to explode."

Oscar gave Trick a condescending glance.

"Well, wouldn't you?" Oscar said, gesturing to me. "Look at him."

Then Oscar stepped back and let his gaze drift down my body and back up, while I tried to control my reaction to that plain assessment.

"Hmph. He ain't really my type," Trick commented.

Oscar's eyes flew wide. "Not your —"

I laughed. "See? Maybe you're the only one that wants me. I guess I'm lucky I found you."

"Well, you are lucky. But I ain't even gonna believe what Trick says. I've caught her lookin' at you."

Trick snorted in a way that made me wonder if Oscar was right. She had offered her services to me when I'd first arrived at The Angel, when I'd been distracted with worry o'er Oscar's injury. Then again, that was her job.

"I mean, I don't normally go after men who prefer to bed other men. I ain't much into sufferin' the pains of rejection again and again." She cocked her head, eying one of the men talking to Sally by the window. "Plus, I've got my hands full with the men who give me cash. I ain't givin' it away for free these days."

Oscar laughed, and I smiled.

"Although, I'm enjoyin' the break, to tell you the truth. 'Tis nice to get out of corsets for a bit." She straightened the fold of her sleeve where it rested below her elbow and brushed a bit of dirt off the knee of her trousers.

I liked seeing her in them things. They suited her, and since I had fallen for Oscar and met Clarence and Irene, I had an appreciation for people who didn't stick to the normal ways of their sex. It made Trick more interesting to me. And when she dressed this way, it seemed to bring out all her grit and confidence.

"Jimmy?" Oscar said, pressing against my arm and gazing at me all mooney-eyed.

"Yeah?"

"I reckon I could use a bath."

I looked Oscar o'er. His clothes were dark with dirt and sweat, and his hair was plastered to his forehead and neck from wearing his hat all day. He smelled funky, too, but I didn't care much about that. Still, I made a face.

"I reckon that's true. Why don't you head on upstairs, and I'll let Miss June know we'd like a tub of hot water brought up."

"Would you, Jimmy?"

"For you? A course."

"Well, 'tis more for you than me, you know. Since I'm gonna be all over you tonight, you'll want me to be clean."

* * * *

Sure enough, Miss June had two of the girls bring a tub of hot water up for Oscar. He stripped off his soiled clothes and stepped into it while I reclined on the bed and watched him.

"Oh, it feels so good. 'Tis so warm." Oscar groaned as he sank down into it. "Gosh, I'm gonna stay in this bath all night."

I smiled, snaking my hand into my pants and wrapping my fingers around my cock. I was randy as a rooster, and I was hoping for some sweet relief. I was feeling good, and I needed to take care of my husband and look after myself in the process.

"You'll get awful cold and lonely, then." My breath hitched as I stroked back and forth and stared at Oscar's bare back and shoulders.

He turned his head and fixed his gaze on my trousers where my hand was concealed.

"Are you — ? Jimmy, are you playin' with yourself?"

"Uh-huh."

"Well." Oscar seemed taken aback. "You're just gonna sit there and play with yourself and watch me?"

"Uh-huh," I murmured, feeling relaxed and excited at the same time. "Seems like a good idea."

"You better not spend, Jimmy. I've gone days without havin' you inside me, and I don't care whether you put it in my mouth or my ass, but it better be good and hard."

I laughed at how indignant he sounded, like I had the last piece of cake or pie, and he wanted it.

"Settle down. I ain't gonna spend."

"You sure?"

I shrugged, feeling lazy and aroused – and not particularly caring of what happened.

"If I do, you'll only have to get me all hot and bothered again."

"Wait. Don't you dare waste that stand on your own hand, you hear me?" Oscar said, swooshing himself down into the water to rinse, then surging up and grabbing the towel from the floor.

Chapter Fourteen

Shenanigans

"Oscar, you ain't rinsed," I said. My words sounded breathless and broken as he rose from that water like a vision from the depths sent to temp me to my doom.

"So?" he said, stepping onto the colorful rope mat and swiping the linen towel o'er himself with undue haste. "What's a little bit of soap gonna do? I'm cleaner than I was, that's for certain."

I attempted a laugh but was too caught up in the desire surging through me as I watched him and continued to attend to myself in direct defiance of him. It amused me when Oscar got bossy, since I was the one usually telling *him* what to do.

He gave his hair—which he *had* rinsed, thank goodness—a shake and a rough drying with the towel, then threw the damp cloth aside and stalked to the bed, an angry look on his face that only made me more lost to him.

He crawled onto the mattress and braced himself o'er me, giving me a meaningful stare then taking the sheet in his hand and pulling it down to expose me. His gaze slid o'er the stitches in my healing injury as I stopped moving. He dropped the sheet below my knees and knocked my hand away, then bent to take me into his mouth with a speed and efficiency I wasn't prepared for.

My head fell back against the wall as my cock was engulfed in warmth and wetness.

"Christ," I gasped.

Oscar moaned, sending vibrations through my dick as my need increased and I thrust against him. He pinned me with his elbows on my hips, careful to avoid my stitches, and went at me even harder, the sounds of slurping and whimpering and heavy breathing the only noises in the room.

It didn't take long. I'd been anxious and frustrated all day, and watching him bathe and emerge like a sea-god from that tub had left me wild for him.

I shouted as I emptied down his throat, his technique so practiced and attuned that it always left me defeated, in the very best of ways. My gasps rang out as I rode the delicious waves of a much-needed release, and Oscar made choking noises as I emptied into his throat.

He let me slide out then proceeded to tease and torment my shrinking, sensitive cock as I lay helpless on the bed, the sheets twisted and my protests unheeded.

He grabbed my wrists and held me still as he nipped and sucked my balls and tickled my over-sensitive cock. Even still, remnants of my pleasure spiked and combined with the pain as I let him have his way with me.

Finally, he tired of this game and surged forward, taking my mouth with his and sliding his lips o'er mine so that I tasted my spend on him, still careful to avoid my healing injury.

I broke from the kiss and took his face between my palms, my gaze raking o'er his swollen lips and bright dark eyes.

"Did you really kill that dog with one shot?"

"Yes, sir, I did. Felt bad, but there weren't nothin' else anyone could have done. That thing was out for blood, I reckon. Must have been diseased — or so badly treated it lost its mind."

"Well, I'm real proud of you, and that's a fact."

Oscar seemed to go all soft at my praise, but he surged forward and kissed me again, desperate and hard and needing some relief of his own. He pressed his cock against my hip as he surveyed me with unbridled hunger.

"What do you want, pretty boy?" I said in a low voice, as an urgent need rose in me. I grasped the globes of his ass in my hands and pulled them apart, making him squeak in surprise and moan with abandon.

"I wanna ride you, Jimmy."

"What?"

He smiled a devious smile and glanced down at my cock. I could feel that 'twas already swelling with renewed hunger. The injury from my fall had not dimmed my ability to get hard for this man, that was certain.

"Well, you oughtn't to strain yourself if you wanna ride out with us tomorrow. So, I figure, once you got your stand back, I'll get onto you and do all the work." He grinned wider. "Then you can watch me."

"Okay."

"Okay?" he laughed, raising his eyebrows. "That's all you got to say?"

"No. I mean, I would like that"—I swallowed thickly, picturing it—"very much."

He flashed me a sly look. "Okay. But first I gotta get you hard again, don't I?"

"Won't take long, I reckon. I'm already halfway there."

"Good," he said, and shuffled back on me, taking my cock in his hands and bending down to use his mouth again.

I groaned as I watched this charming, wild boy, who had killed a mad dog with one shot, treat my cock like 'twas the most precious thing in all the world, teasing it and licking it, bringing it to a solid stand in a matter of moments. The sight of it did as much for me as the touch. Oscar crouched on the sheets, his ass in the air, swaying wantonly back and forth like he was imagining what 'twould feel like to have my cock inside him.

"You know what would really get me goin' again, you naughty thing?" I said, gazing down upon the top of his head as his gaze flicked up to mine and held it. "You, ass up, o'er my knee."

Oscar groaned, then let my cock slide from his mouth, as he rutted against the mattress.

"But, Jimmy," he murmured, his lips shiny with spittle, "what do I gotta get punished for?"

"Oh, I'm sure I can think of somethin'."

"Fine," he said, pretending to be put upon, as if the thought of it was so trying and he was doing me a favor by cooperating, when I could tell by the way his cheeks pinked and his breathing quickened that he wanted that spanking more'n anything.

"O'er my lap, then. Hurry up," I said, with a sternness I knew he'd like.

"Yes, sir," Oscar breathed out. He gave my cock a final lick and climbed atop me, arranging himself on hands and knees above my lap. "I ain't gonna lie on you, 'cause that might bother your healin', so you'll have to figure it out like this," he said, gazing at me with innocence as my hand went to his smooth, plump bottom and cupped it, my breathing speeding up with the anticipation of it.

"All right. I can work with it."

I played my fingers along his cleft, sliding them and brushing the tips o'er his hole as he shuddered and moaned.

"Come on, Jimmy," he groaned, licking his lips.

"I'm gonna take my time with you, Oscar," I murmured. "We got all night."

"All night! Ain't we gonna get some sleep?"

I sighed, slipping my hand under him to play with his stand as he slitted his eyes and groaned again.

"I suppose we might…but not for a while," I said, giving him a light slap to start things off.

Oscar closed his eyes and moaned. "Harder."

I slapped his ass again.

"Oh fuck. Like that. Oh, Jimmy."

I loved him this way — wanton and wild. His face went through so many emotions as I pinked his ass up good that I sent another prayer of thanks to whatever deity had blessed me.

"You're my naughty boy, ain't you? You like to tease me past the point of tolerance…"

"I do. I love to tease you…so much."

His words were punctuated by the sound of my palm making contact with his ass, and his breath hitched with each spank, making him sound broken and desperate. I grabbed the jar of saddle grease from the side table where I had put it when Oscar had gone into the bath.

"All right, stay still. I need to get you ready."

"Oh!" he gasped, panting as he held himself o'er me. My cock was at a full stand again.

I scooped some grease with two fingers and slid them into Oscar's crack, finding the wrinkled skin of his hole and teasing him as I prepared him. Oscar, randy and wanting, arched his back and pressed up against my touch.

"I'm gonna finger you first, 'cause I know you like that."

"I do. I *do* like it," Oscar panted, turning his head to give me a half-lidded glance. He was gone already, into that place where he was nothing but need and wantin' — and a slave to whatever I told him to do.

I put my dry hand on his shoulder to stop him swaying.

"Be still now."

"Yes, sir."

"And don't yell out. We don't want the rest of the place to know what I'm doin' to you."

That made him hitch his breath. I knew the thought of others being close by would make him crazy. Having to obey me and try to be quiet when he was out of his mind with desire was something Oscar enjoyed.

I watched his face as I breached him with slippery fingers, pushing all the way inside in one smooth motion. His eyes flew wide as he gasped then uttered a low, soft moan.

A surge of lust caused my cock to thicken even more as Oscar reacted to the invasion. As I pushed my thick fingers in and out of him, brushing them against that special spot, Oscar closed his eyes and dropped his head onto his arms, keeping his ass in the air and giving himself up to me.

"Good boy," I said. The praise caused a wail to come from Oscar. "Shhh, be still. I don't wanna have to tell you again."

"Oh…God. Yes, sir."

His words were so quiet. He didn't say anything else as I fucked him with my two fingers, then added another and worked him until he could barely handle it.

"Jimmy…Jimmy…" he pleaded, his cheeks ruddy and his drying hair all tossed about.

"You wanna ride me now?" I asked.

"Yes. Yes!"

I slipped my fingers out of his ass and helped him to move so that he was positioned o'er my stand.

"You need help, or are you gonna do it all, you talented strumpet?" I said, giving him a look that said I knew he could fuck me all by himself and probably wanted to.

He gasped at the word 'strumpet', and I could tell he liked me calling him that.

"I'll do it. Give me some of that grease."

I grinned and slapped two fingers of grease into his outstretched hand, wiping them into his palm. He reached behind him and found my cock, slicking me up good before spreading his cheeks and lining up his greedy hole.

I almost died as he rubbed the tip of my cock against his pucker, back and forth, to tease the muscle into opening for me. When the head of my cock slipped in, I grabbed his hips to keep him still while I got used to it, or 'twould have been done before it started.

He groaned and pushed down, past the resistance of my grip as he sank onto me with the ease of a well-trained whore. The thought gave me a twinge of guilt, because Oscar wasn't a whore, and I'd never truly think of him that way, except he was so at ease with everything and skilled at it that I was the luckiest man on this earth.

"Oscar," I said, as he moved on my poor, desperate cock. "Oscar!"

He glanced at me, as if he knew what I was begging for but didn't give a hot damn. He was gonna get what he came for, whether I lost control or not, so I simply held on for dear life.

The sight of him was enough to tip me o'er, and I had to grit my teeth to avoid it. Whenever he mounted me, something took him—a wild, crazed need to subdue me, I supposed—and it always worked. I was helpless under his assault.

I lay there, the muscles in my legs clenching with the effort to hold back. The muscles near my injury throbbed but 'twas worth it and 'twas nothing compared to the way my cock felt as Oscar moved, his body twisting and sliding back and forth, up and down, until my vision went hazy, and I got so close I could taste it.

I wrapped my hand, still slick with grease, around his bobbing cock and started to stroke him, determined to make him come before I lost my own battle.

"Now be a good boy," I panted, a whimper escaping, "and come for me."

Oscar's dark-eyed gaze met mine as I worked him. His pace increased, and he opened his mouth with a cry as his cock shot spurts of white onto my chest. My climax took me at that moment, and I held him still as I emptied into him, my head falling back against the wall and the most primal, satisfied sound coming out of me.

It didn't stop, the sound or the climax, for several moments, and the intense waves of pleasure were worth all the hardships of the past few days. Oscar was safe, spent and in my arms—and that was all that mattered.

Chapter Fifteen

Caliope

Despite our enthusiastic coupling, I barely noticed my injury on waking in the morning, which was very promising as I needed to pass inspection by Miss June before I was 'permitted' to ride out. Problem was, if she tried to forbid me and told me I needed to stay at The Angel for another day, I'd have to tell her that, with all due respect — and I had a lot of respect for Miss June — I wasn't prepared to sit on my ass again while Oscar and Trick went out together.

It didn't come to that.

After we got some breakfast — in the kitchen this time — Miss June gave the stitches a look o'er and declared me fit to ride. I was so happy that I hugged her.

"I know it's been a rough few days, Jimmy, but you've been a good patient."

"Thank you for the excellent care, Miss June."

"Now, you promise to rest when you can, although the wound is healing up real nice. I'll take the stitches out next week."

Now that I was well enough to go, I half expected Miss June to keep Trick back. But Trick was waiting for us in the stables in her boots and trousers and shirt, just the same.

"Well, well, well," I said, looking her over. "I get to ride out with the infamous Trick, do I?"

"Infamous? What does that mean?" Oscar said, and I reckoned Trick wanted to know, as well, since she looked at me with curiosity.

"It means she's known for committing some questionable and immoral acts," I said, wagging my eyebrows.

Trick grinned and nodded. "Yes, sir. That's me, all right." She touched the brim of her hat and took a bow.

Oscar doubled o'er laughing.

"That really what it means, Jimmy?"

"Well, usually 'tis referrin' to violence or some such thing. But I suppose there's a few people would think what Trick gets up to with her clients was plenty wicked."

Trick gave me a wink. "I reckon you don't know the half of it."

Oscar's eyes bugged out of his head.

"What the hell does that mean?" I asked.

"It means, Jimmy Downing, that I got me a trunk of treasures upstairs that would blow your damn mind."

"Fuck," Oscar exclaimed. "Like what?"

"Well, now, that's my secret. If you ask nice, I could show you sometime."

I rolled my eyes. "Oh, Christ. That's all he needs."

Trick glanced at me as she adjusted the length of her stirrup and patted her horse's brown neck. "Oh, there's some things in there for you, too, Jimmy, that I reckon you'll find to be very, very interestin'." She cocked her head, gazing at Oscar with contemplation. "And practical."

My cheeks flushed. I wondered what she had in that treasure chest. But 'twas no matter at the moment, because we needed to go.

"Where did you get another horse?"

"This is Juniper, Gus's mustang mare. I've ridden her before, on occasion. She's a tough old girl, but I can manage her."

As we rode out of the stables, clouds had gathered, and it looked like we might get some rain. But after a little while, the sun broke through and shone its warmth down on us. I was glad that riding didn't seem to strain my injury. 'Twas nice to be outside and with Oscar and Trick, riding through the countryside with the mountains looming on all sides. We were used to feeling small in the wilderness of northern BC, and in some ways, those mountains made me feel safe and protected.

The town of Agnes Hill was about nine miles south of Telegraph Creek. 'Twas a little village on the edge of where the creek widened and became a more significant waterway. 'Twas a charming place, about the same size as Port Essington and on the water, so it made me ache for home.

"Do you think Cal lives in the town? Or maybe has a place nearby?" I asked.

"The fella we spoke to said she was dressed like a farm wife, so I figure she lives out in the country nearby," Oscar said.

"That's right. Although we can perhaps ask some of the folks in town if they've seen her. And that's assuming it is the right person."

We tethered the horses outside the mercantile and spent the better part of an hour on foot, asking anyone we came in contact with if they'd seen or heard of a person named Cal who lived anywhere close. Nobody that we spoke to had heard of or seen her, so in the end we decided to head out in one direction and start visiting the local homesteads. The farms were scattered about, none within easy sight of one another. We only managed to cover a small area that first day and went back to The Angel with no new leads.

The following two days passed in a similar fashion with no progress. 'Twas disheartening and exhausting, but, on the bright side, I was with my husband and his very entertaining friend. Trick turned out to be a highly amusing companion. Her off-color remarks and ribald statements made the time pass quickly, and she had us in absolute stitches on more than one occasion.

At the end of that first day, my wound was aching a bit, but by the third day, it seemed to stop complaining, and my muscles were getting used to strenuous activity again. Miss June said she would take out the stitches on Sunday, when we'd promised to take a break from our searching, whether we'd found Cal or not.

'Twas while I was waiting outside the saloon in Agnes Hill for Trick and Oscar, enjoying the morning sunshine on my third afternoon out, when I saw a tall woman in a rough brown skirt and a flowery blouse, with a wide hat pulled low o'er her eyes, walking toward the dry goods store, that something made me take notice. I don't know if 'twas the body type or the gait, but something screamed out to me that this was Cal — or that it might be.

I quick left the stoop in front of the saloon and paced toward the woman. When I got close enough, I tapped her on the shoulder. She started for sure, but instead of stopping and addressing me, she tucked her head to her chest and walked faster, holding her skirts so I could see her black-buttoned shoes making dust in the dirt of the street.

"Cal?" I said.

The woman stopped then and waited, not looking my way, as if deciding whether to acknowledge my address.

"It's Jimmy," I said, in a kind voice, as she seemed a bit spooked and like she didn't want no attention from anyone.

The woman straightened and squared her shoulders, tipped her hat back and turned.

I recognized Cal's familiar face, with its shadow of stubble, though it seemed she'd tried to hide that with subtle face paint, and I couldn't blame her. If she was hoping to pass as female to the general public, she needed to cover up some of the most obvious disparities.

"Cal! We been lookin' all o'er for you!"

I moved toward her, but she took a step back and regarded me with distrust and a deep-seated wariness, so I stopped and stood there.

"Jimmy? Is it—? Is it you? Truly?" Cal's voice quavered as she looked me up and down and squinted as if she were trying to see through some sort of fog. I held myself back, because the last thing I wanted was to scare her off. Sure, we used to be friends, but a lot of time had passed.

"In the flesh and all the way from Port Essington." I smiled like that was no big deal. "Miss June is awful worried about you, Cal."

"Is Oscar with you?"

"He's in the saloon with Trick. We're all out here lookin' for you."

"My goodness," Cal said, as if she couldn't quite believe it.

She looked...well, not that good, if I were being honest. Her skin was pale and patchy, and the features of her face were gaunt, as if she wasn't eating well.

"Are you all right?" I asked.

She stared at me for a long moment, then smiled and said, "Sure, I am. Why?"

The smile didn't reach her eyes. 'Twas a good act, but that's what it was. Still, I wasn't about to call her out about it. Not yet, anyway.

"Miss June says you left The Angel to get married. Did you? Get married, I mean?"

Cal glanced away, then quick as anything returned her gaze to mine and kept that stilted smile on her face. "Yes, sir, I did. I'm a married woman now."

Her voice wobbled and her forehead creased. She was about to say something else when a whoop interrupted us and Trick burst upon the two of us like a rogue wave.

"Cal! Oh, Cal, 'tis you!" Trick yelled as she ran up to Cal and took her in a hearty hug, lifting her from the ground.

Cal made a noise of terror, and I put a hand to Trick's arm.

"Careful there. You'll spook her," I said.

I didn't know what was wrong with Cal—whether 'twas simply a need to be inconspicuous and we were calling all this attention, or whether 'twas something more worrying.

Oscar came up and hugged Cal next, and he was a mite gentler, and Cal seemed to relax and let him hold her for a brief moment before pulling gently away.

"I'm so glad we found you," Oscar said.

"I've been busy, that's all. My...husband keeps me very busy," Cal said, her voice trembling and her gaze darting around.

"Oh, I see," Oscar said with an implied meaning, and Trick said, "My, my, my, does he?"

Cal huffed a nervous laugh. "Well, yes, he does. He's...he's a beast between the sheets."

Trick and Oscar laughed, and I smiled. But there was something not right here, and I aimed to figure it out.

"Where are you livin' now?" I asked.

Cal shrugged. "Oh, out of town a ways...on Albert's farm. We've got twenty acres. And fruit trees. And the house is lovely, so big. Takes my breath away every time I see it!"

"Really?" Oscar said. "We got a house now, too, Jimmy and me. In Port Essington."

"That's good to hear."

"Yep. My uncle had passed, but he'd left his land, and we built a house on it — with a sitting room and two bedrooms."

I glowed at how proud Oscar sounded of the house we'd built with help from our friends. I missed it with a fierceness that surprised me.

"How come you ain't been to see Miss June, Cal? She said you promised to go see her and let her know how you was gettin' on," I asked, giving Cal what I hoped was a look of expectation.

"Oh, I meant to. I kept meaning to. We're so busy, you know. Not only with *that*," she said, at the ribald look Trick gave her. "With practical stuff, too. We got some farmhands we need to feed, and I help with all the field work. 'Tis tiring being a farmer's wife, but I wouldn't trade it for the world."

I watched Oscar as he listened to Cal, then met his gaze when he turned to me. I shrugged. Who was I to say 'twasn't so — or he or Trick neither. If Cal was lying — and part of me figured she was, or at the very least she was pretending everything was all right when 'twasn't. But there was nothing we could do until she decided to trust us with the truth of it. We just had to let her know we cared about her, and we were here if she needed us.

"Won't you come to the saloon for a minute?" Oscar said, "We'll get you a drink and a bite to eat."

"Oh, no thank you," Cal said, turning in the other direction. "I need to go. Albert worries when I'm gone too long."

"Cal," Trick said, "we'd love to meet your husband and see your home. Won't you have us over? You don't gotta feed us or nothin'. We only want to see this fine house and land of yours." Trick's gaze was calculating, and I knew she was trying to figure things out, like I was.

"Oh, well, I...I have to ask him if that's all right."

"You do?"

Cal laughed, and it sounded on the verge of hysterical. "Oh, he'll say yes, I'm sure. But I need to make sure he knows to expect you. He's very private, my Albert. He don't like to be with other folks too much."

That there gave me warning bells in my head. I supposed it could be true that he was simply a loner who loved Cal dearly and owned a big house and fine land—but I had my doubts.

"Anyway, 'twas lovely to see you all," Cal said, gathering her skirts again and heading away from us and the dry goods store. "I have to go. Maybe I'll see you again when you're in town... Say hello to Miss June, tell her I'm fine and she don't need to worry no more," Cal's voice broke on those last words and she turned away, hastening her step, then disappeared behind some buildings.

The three of us exchanged glances, in which our unease and unwillingness to accept what Cal had told us, was evident.

"Do you think she was lyin'?" Oscar asked.

Trick spat in the dirt. "Sure, she was. I don't think everythin's fine at all." She scuffed her boot in the dirt and handed me the reins of her horse. "I'm goin' after her."

"I don't think that's a good idea," I said, worried we might scare Cal off and she'd hide herself away even more than she already was. "I know you want to find out what's what, but I think we need to give Cal the benefit of the doubt. 'Tis possible she was telling the truth."

"I wanna see where she goes, so's we can find her another time," Trick said, stepping away from us. "I promise I won't get close. I'll only see what direction she takes when she heads away from town."

"Fine," I said. "Don't let her see you. She's bein' cagey, and I don't know why. She must have a good reason."

Trick bobbed her head once and walked in the direction Cal had taken.

"We ain't gonna just go back to The Angel, are we?" Oscar asked, his expression showing concern.

"Well, we need to give Miss June the message from Cal and see what she makes of it. At least we found her. We know she lives around here someplace."

"Sure, but where?"

"She was on foot, so it can't be too far. Trick'll find out the general area and we'll ride out there tomorrow, see what we can see.

"All right."

After about ten minutes, Trick rounded the corner of a building and came toward us.

"Did she see you?" Oscar asked.

"Nope. I said I'd be careful."

"So?" I asked.

"She went East, toward Wildman's Creek." Trick shrugged. "I could have followed her all the way home."

"I know. But let's give her the respect of believin' her for now. Tomorrow, we'll start searching, and if we find her and everything's as she says, then perfect."

"And if it ain't?" Oscar said.

I shrugged and exchanged a look with Trick.

"Then we'll have to figure out what needs to be done," I said. "If Cal is lying, I'm sure 'tis not because she wants to. 'Tis because she feels she has to, and I wanna know why."

* * * *

Miss June was thrilled to hear we'd found Cal, but she was as concerned as we were, when we described how Cal had been acting and what she'd told us.

"I don't like this one bit," she said. "It doesn't seem like Cal at all. I wonder if that man who took her and married her is keeping her under his thumb. Especially since he knows Cal has a secret to keep, it gives him something to manipulate her with. I believe that if Cal was free to do as she pleased, she'd have come and paid us a visit. And she would have been happier to see the three of you, and maybe even invited you over to show you her *big house and fine property*. Hmph. I don't like this at all."

"Me neither," Trick said. "Doesn't seem right."

Miss June glanced at me. "How are you feeling, Jimmy?"

"Fine. You got magic hands, Miss June."

"You're not the first person to tell me that, Jimmy."

Oscar got her meaning and whooped a laugh, slapping me on the back. "Now, now, Jimmy. Don't you go seducing Miss June. You got your hands full already."

'Twas a good break from the serious events of the day, and we laughed.

"Well, you rest now, Jimmy," she said, "since you're back early. And tomorrow the three of you can ride out and see if you can find Cal's homestead—maybe have a talk with Mr. Webster."

I frowned. "That her husband? She mentioned someone named Albert."

Trick snorted. "Yeah, that's her husband. I told her not to trust the bastard."

"You did?" Oscar said. "Why?"

Trick shrugged. "Had a feeling, that's all. He was awful nice to Cal when he was purchasing her services. A little too nice, you know? I had my suspicions."

Miss June sighed and put a hand to Trick's shoulder. "As did I. And I told her to be careful, that sometimes the things men say to a woman when they want something aren't entirely sincere."

"I think," Trick said, playing with the brim of the hat she held in her hand, "she was so happy to have a man who accepted her the way she was, bein' that she had...you know, those parts that a woman ain't supposed to have."

"No, he didn't mind that. Paid for the pleasure many times," Miss June said, her eyebrow arched. "But Cal was in control of it, and she could have denied him. I wonder if, as soon as she left here, that man took her over."

Trick nodded. "And now he's got Cal all to himself, he don't have to pay for it no more, and he can hold that secret over her to keep her loyal. 'Twas a suspicious business all along, if you ask me."

Miss June looked miserable. "But we did what we could, didn't we? We couldn't have forbidden Cal to take a chance at marriage and a respectable life."

"No, that's a fact. She'd have gone anyway and never spoken to us again."

They exchanged a glance and Trick said, "Though she ain't speakin' to us now. Didn't sound like she was gonna come by."

"It almost seemed like she was more upset to see us than anythin' else—and that she would rather not have," I said.

"Which don't make any sense at all," Oscar stated. "We were her friends, and we'd come all this way to see that she was all right. If she was really all right, wouldn't she have laughed, apologized for causing us all that trouble and come back with us to see Miss June?"

"I reckon that would have made more sense."

"Something's not right about this," Trick said. "And I aim to find out what. We ain't gonna give up on Cal, not now. I reckon she's in some kind of trouble and needs our help, but she's too scared or ashamed to ask for it."

Chapter Sixteen

A Strange Discovery

The next day we were even more eager to head out. We were convinced there was something up with Cal, and we wanted to know what it was. Her behavior had been suspicious and uncharacteristic.

Trick came up with a plan. She knew the area a little, whereas Oscar and I were less familiar with the surroundings.

"Let's head out toward Wildman's Creek and start there. There's bound to be some homesteads in that area, though I doubt there are any grand ones. From what I know, 'tis where a lot of poorer folks are set up as best they can. If we don't find Cal's place, we'll ride out along the road where the wealthier folks live. Maybe Cal was tellin' the truth, and she lives in a fine home with a loving husband." Trick sounded doubtful.

"All right," I said.

I watched as Oscar swung up on his horse and brought Onyx around to face the direction we wanted to go. He had good form, and the two of them seemed right out of a horseman's catalogue. He had gained in confidence, and it looked real good on him. 'Twas a fact that I might have coddled him in the past, because we both enjoyed it in the sheets. But maybe 'twas time I treated him like a man when we were in public. That had been a difficult thing to wrap my head around back in Port Essington, but 'twas getting easier. Oscar was clever and capable, and I had a mind to remember that.

"What?" Oscar said, noticing the way I was watching him. "You're lookin' at me all queer."

Trick glanced my way as I smiled and shook my head.

"Simply admiring the view is all. You're a handsome fucker, you know."

"Aww, shucks," he said, acting shy. But there wasn't anything at all bashful in the look he threw me.

"Now, now," I said, bringing Dixie alongside Oscar and Onyx. "Don't get me all worked up when we got a long day of riding and searching ahead of us. I need to concentrate," I said.

"You started it. Maybe keep your eyes on your reins and not my ass," Oscar said, and Trick guffawed.

"Yeah, Jimmy. Jeez," she said. "Try to control yourself now."

I grinned, and we headed out toward Wildman's Creek with hope and humor. The good feelings only lasted as long as it took to reach the first broken-down homestead.

"I told you," Trick said, pulling Gus's horse up and nodding toward a woman who was hooking a tired old mule to a plow, in clothes that had seen better days. "This ain't the finest area. Lotta folks struggling."

"No doubt," I said.

"We should ask her if she knows Cal, though. Even though I sort of hope she don't."

I nodded toward Trick.

"You should go. E'en though you're dressed mannish, I reckon you're less intimidatin' than we are."

"Only because she don't know you," Oscar said with a grin.

We watched as Trick rode up to the woman, and they had a conversation. Wasn't long before she rode back to us.

"Nah, she says most folk around here keep to themselves. She don't know her neighbors and don't want to. She got enough problems of her own, she says."

"I reckon that's true," I said, gazing at the ratty looking home and the small barn. More and more, I appreciated the fine house Oscar and I had built with the help of our friends in Port Essington and understood how lucky we were. Not everyone was so fortunate.

We rode on and approached a few more people, with no luck and increasing feelings of melancholy at the sad state of most of the dwellings.

"This ain't the kind of place where I'd want to have a home," Oscar muttered, as we got back to the dirt road after speaking with a very thin man holding a gun, who'd spit on Trick and told us to leave him be, that they didn't need strange folks snooping around. I'd had my hand on my rifle in case things had gotten ugly, and I had to admit, I was ready to call it a day and head back to The Angel.

But as we rode past a large stand of conifers that opened up to a large field containing a barn with what looked like a weathered homestead tucked in behind, a small child darted out from behind the trees and headed toward us, a bold grin on the tyke's dirty face and laughter bubbling from his lips.

We pulled the horses up and watched the wee thing run. 'Twas wearing a pair of ripped dungarees that were held up with one strap, and its small, filthy feet were bare. The child's torso looked as begrimed as his face.

"Samuel! You get back here right now!"

The tone and timbre of that voice sent a chill up my spine, and I watched as a woman with dark hair almost to her shoulders came running, her skirts in her hand and her stride quick as she chased down the young runaway.

"It's Cal," Oscar said, before any of us could.

Cal glanced o'er and hesitated for a split second before surging forward and grabbing the child from the ground and swinging him up into her arms.

"Sam, I told you not to go near the road," she said with some strictness, but the way she held the boy and the tenderness with which she patted his cheek and chuffed his chin, spoke of a care I wasn't surprised to see from the woman we had known.

The child wiggled and pointed.

"Horsey!"

Cal glanced o'er again and kept her gaze on us, nodding to the child and holding him still.

"Yes, that's right. Nice horseys. But you need to stay away from strangers, Sam. It ain't safe." Cal said, giving us a glare that surprised me with its ferocity, before she turned and headed back toward the trees.

"Caliope!" Trick said, in a voice that held a contempt and anger that I felt in my soul. "Don't you dare hide from us. We *seen* you."

And Cal shriveled, hunched herself o'er the child, and stood stock still as if hoping to disappear.

Oscar and I exchanged a glance as Trick dismounted and strode up to Cal and the child, who peeked from behind Cal's arm with wide eyes and a look of fear on its plump face.

"Cal, I'm sorry," Trick said carefully. "I didn't mean to yell, only I want to talk to you."

Cal kept looking at the ground. Then she shuddered and turned as she straightened, presenting to us a carefully constructed expression of surprise with an underpinning of annoyance and fear.

"I'm sorry. You startled me," she said, reassuring the child, who struggled to be put down. Cal clicked her tongue. "You hold my hand, Samuel, and I will put you down. You gotta stay with me."

Samuel grinned, and Cal set him down on the grass, holding tight to his small hand and gazing at Trick and Oscar and me.

"He likes to run. I'm tryin' to teach him to stay where it's safe."

Trick smiled. "I reckon that's a tricky one for a child his age. How old is the little one?"

"Almost two."

"Where's his momma?" Trick asked.

Perhaps the question was insensitive, for Cal pulled herself up and said, "*I'm* his momma," in a voice that brooked no argument.

"Momma," Samuel repeated, swinging their joined hands and grinning.

"Oh," Trick said, with a smile. "Well, then. All right." She glanced our way as if she wasn't sure where to take the conversation.

"This your homestead, Cal?" Oscar said, swinging down from Onyx and walking toward her. "We been ridin' all mornin', lookin' for you."

Cal held tighter to Sam's hand and seemed like she wanted to run. Oscar stopped walking and scratched his chin.

"I'm awful thirsty," Oscar said. "Do you think we might come in for a bit?"

"Tirsty!" Samuel said, tugging on Cal's hand.

Cal took the measure of us. "My husband's not home, but I s'pose it'd be all right."

"Thank you, Cal," I said. "It'd be mighty kind of you. I'm a bit parched myself."

Cal nodded, and I saw a flicker of something, perhaps a memory of the friendship we used to have, before she turned and started toward the stand of trees.

We glanced at each other and followed.

The house, when it became visible, was barely more than a sizeable shack, with walls that needed shoring up and a roof that probably leaked when it rained or snowed hard. As if she knew how bad it looked, Cal kept her head down and took her time, reluctant to take us there, I supposed. But now that I was aware of it, I wanted to see inside. I needed to see how bad it was and what kind of a situation Cal was in, through no fault of her own.

"This is fine land, Cal. What do you and Albert grow?" I asked. The fields looked like they'd been abandoned and not tilled for a while, but I thought I'd ask, in case I was missing something.

"This is the house, here," Cal said, ignoring my question and stating the obvious, in a morose tone of voice, as the door opened and a girl child of about six or seven peeked out, strands of brown hair escaping from uneven braids.

"Elizabeth," Cal said, "where's Peter?"

The girl gaped at us while she answered Cal. "He's out back, tryin' to fix the washing line."

"Can you go get him please? We got some visitors."

Elizabeth gazed at us with wide eyes and shrank behind the open door.

"It's all right, Lizzy. They're kind folks. They only want a drink."

Lizzy looked as if she didn't truly believe Cal, but she nodded and pulled the door wider as Cal took Samuel in, and we followed.

As we stepped inside the dark space that smelled like spoiled milk and urine, Cal sighed. "It ain't much, but it's ours."

"Sure," Trick said, gazing about us at the sorry state of Cal's home. "Better 'n I got."

Cal's gaze flashed to her, assessing. Did Cal regret not being at The Angel? The Angel was more comfortable, and cleaner by far, than this place, and didn't have the demands of three children and an absent husband to worry her. But Cal had worked hard while she was there, and 'twasn't necessarily a life to strive for either.

"Get Peter, please," Cal reminded Lizzie with a gentleness of manner I remembered.

"Yes, Momma," Lizzie said, her eyes huge and her manner subdued as she slipped into the kitchen and out of the back door.

Chapter Seventeen

Dire Straits

The setting was shocking, for certain, but the way Cal was with these children reassured me that she hadn't lost her warmth and kindness. She was giving it all to them and maybe didn't have any left for the rest of us.

"You look after all them kids on your own?" Oscar asked, gazing about the place and trying not to show any kind of judgment in his expression.

Cal stood and reached for a soiled cloth, using it to wipe away some food that had spilled on the floor. "I'm their momma now."

"Where'd your husband go?" I asked, curious about the state of the place and Cal's obvious lack of help.

She didn't look at me, only nodded. "Oh, he had to travel for some work is all. He sends us money when he can, and he'll be back in a few weeks…hopefully."

Cal didn't look all that hopeful.

"Hmm. You got enough to eat?" Trick asked.
"Sure."

At that moment, Lizzie came back with Peter, who looked about eleven or twelve, with a shock of shaggy black hair and a spatter of freckles on his cheeks. He gazed at the three of us with suspicion and alarm.

"Peter, these are my friends. I used to know them, back before I—I came here. Can you please get some water from the well so's everyone can have a drink?"

"You got no pump in the house?" Oscar asked, and Cal's eyes darkened.

"We got a good well. And I got a good boy who'll go get me water when I need it, ain't that right, Pete?"

Peter beamed at such praise and nodded, still eyeing us warily. "Yes, ma'am. I'll go get some."

"I'll come, too," Oscar said, "I need to use the privy."

"I'll show you where that is," Peter said, as if glad to help with something else. And if anyone could win him o'er, it'd be Oscar.

Lizzie crossed her arms. "I can get water, too. I'm strong, and I like to help Momma!"

Trick smiled and crouched near the child. "You do look strong, Lizzie. I'm sure you help your momma out lots."

Lizzie smiled as she looked Trick up and down. "You wear boys' clothes."

"Well," Trick said, "these are my clothes, and I ain't a boy. So they ain't boys' clothes a'tall." She looked down at herself. "I reckon anyone can wear these, if they want."

"I like dresses," Lizzie said.

"Well, that's fine. I wear dresses, too. But for riding a horse, trousers make more sense."

"I suppose," Lizzie muttered. "Only I ain't got a horse."

"That's too bad. Did you want to ride mine? I can lead her around if you wanna try it."

Lizzie's head swiveled, and she gazed imploringly at Cal. "Can I, Momma? Please? Can I ride a horse?"

Cal gave Trick a look of resignation. "Sure. But be careful."

"Cal, you know I won't let her come to any harm," Trick said.

"All right."

Trick took Lizzie by the hand and led her out front to where the horses were hitched.

Little Samuel pulled at Cal's skirts.

"Milk, Momma. I want milk," he said, his face scrunched up.

Cal looked helpless as she stood by the dirty sink. "We ain't got milk, Samuel. I told you." Her voice was barely audible.

Samuel started crying as I tried to figure out what to do. 'Twas plain to see that Cal and these children were not in a good situation, but Cal was telling us that everything was fine. Did children this young need milk or was water good enough? Darned if I knew, but Miss June might.

"Here, Samuel, you want to play with my watch?" I said, pulling the trinket out of my pocket and handing it o'er. Sam wrapped his pudgy fingers around it as he grinned with delight.

"It'll only go in his mouth, Jimmy," Cal said in a resigned voice. "Give it to me, Sam." She took the watch from the child and handed it back to me. Samuel started to cry, and Cal put a hand to her forehead.

"It's real nice to see you," she said, without any real conviction. "But I have a lot to do here, so I can't sit around and visit. You best be on your way."

I watched as she lifted the wailing child and shushed him.

"Cal. We...we want to help you."

"I don't need help, Jimmy. I told you. Albert sends money when he can. We'll get more soon, I'm sure of it. But thank you for checking in."

I knew it'd be pointless to argue. "All right. Sure."

The children seemed bright and mostly healthy, even though their clothes had seen better days, and the house was a mess. Maybe Miss June could send some of the girls to help Cal out until her husband got back? If she'd even accept assistance. Somehow, I doubted it.

But I hated to see her in this situation. She was in o'er her head, and she knew it. So why wasn't she more friendly? I supposed there was some pride involved — and not wanting to admit she'd made a mistake. At least now we knew where she lived, and we could check in, even if it seemed Cal didn't want us to.

And once we'd let Miss June know where she was, Oscar and I could think about going home. We'd accomplished what we'd come to Telegraph Creek to do. But this whole situation with Cal gave me an uneasy feeling, and I felt like we should hang around a bit longer. Maybe Miss June could get through Cal's defenses to find out more. 'Twas worth a try. I knew she'd want to pay Cal a visit once we told her everything we'd seen.

Cal sighed. "I know it don't look like much, Jimmy, but 'tis my life now — and I don't regret it."

"That's good," I said. "I never pictured you with children, to be honest, but you got a way about you that's very motherly."

For the first time, Cal's smile seemed genuine. "Thank you. These children mean more to me than" —

her voice hitched, and something dark came o'er her face, but she got a hold of herself—"than anythin'. They're my children, now, and I love them so much."

"That's plain to see," I said, and I meant that.

"It ain't easy. But 'tis better than—" Her gaze flashed to mine, and I wondered what she'd been going to say. "Well, anyhow, I'm tryin' to do right by them."

"I know you are. You're a good woman, Caliope, and I'm pleased to know you."

We heard a door creak and the scuff of bare feet and boots on the floor as Oscar and Peter came in through the kitchen. Peter put a pitcher of water on the counter and grabbed a tin cup.

"Not that one, Pete. Get a clean one out of the cupboard."

"Have we got a clean one?" Peter asked, with some frustration. "I thought Lizzie was supposed to wash the dishes."

"She was busy helping me with the clothes. You and I can do them after lunch."

"Sure, okay."

Cal let go of Sam, who'd settled down, and opened the cupboard door, then froze stock still. I wondered if they had any clean cups or dishes, which seemed doubtful, looking at the dirty ones piled on the counter.

"We'll use this one," she said finally, bringing out a large mug made of stoneware. 'Twas black with speckles on it, and for some reason Cal was looking at the mug with trepidation.

I glanced at Pete, who also had his gaze fixed on the mug.

"But that's—" Pete started to say, in a very quiet and alarmed voice, as his gaze shifted to Cal.

"Don't matter," Cal said quickly. "Now be quiet and get our guests something to drink."

The water from the well was cold and fresh, so at least they had that, even though they had to fetch it.

"You've got quite a bit of good land here," Oscar said. "You got some help farmin' it?"

"Albert was doing that, but it never amounted to much. So he's...gone to find work. There's jobs out there, if you can find 'em."

"That's true enough."

"And I ain't got the time, what with lookin' after these three," Cal said. "And we ain't got any animals. We can't afford to feed them, anyway."

"There's plenty of space for a chicken coop. Then at least you'd have fresh eggs."

Cal gazed at Oscar like he was from another planet. "Whose gonna build a chicken coop?"

"We could," Oscar said, glancing my way. "We built our own house in Port Essington — with some help, of course. But I reckon we could build a coop for you. We could even get you some chickens to start you off."

Peter looked at Cal with hope in his eyes. "I could look after 'em, Momma. And Lizzie would help, I'm sure of it."

Cal chewed her bottom lip. "I don't know. I got my hands full already."

"Come on, Jimmy," Oscar said. "Let's get these dishes cleaned. I'll show you where the well is, and we can bring back a tub of water for washing."

"Here," Peter said. "This is what we use to get lots of water if we need it."

He picked up a big pot from the floor beside the stove and passed it to me. 'Twas clean enough, thank goodness.

"Thank you," Cal said, though she seemed awful anxious for someone who had some unexpected help she desperately needed. 'Twas so far from how I remembered her that it made me awful sad. Her life should have been better now she was married and not charging strange men for the pleasure of her intimate company.

Sure, she had the children, but they came with a lot of problems of their own.

Oscar and I walked together to the well and filled up the big pot. We could see Trick leading Willow along with Lizzie perched on her back. The child clutched the horn of the saddle as she grinned with pure joy.

"This is bad, Jimmy," Oscar said, as we walked to the well. "Cal ain't telling us the truth. I ain't so sure this husband of hers is comin' back. And maybe they don't want him back."

I frowned. "We gotta take her at her word, I reckon. Maybe Miss June can come and get the truth out of her."

"Maybe." Oscar kicked at the dirt. "I suppose, for women, marriage ain't all sunshine and roses."

I nodded. "I reckon that's true. Not always, anyhow."

We filled the pot and brought it back to the house, then set it in the sink and washed all the dishes with Peter's assistance. When Trick and Lizzie came back, they helped, too.

Cal looked on with resigned acceptance while she kept Samuel busy and fed him peanuts from a bowl.

"You got food in the house?" I asked, worried Cal wouldn't like my question, but knowing I'd hate myself if I didn't ask it. "Enough for you and the children?"

Cal sighed. "Yes. You can look in that cupboard and see what I got. There's a bag of potatoes in the cellar and some apples. You can check if you want."

I was hesitant to do that, but Trick came right over and opened the cupboard Cal had pointed to. There was a loaf of wheat bread, a block of cheese, what looked like strips of beef jerky and a jar of pickles. 'Twasn't much, but at least 'twas something.

"All right," I said. "We're gonna be on our way then. But I reckon Miss June is gonna wanna come and see you and the children, now that we found you."

"All right." Cal seemed resigned to this, but she didn't seem at all happy about it, which was another strange thing.

"When do you expect your husband back?" I asked.

Cal shook her head. "Don't know. Maybe a week. Maybe a month. Ain't much for him to do here, and he's gotta get us some money. I expect he'll wire some in a few days."

Trick stared at Cal, and I figured she was trying to suss out if Cal was being straight with us.

"What'll you do if he don't?"

"He will. It'll be fine."

"All right."

"Do you have to go?" Lizzie asked, pulling on Trick's jacket. "I wanna ride Willow again!"

Trick knelt down and smiled at the little girl. "We'll come back. Don't you worry. It's a good idea for you all to learn how to ride, I reckon, if your momma says it's okay."

Cal looked out of the window. Seemed she was done with us and wanted to be left alone.

"Bye, Cal," Oscar said, gazing at his onetime friend with a sadness I could feel, since it echoed in my own heart.

"Bye," Cal said, but she didn't look at us as we took our leave — simply held little Samuel close and stroked his back as he gazed at us o'er her shoulder with droopy, sleepy eyes.

Chapter Eighteen

Miss June to the Rescue

We didn't speak much on the ride back to The Angel. I supposed we were reeling from the discovery of our old friend, living in a hovel with three children who called her 'Momma' with no man around and pretending everything was fine, when it clearly wasn't.

We stabled the horses with William and went to see Miss June. She wasn't in the parlor so we headed to the kitchen, where she liked to spend her time during the day, chatting with Cook, sewing or doing a number of other things that contributed to the effective running of The Angel.

As we walked down the hall, she came out of the kitchen and saw the three of us. Her eyes flew wide, and she stopped in her tracks.

"Did you find Cal?"

"We found her," I said.

Miss June's hands flew to her cheeks, and she gasped. "Well? Is she all right?"

"Well, she is and she ain't," I said, and glanced to Trick for some assistance.

Miss June ushered us into the kitchen, and we sat around the big wooden table. Cook continued her business at the stove but she had one ear on our conversation, I reckoned.

"She's livin' on a small" —I glanced at Oscar. Could I even call it a farm? —"farm…in the Wildman's Creek area."

"Cal says her husband's away to look for work, that he sends her money when he can and that she and the children are fine," Trick added.

Miss June blinked. "The…children? Cal has *children*?"

"Sure. I don't know where the original momma is, but Cal's their momma now."

Miss June blinked, absorbing this news. She huffed a laugh, and I could see she was taken aback at this news. "Goodness."

Oscar smiled. "That was the only comfortin' thing about any of it. You should have seen Cal with those young uns —like she was born to it or somethin'. They called her Momma, and she was real good with 'em."

"That's a fact," I said. "They were good kids, too. They helped us to clean up a bit. The place was a shambles."

"Oh dear."

"I reckon Cal's in over her head," Trick said, "though she wouldn't admit it."

"How old are the children?"

I glanced at Oscar and Trick for help. I didn't know much about children, but neither did they. Nobody said anything, so I took a shot answering.

"Well, the smallest one, he's only a baby still, though he's walkin'…well, runnin', I should say. That's how we found them. He was tearin' toward the road, and Cal came out from behind some trees to get 'im."

"Oh my," Miss June said, putting a hand to her mouth.

Trick chimed in then. "I asked Lizzie how old she was, and she said she's seven, Samuel's one and a half and Peter's ten."

I'd assumed Peter was older than that, simply because he'd acted like he was in charge of things. But he was pretty young, too.

"They're smart, they looked healthy and they love Cal. You could see it," Oscar said.

"Sure," I said. "That's true."

Miss June was silent for a long while, gazing at all three of us.

"Well," she said finally, clasping her hands together. "I'm going to want to pay Cal and the children a visit tomorrow. Do you three want to come with me?"

I glanced at Oscar. "Might be best if you and Trick go. Cal didn't seem to want Oscar and me in her home. She don't seem to think you needed to get us to come help."

"Yeah, because everythin' is fine and dandy," Oscar said in a sardonic voice. "'Cept it ain't. For sure, it ain't. But she won't tell us the truth."

"No, I want you to ride out with me…and Trick. But the three of you can wait outside while I go in and speak to Cal on my own. Perhaps you can entertain the children."

"Sure," Trick said. "They like the horses. And Cal seems to trust us with 'em."

"All right. Gosh. I don't think I'll sleep well tonight, but we'll ride out early tomorrow, and go pay our dear Caliope a visit. I want to get to the bottom of this."

* * * *

We left The Angel at ten the next morning and rode out to Cal's place. Miss June borrowed a horse from one of her regular clients, who was given some extra time with his favorite girl as a trade.

"You have a lot of skills, Miss June," Oscar said, watching her handle the unfamiliar beast with ease.

Miss June smiled at him. She'd kept her skirts on but had hiked them up so we could see her bloomers as she rode astride the black gelding. Her hair was wrapped neatly around her head, although a few tendrils escaped in the breeze. I reckoned she'd been mighty handsome when she was young.

"Yes, I do — more'n you'll ever know."

Oscar laughed. "More'n I'd wanna know. Though I figured, since you're runnin' a cathouse."

"I always said, the best two skills a girl could have were how to ride a horse and how to ride a man."

Trick cackled.

I felt my cheeks heat at the thought of my beloved Miss June spreading her legs for someone, but there was a question I wanted to ask. "You ever work — that way — anymore?"

Miss June snorted. "What? No. The men who come to The Angel want the young 'uns like Trick and Sally. They don't wanna pay for my old ass."

"Aw shucks, Miss June. You're still pretty and allurin'," Oscar said, waggling his eyebrows. "And you got the experience of many years of tumblin', I reckon. You could charge a fortune for your services." He grinned, playing with her.

"I doubt that. Anyway, I'm busy enough running the place and keeping my girls safe."

Trick was shaking her head at the turn of the conversation.

"Now, I'm not saying I haven't been propositioned once or twice," Miss June admitted. "But I always pretend they're joking and send them one of the younger girls. This old body ain't up to it no more."

"But don't you ever…" Oscar said. "Don't you ever wanna…get up to somethin' with a man? You ain't that old."

"Well, thank you, Oscar. It's nice to hear someone say that now and then," she said. "As to your question, sometimes I do," she admitted, with a sparkle in her eye. "But I've got ways to satisfy that urge all by myself."

Oscar's eyes flashed wide, and I gave a hearty laugh. 'Twas a good, light conversation, to relieve some of the tension we felt heading into a bad situation.

Miss June's expression sobered as we rode into the Wildman Creek area, and she took in the state of the homesteads.

"This doesn't look very promising, now, does it?" she said.

"No, ma'am. It ain't the best place to be raisin' children, I don't think."

"Perhaps not. But I reckon most of these folks don't have a choice about where they've got to live."

"True. But they don't have to be so churlish when approached by a stranger," Oscar muttered, referring to those efforts we'd made to speak to several of the local residents.

"This is the place," I said as we got closer to Cal's homestead. "Just behind those trees, there."

"It's a pretty spot," Miss June says, her forehead creased with concern.

"Sure," Oscar says. "Fine piece of land, but nobody to work it with Cal's husband gone. She's got her hands full."

"I'm sure she does," Miss June says. "Three children are a lot to look after."

"Did you ever want wee ones?" Oscar said, looking at Miss June with an eyebrow raised.

Miss June snorted. "I'm the second oldest girl in a family of twelve. I've already looked after enough children for my own satisfaction, thank you very much." She gazed at Trick. "Now I'm a momma to the grown women in my care, and that's much more rewarding."

We rode around the trees and up the gentle slope toward the house. Miss June noticed the small barn.

"Do they have any animals?"

"Not even poultry or a milk cow," I said. "Things seem pretty desperate."

I took off my hat and swiped it against my leg. "I'm not sure Cal's husband is much of a worker, to tell you the truth, whether 'tis here at home or out and about."

Trick spat into the dirt. "I agree. I wouldn't be surprised if Cal's lyin' through her teeth about him sendin' any money. I don't think he's comin' back."

Miss June contemplated this. "Why wouldn't she tell us? If she was so desperate?"

"Pride," I said.

"Shame," Oscar added. "She left her security at The Angel for a dream that didn't turn out so good, seems like."

Miss June gave a nod as we dismounted.

"I'll go in by myself and see if I can persuade her to send the children out to see the horses. And you keep them busy, all right?"

"Of course," I said. "I wanna have a look in that barn and see if 'twould be all right for stock, if Cal had any."

"All right," Miss June said, nodding with approval.

I figured maybe we could get Cal a cow or some chickens. Peter and Lizzie were old enough to help with milking and feeding, and at least they'd have fresh milk and eggs to eat, without having to spend on anything but grain and hay. I was willing to build a coop, but a cow would need the barn.

We waited with the horses until the children came out of the house. Peter led little Samuel by the hand, with Lizzie following.

When they got near to us, Trick crouched down and extended her hand to the little girl in the ratty dress that was a mite too short.

"Hey there, Lizzie, you wanna feed Willow a carrot?" She took the vegetable out of her pocket and held it up in front of the approaching children.

They stopped, Peter and Lizzie's eyes going wide as they homed in on the huge orange root in Trick's hands. Samuel started to cry. Lizzie whispered something to Peter, who nodded and straightened up, giving Trick a sober stare.

"We ain't had any breakfast," he said, in a small voice, as if he was too scared to ask for the carrot outright.

Oscar and I exchanged a glance as Trick lowered her hand.

"Well now. You know, Willow had some grain back at The Angel. So, I reckon she don't need this here carrot," Trick said, holding it out to the children. "You want it?"

"Yes, ma'am. I reckon 'twould hit the spot," Peter said, taking it from her like 'twas made of pure gold.

He held it carefully, blinking at it, as if he couldn't believe he was holding a whole carrot in his hands and was only waiting for someone to snatch it away. When that didn't happen, he took a deep breath and broke it into three pieces. He gave the long, narrow end to Lizzie, the fat end piece with the greens on it to Samuel, and he took a bite from the middle piece.

Peter's eyelids closed as he chewed, as if he hadn't had a solid piece of nourishment in weeks.

Chapter Nineteen

The Old Barn

Watching the children eat a carrot with such reverence and gratitude pulled at my heartstrings.

"You got any more?" I whispered to Trick. "They're plumb starved."

"I only brought the one."

Oscar must have heard us or figured out what we were talking about. He opened the flap on Onyx's saddle bag.

"I got some bread and cheese," he said.

I nodded. "They'll want that, too, I reckon."

So we had a little picnic with the children out there on the sun-warmed grass, while Miss June spoke to Cal in the little house. When they'd eaten all their shrunken stomachs could handle, Oscar and Trick took turns leading the horses around the field with Peter and Lizzie enthusiastically astride, while I took Samuel with me to look at the barn.

He came with me all right, until we got close and he realized where we were going. Then he screamed and pulled against my hold. It startled me, but I didn't let go, because the last thing I needed was for Cal's youngest to be running loose when she'd trusted him into our care.

"What's wrong, Sam? You don't wanna go to the barn?"

He screamed again, his cheeks red and his eyes wild, and I had to hold his arm real tight. I worried I was hurting him. I glanced to the others and saw Peter slide down from Onyx's back with Oscar's help and start running o'er to us, a stricken look on his face.

"Don't take him in there!" Peter yelled.

I blinked in confusion at the older child as he reached us and scooped Samuel into his arms, gazing at me like I should have known better.

"He don't like it. None of us do."

I peered at the seemingly innocent structure, made of rough wood and nails.

"Why?"

Peter regarded me for a long moment. He looked toward the house, then frowned at the ground, his face going red. I couldn't tell if 'twas shame or anger.

"Momma don't want us to tell."

Peter's voice was so low I barely made out the words. Oscar and Trick had approached with Lizzie, who ran toward Peter and threw herself into her brother's arms. The older child held her as she started to hiccup with silent tears.

Oscar and Trick and I gazed at each other with looks of puzzlement.

"What's all this about?" Oscar asked, watching the children and raising his eyebrows at me.

I shrugged. "I don't know. But they sure don't wanna go in there." I crouched down to get to Peter's eye level. "Peter," I said in an even, neutral tone, "is it all right if Oscar and I go into the barn?"

Peter stared at me with a serious expression, then nodded once.

I glanced at Trick. "Stay with them."

"Sure," she said, frowning.

Whatever was in the barn, or whatever had happened in there, had traumatized these children. Had their daddy beat them in there? Didn't seem like that would have made them react the way they had, but I supposed 'twas possible. Maybe 'twas best he'd gone, if that was the case.

"Come on," I said to Oscar, who seemed hesitant. "Let's have a look."

He glared at the barn, then looked at me, and I thought he might be sick.

"I —" he said.

"Here, you stay with the kids," Trick said, moving forward and joining me in front of the barn door. "I'll go with Jimmy."

Oscar nodded with relief. "Okay."

He stepped back to stand beside Peter and Lizzie. Peter was still holding little Sam, and Lizzie was plastered to Peter's side, an expression of pure terror on her face.

I reached for the handle of the door, and Sam started wailing again, as if I was about to release the devil or some such thing.

"'Tis all right," Peter shushed him. "We ain't goin' in there. They are...for a minute."

That made me feel better, as Peter didn't seem worried about us going in the barn. There likely wasn't anything out of the ordinary inside it. But something had happened there — something that they didn't want to tell us. Or that Cal didn't want us to know.

I tugged the door open a bit and peered inside, in case there was a dead hog or something. But the kids would have told us if 'twas something so ordinary. And we'd have smelled it.

Sunbeams slipped between the rafters through the unsound roof of the outbuilding, making dust motes in the air. There was straw on the floor that looked pretty fresh, even though Cal had said they didn't use the barn. Trick and I looked around at the ramshackle walls then meet each other's gaze.

Trick shrugged.

"Looks like a plain old barn to me."

"Yep," I agreed. I gazed at the open door behind us, then back at her. "But there's a story here of some kind."

"Sure enough," she said. "I suppose we'll have to ask Cal about it, though she might not tell us."

I nodded. "Not today. Let's see what Miss June finds out first."

"All right."

We went back out into the bright daylight and smiled at the children, who still seemed unsettled.

"What a boring old barn," I said. "Ain't much of anythin', is it?"

Peter seemed to sigh with relief, and he gave me a hesitant smile. "No, it ain't much."

Lizzie flashed her gaze to him and back to me.

"You want to try ridin' Dixie?" I asked her. "Or maybe Oscar will let you ride Onyx."

Lizzie's eyes went wide, and she smiled, all her fear about the barn gone in an instant.

"Onis! Please, can I ride her? Please!"

Oscar and I exchanged a relieved glance, even smiling at Lizzie's twist on Onyx' name.

"Of course you can. I reckon Onyx will be happy to have you up there," he said, holding out his hand to Lizzie, who rushed over and clasped it.

I met Oscar's gaze as we walked back to the horses and smiled. He was good with them kids, and it made me happy to see it. Didn't seem like he'd had much parenting when he was small, but he knew how to do it, sure enough.

I glanced back at Peter, who had let Samuel down so the little one could follow us on his own. Peter stood stock still and stared at the barn, as if he couldn't let go of whatever 'twas that it meant to him.

"You comin'?" I said, wanting to break him out of the spell. Maybe, if Cal refused to tell us what had happened there, I could get it out of Peter.

"Sure," he said in a quiet voice, and moved to follow us.

We led the children around the field on the horses, steering clear of the barn, until finally Miss June came out of the house with Cal, and they walked toward us.

Cal's face was red, like she'd been crying, and Miss June seemed concerned.

"We'd best get back to The Angel," she said.

Cal barely glanced at Oscar as she scooped her daughter off Onyx's back.

"Momma, I'm learnin' to ride!"

"Did you thank Mr. Yates?" Cal said.

"Who's Mr. Yates?" Lizzie said, truly puzzled.

"That's Oscar's last name, though you don't gotta be so formal," I said.

"Thank you for letting me ride Onis," Lizzie said. She stepped forward and wrapped her arms around Oscar, holding him tight.

Oscar gazed at me with surprise, as he put an affectionate hand on Lizzie's head. "Of course, Lizzie. You'll be a fine horsewoman someday."

"I told Cal we'll be back tomorrow with some of the girls, and they can give Cal's place a thorough cleaning. And we'll bring a picnic lunch for the children."

I smiled, relieved. Miss June always knew what to do.

Cal seemed wary, but she nodded. "Thank you."

Miss June laid a hand on Cal's back. "We're happy to help you, Cal. We're so glad we found you, but I do wish you'd told us what was going on. It's not right for you to be out here all alone in such straits."

"Yes, ma'am. Thank you."

Cal let Miss June give her a hug, and she hung onto the older woman for a long moment, her face pressed into Miss June's soft neck. Then she forced herself away and gathered the children.

"Come on. We gotta go inside."

"We'll be by at noon tomorrow, Cal," Miss June said. Cal didn't answer, and Miss June and I exchanged concerned looks.

* * * *

That night, after we'd grabbed a quick supper downstairs, and the girls were busy with clients, Oscar and I retired to our room. I must have looked a bit morose, for Oscar told me to cheer up, and that he'd be back in a minute.

I picked *The Call of the Wild* up off my bedside table, and I guess I read about half a chapter before the door opened and Oscar slipped inside. I didn't look up right away, because 'twas the middle of a dramatic scene, and I wanted to finish my paragraph.

I heard his footsteps then the mattress shifted, and the edge of a black silk sleeve fell onto the page as Oscar slipped the book from my slack grasp and laid it gently on the table. I gaped at the lovely vision before me.

"Oh, Oscar," I said as he smiled and batted his lashes.

His luscious, slim form was wrapped in a peignoir of black silk with bright orange trim and a fierce gold dragon embroidered on the left side. As I watched, he kneeled up and pulled the end of the tie that kept it closed. The delicate fabric fell open, revealing the scintillating lace underthings that Oscar wore beneath it.

"Oh my God," I whispered, my gaze caressing him as I took in the stunning vision of Oscar in an ebony satin basque and midnight black silk bloomers that outlined his boyish curves and made him look like a girl in all the best of ways.

I grabbed his hips, and I held him still, so I could take it in, my cock already a hard rod in my trousers and my cheeks flushing with excitement.

"Where did you get this stuff?" I asked, breathless and amazed.

Oscar rolled his eyes and trailed the end of the tie from his peignoir across my lap.

"Where do you think?"

I grinned. "From Trick?"

He nodded. "The one and only. Jimmy, she's got a treasure chest in her room!"

"What? Trick's hoardin' treasure? Does Miss June know?" I mocked him.

He slapped me playfully on the shoulder.

"I don't suppose 'tis gold, but she wouldn't let me look! She says I gotta bring you sometime, and we can go through it together."

Interesting.

"Sure." My forehead wrinkled. "Wait a second! Ain't Trick entertainin' right now?"

Trick had been taking a break from her whoring, but when we'd got back from riding out, one of her regular clients had been in the parlor, and his eyes had about popped from his head to see Trick in her masculine get-up. He'd made a very polite request for a couple of hours with her, and Trick had agreed after doubling her price like the shrewd businesswoman she was.

Oscar chuckled. "Well now, she did have Mr. Clark in her room, but he didn't seem to mind watchin' her dress me in these fine things."

My chin dropped. "Well."

"Didn't take very long, and he was only sittin' on her bed and lookin'. Trick figured 'twould make his visit extra special to watch us."

I thought back to my days visiting cathouses, and, yeah, I supposed if something similar had happened, featuring a young man of Oscar's looks and delicacy, I probably would have enjoyed watching, too. I reckoned a lot of men were more open about certain things than society at large had us figured for.

I grinned, my gaze running o'er Oscar in his seductive ensemble.

"I suppose that makes sense. Who wouldn't want to look at you gettin' outfitted in all this finery, you pretty poppet. Long as he stayed on that bed and didn't come near you."

Oscar grinned, stretching and bending this way and that, so I could see the way the fabric encased him so perfectly, his small brown nipples peeking o'er the edge of the boned corset.

"Oh no, Mr. Clark stayed right where Trick told him to. I think he likes bein' ordered around, ye see," Oscar said. "Like I do."

"Oh," I said. "Well, that's fine, then."

"Do you like the way I look?" Oscar said, reaching his hands toward the ceiling and arching his back so's I could appreciate him.

"Oh, Oscar," I said, gliding my hands along his hips and up the sides of the basque, my fingers trembling with the pleasure of it. "'Course I do," I said, breathing hard. "You look...you look so charmin' and like a perfect gift that I'm gonna unwrap and do terrible, vile things to."

Oscar shivered and rocked his bottom against my thighs, gasping. "Jimmy, that's all I want."

I tugged him against me, then ran my hands up his back and found his mouth with mine, taking him over and making him pant and moan. He tasted of mint and chocolate, and I wondered who'd been feeding him this time.

"You been...eatin' chocolate..." I murmured, between hearty and desperate kisses.

Oscar huffed a laugh, and I truly loved that sound from him. "Yes, sir."

I slid a hand under the laced edge of his drawers, and slipped it underneath to cup his smooth buttock, as he clenched and rubbed up against me.

"And who gave it to you? Mr. Clark?"

"Well, Jimmy, ye see," Oscar panted, "he had all sorts of goodies that he'd...brought for Trick, and he...and Trick thought I ought to have some."

I grunted with mild displeasure.

"What was I supposed to do?" Oscar panted, pulling back to frown at me. "Decline?"

I grinned. "A good boy would have said 'No, thank you.'"

Oscar stared at me. I supposed he was trying to figure out whether I was being serious. He gave me a wry grin and shrugged.

"Well, then, I guess I ain't a very good boy."

I slid my hand out of his bloomers and yanked them down, causing another gasp from Oscar as his eyes flew wide and his cock bounced free of the silk, looking especially fetching as it rose against the lower edge of the corset.

"Oh, fuck," I said, my own eyes going wide at the way he looked, with the peignoir falling off his narrow shoulders and the bloomers under his balls — a creature that was the perfect mix of masculine and feminine, so divine it made my cock weep. "You are just perfect, Oscar Yates. My perfect boy. Naughty and brave and free and so, so, *very good*."

I grasped his waist and rolled him o'er, so I could strip those silk bloomers off him and spread his legs, gazing at the place I was going, and at his swollen cock that was red at the tip and looking so beautifully engorged for me.

"Jimmy!" he cried out, then laughed, then groaned. Oh, God. Fuck me in my peignoir and corset. You got to. *Please!*"

Instead of answering him, I laid him out beneath me and peppered his exposed skin with kisses and small bites, while he lay spread on the bed, a debauched sacrifice to my raging appetites. He whimpered and moaned and gasped as I ravished him and cried out when I finally pushed inside him with the aid of the oil Trick had given us.

I fucked him slow, steady and determined, until I'd wrung everything from him, then spent into his heat with a roar and a curse. I sorely hoped that Trick would let Oscar keep these items of clothing so's we could do this at home in our own private bedroom, because if I never got to see Oscar dressed this way again, 'twould be a goddamn sorrow.

Chapter Twenty

A Picnic with Friends

Turned out that Miss June didn't have any trouble getting a crew of four of her girls together to help Cal out. The following day, she had Cook put together a picnic basket for Cal and the children, determined to treat them to a good meal and a pleasant outing.

The day dawned clear and warm. Oscar and I had bathed and shaved after our surprising encounter the night before, and first thing that morning, Miss June has taken out my stitches and declared me healed. I barely noticed the injury anymore, except for some itching on the surface now and then. Miss June had said that was from the new skin growing, so 'twas a good sign. I'd have a scar but 'twould be small and even, thanks to her expert care.

Once we got this thing with Cal sorted, Oscar and I could be on our way home. I missed Port Essington like I'd not missed any place in my whole sorry life. The winter we'd spent together there, with Clarence and Irene close by, and building our house with Tim and Carson in the spring, had been the most rewarding eight months I'd ever spent, anywhere. I reckoned Oscar was missing our home and our friends as well.

We had Gus hitch up Willow and Dixie to the wagon that Miss June kept for emergencies. Oscar rode Onyx, and Trick and I went in the wagon. I figured little Lizzie would shed some tears if she couldn't have another ride on Oscar's sweet black horse today.

When we got to the homestead, Miss June and the girls went inside and me, Oscar and Trick hung back by the horses. After a few moments, Cal emerged from the house with the children, regarding us with a caution I still found difficult to fathom.

Cal should trust us. There was no reason, that I knew of, for Cal to be so wary—which made me sure that something had happened, and she wasn't owning up to whatever it was that had made her like this and had traumatized her children in the barn. But 'twas a delicate situation, and Miss June had said to let her handle it, so we would pretend everything was fine and treat Cal and the kids to a lovely outdoor lunch on this gorgeous summer day.

Miss June came outside once she had got the girls working and joined us. Lizzie was already clamoring to ride Onyx, so Oscar lifted her onto the mare's back, while Miss June and Trick laid out the checkered picnic blanket on the grass. We set up by the stand of trees, so we weren't anywhere near the cursed barn.

Cal settled herself down on the blanket, with Sam in her arms and Peter beside her, and eyed the substantial wicker basket with interest. Miss June and I exchanged a glance. I reckoned Cal was hungrier than the children, for 'twas obvious she put them first and herself last, which was what a good parent was supposed to do.

Samuel squirmed, cried and seemed to want to get out of Cal's grasp. From what I knew of children, which wasn't much, he was at an age that meant he didn't want to be still. But once Miss June opened up that picnic basket and started unwrapping all manner of foodstuffs, that child got quiet, his eyes went big as saucers and drool dripped down his tiny chin. He gave a little whimper and sat down hard on the blanket beside Cal, his mouth open, as if he couldn't even comprehend what was being laid out in front of him.

'Twas the saddest thing I'd ever seen, apart from the way that Oscar had wolfed down that supper I'd provided him, when he'd been down on his luck in Dawson City. Although there were things about my past I would have liked to have changed, I was grateful that I'd never gone through periods of intense hunger. There had always been something, even if 'twas criminal acts that had provided the means for the grub we ate.

"*Cheese*, Momma," Peter said, in a hushed voice, gazing at the slab of cheese that Miss June put onto a plate with grapes beside it. There were three big loaves of wheat bread, too, a jar of olives and some cured meat.

"Would anyone like some lemonade?" Miss June asked, as if throwing picnics was her line of work. She held up a steel flask that glistened in the light of the sun.

Three hands rose into the air, so I figured these children had been to school on occasion.

Miss June smiled and poured the lemonade into a tin cup that she passed to Lizzie.

"Have a few sips and give it to your brother, Lizzie. Then I'll fill it again, and Cal can give some to Sam and have some for herself."

"Thank you," Lizzie said as she wrapped her hands around the cup and took a sip. Her eyes flew wide, and she tipped the cup, drinking down every drop before she knew she was doing it. Her expression faltered when she lowered the cup and realized 'twas empty, but Miss June only smiled.

"My, you were thirsty, weren't you?" she said. "Give the cup to Peter now, and I'll fill it for him."

Lizzie did as she was told, licking her lips with a dazed expression on her doll-like face.

Oscar and I had a metal flask of our own, with something nicer than lemonade in it, which we shared with Trick.

Peter drank the lemon and sugar concoction carefully, with his eyes closed. When he lowered his cup and opened them, they held more delight and happiness than I'd ever seen.

"That tastes like sunshine," he said.

I glanced at Oscar. Oscar had made the same comparison about the oranges we had at Christmas at Clarence's and Irene's, and the memory of that fine day came back to me. We hadn't expected to spend the holiday with anyone, but Irene had invited us, and we'd ended up forming a strong friendship with the two of them. I missed them terribly.

"Is your lemonade as good as this?" Peter asked, nodding at the flask Trick was swigging from.

She passed it to me with a smile. "Oh yeah. Our lemonade is real good, too. Might be a tad stronger than the stuff you got."

Oscar grinned as I took a swig, the soft burn of the whiskey going down my throat.

"Here, give me some of that tasty, strong lemonade, Jimmy. I need to wet my whistle," Oscar said.

I wanted to say something saucy back to him, and Trick seemed to be expecting it, but I remembered in time that we were surrounded by innocent ears.

"Here, then. Don't drink it all."

Peter laughed, and Oscar rolled his eyes.

"See what I gotta put up with?" he said to Peter. "This man thinks he's my pa or somethin'."

I laughed but stopped when I saw Peter's reaction to that word. The boy cringed, and Cal put a hand to his arm for comfort.

"Jimmy would make a fine pa," Cal said, gazing at me out of soulful eyes with more affection than I'd felt from her since we'd got reacquainted.

"Oh, I can vouch for that," Oscar said, with a wink at her.

And Cal almost smiled, but she caught herself and looked down at her lap. 'Twas good to see a flash of the old Cal there.

The Caliope we'd known had been sweet and saucy, and used to delight in the ribald comments Oscar would make. She'd even dressed Oscar up in bloomers and a corset one time, like Trick had done this time, to surprise me. 'Twas hard to believe that the Cal we'd known and the Cal who sat near me on the picnic blanket were the same person. Whatever had happened here, it hadn't been good, and it hadn't been what Cal had expected when she'd left The Angel. I could guarantee it.

But she'd become attached to these children, that much was obvious, and they to her, and Cal couldn't come back to work at Miss June's with them three to look after, and God only knew where their pa was. So I didn't know what to do, except for what we were doing now, which was to feed and help them, so maybe Cal would trust us enough to be truthful.

Chapter Twenty-One

A Fresh Start

We ate the picnic and drank the lemonade and whiskey and had a pleasant time out there on the grass, in the sunshine. A fragrant breeze kept the sun from being too hot, and, anyway, we were in the shade of the tall pines. The humming of insects and the twittering of birds provided a peaceful backdrop to our picnic.

The only downside was the mosquitoes. Cal and the children barely seemed to notice, and they never bothered me too much, but Oscar seemed irresistible to them. First he twitched and cursed, then swatted at them, until he stood and performed his silly dance again. I couldn't help but laugh at the image of him twisting and swatting and cursing.

Peter was watching, too, and he laughed when I did. Then Lizzie, her face a mess of blueberry jam, started, then Trick noticed.

"Good grief, Oscar. 'Tis only a few mosquitoes," she said, blowing one away from her face with a casual puff of air.

"They won't let me be," Oscar whined. "Goddamn fuckers!" he said, as he twirled around and tried to slap himself on the back.

I glanced at Cal, but she didn't seem to mind the cursing. Oscar turned back, his cheeks flushed with the heat and now embarrassment.

"I'm sorry, Cal. I didn't mean to curse in front of the children," he said.

"Never mind. They've heard worse," Cal said, then shifted her gaze away from mine.

"You're so funny!" Lizzie said, seeming more carefree and alert now that she'd had some good nourishment. "Is that the mosquito dance?"

Oscar narrowed his eyes at her, but he was smirking, too. "Why, I suppose it is, Miss Lizzie. You're lucky you don't have to do it. They seem to be in love with me."

"Why, who wouldn't be in love with you?" I said, with sincerity.

"I don't care who'd be in love with me, long as they don't buzz around my head and bite me on the ass."

The children laughed, and Cal smiled.

"*You're* in love with Oscar," Lizzie said, peering at me in a way that made me feel transparent and stating it as a fact and not a question.

I sighed and popped a cracker into my mouth. "Yes, miss, I am. I can't deny it, and why would I?"

It felt good to be honest and plain with these young 'uns who, God willing, would grow up and remember me and Oscar, how in love we were and realize that whether 'twas two men loving each other or two women, it didn't make a hell of a difference.

Cal looked on silently. She had eaten some bread and cheese, and a few of the grapes, and seemed more energetic and amenable. Now she was peeling slices off a nectarine with a paring knife, passing them out to the children and having some as well.

'Twas a pretty sight, and it warmed my heart.

Cal's eyes shone brighter, and her cheeks had more color. I was reminded of an earlier time, when I'd brought Oscar to The Angel out of desperation, and I'd seen a lovely young man dressed in women's underthings who'd primped and preened like the other girls. Later, Cal had told Oscar and me that she felt she was a woman who'd been born with the wrong parts, and she'd prefer us to use 'she' and 'her' instead of 'he' and 'him' when we spoke about her. All the people at The Angel respected Cal's wishes, even young William, who worked in the stables. We hadn't met anyone yet who was born to the wrong sex through no fault of their own. Then we met Clarence and Irene in Port Essington, and discovered Clarence was different to most other men in that same respect — and lived his life quite happily in trousers and boots.

I knew that there were all sorts of people in the world. Maybe to make up for the fact that I'd met all the wrong people during the first part of my life, I seemed to be meeting all the *right* people now. Falling for Oscar, though overwhelming and alarming at first, had been the gateway to a better circumstance for me. My world was chock full of kind, warm-hearted folks, and what they had or didn't have between their legs didn't concern me in the least.

Cal didn't give us any more information during our picnic, but at least she and the children had a hearty lunch. When Miss June's girls were done with the cleaning, they came out to join us, and afterward, we went to have a look at the results of their hard work.

The children made sounds of surprise when they saw the swept floors and the extra space that had been created with some ingenuity and hard work.

"It smells funny in here," Lizzie said, as she stepped inside and gaped at the walls that had been wiped clean, and the floors that had been swept and mopped.

"That's the cleaning solution," Mabel said.

Mabel had pale, freckled skin and dark red hair that was piled atop her head in a haphazard way. She was tall and slim, and she had a way of moving that was graceful and efficient.

"Don't it look nice? Your poor momma ain't got time to do a big clean like this, so 'tis as well Miss June brought us in."

She held out her hand to Lizzie. "Wanna see in the cupboards? We cleaned those out and washed all the dishes. Everything's good now."

"Yes, please!" Lizzie said. Mabel lifted Lizzie so she could peer into the clean cupboards.

"You did a fine job, girls. Thank you," Miss June said, placing the leftover food that was shelf stable into one of the cupboards and giving the rest to Sally to put into the larder.

"It looks so good in here, don't it, Momma?" Peter said, looking to Cal for confirmation. He appeared worried, as if he was concerned she'd take his compliment as a criticism for the way it had been before.

But Cal seemed pleased and nodded, blinking her eyes as if holding back emotion.

"Yes, it does, Peter."

She sighed and looked around, seeming at ease for the first time since we'd met up again. "Thank you."

Miss June leaned in and kissed her on her cheek. "You're very welcome, Cal. I hope Albert will be pleased when he comes back."

Lizzie and Peter gazed at Cal, as if waiting for her to say something.

Cal's expression went back to looking tortured, but she nodded. "I'm sure."

"Anyway," Miss June said, clapping her hands together, "we'd best be getting back. But I'm going to come check on you all in a few days, in case Albert's still away. We don't mind helping out, truly, and you shouldn't feel beholden to us, Cal."

"Thank you. I do appreciate it."

She gazed at her feet in the scuffed black boots that poked from under her skirts. When she looked up again, her expression seemed open and vulnerable, like she might be ready to tell us what was going on. But at that moment, little Sam started whining, and it looked, and smelled, like he needed a diaper change. Lizzie ran to Oscar, hugged him and made him promise to bring 'Onis' back so she could 'pratis her ridin'."

'Twas sweet to see. Oscar looked taken aback but pleased to be handled so. He glanced at me while the little girl had her arms wrapped around him, and my heart warmed to see him so treasured by a youngster. I couldn't help grinning.

"Oh, we'll be back, little missy. Don't worry about that. We won't be able to stay in Telegraph Creek forever, but while we're here, we'll be sure to visit you often."

"Peter, c'mere," I said, as Cal went to tend to Sam, and Lizzie let Oscar go so she could hug Trick and ask her to bring some chocolate the next time we came.

Peter walked o'er to me, and I gazed down at him with solemnity.

"Now I know you're only ten, but I gotta say, the way you carry yourself and the way you help out your momma makes you seem much older. You're a good boy, and I want you to keep lookin' out for your momma, your sister and your baby brother. You help out as much as you can, all right? I don't care if it's things like washin' or doin' other stuff that some might consider a woman's work. A real man will help where he's needed, and it don't matter how lowly the task."

"Yes, sir," Peter said, watching me with respect and maybe a bit of awe. I glanced at Oscar, who was watching me with an odd expression on his face. I turned back to Peter.

"Thank you for letting us come and help out your momma. It ain't a sign of weakness to accept help. 'Tis a show of strength to know when 'tis needed and to accept it gracefully."

"Yes, sir," Peter said in a small voice. He swallowed. "We're mighty grateful to Miss June."

"You and me both. When Oscar and I rode into Telegraph Creek almost a year ago, Oscar was injured, and I was desperate. Miss June and the girls took us in and treated us like they'd always known us. Miss June nursed Oscar back to health. Why, she's only just finished helpin' me with a big gash in my side. There ain't no shame or worry in folks helpin' other folks. You remember that, all right?" I chucked him on the chin and smiled. "Maybe Oscar and I'll take you into town someday soon and get you a real cowboy hat and some good, solid boots, so's you can be even more help to your ma."

Peter stood a bit taller, and his eyes widened. "All right." His gaze drifted to my middle. "You gotta big gash in your side?"

"Yeah. You wanna see it?"

Oscar snorted, and took off his hat, shaking his head from side to side.

"Yeah," Peter said, as if 'twould be the most exciting thing in the world. I remembered myself at his age and I supposed injuries were pretty fascinating before they simply became a part of life, and nothing to be amused by.

I tugged my shirttails out of my pants and lifted them so Peter and Lizzie could see the scar of my injury.

"Shucks," Peter said, a little breathless. "How did you get cut like that, Jimmy?"

I laughed and looked at the healing cut, remembering how thoughtless I'd been and in a rush. "Not bein' careful, that's all."

"Slid down the side of a mountain on his ass," Oscar muttered. "Like a damn fool."

Lizzie giggled, and Peter smiled.

I shrugged. "P'raps 'twas foolish. Anyway, I only wanted to get to Telegraph Creek and see your momma."

Cal had finished cleaning up the baby, and she looked o'er when she heard the word. Her gaze focused in on the wound in my side.

"You shouldn't have risked your life for me."

I lowered my shirt tails and tucked them into my trousers, pressing my lips together and shrugging. "Well," I said, "I suppose I'll decide who I'll risk my life for."

AE Lister

"I need a new dress!" Lizzie said, moving in next to Peter and taking his hand. "Please? This one's torn, see?"

I gazed at the little girl's clothes, which were worn, dirty and needed replacing.

"I reckon we can get you a new dress, Lizzie. Maybe we can get your ma some nice things, too — and even Sam."

Cal had gone back to Sam and didn't hear what we promised the two older children. I only hoped she'd allow us the privilege of getting the children something better to wear. Knowing what we knew of Cal's priorities, she was likely to indulge these youngsters that she held so close to her heart.

Chapter Twenty-Two

Trick's Treasure

We rode back to The Angel with lighter hearts, hoping that Cal and the children would be all right for the next few days and that maybe we'd get through to her on our next visit.

"You know, I reckon she almost told us the truth. But then the baby started fussin'," I said, glancing at Miss June as we rode back to Telegraph Creek.

"I think you're right. I'm hoping we'll find out everything when we go back to see her and the children on Sunday."

"You sure you wanna go Sunday?" Trick said. "Ain't we gonna miss the service?"

She was so deadpan, I almost thought she was serious. But Miss June laughed and rolled her eyes.

"I suppose you're right. Perhaps we'd better go another day."

Oscar pulled Onyx up sharp and gaped at Trick and Miss June like they'd plum lost their minds.

"You ain't serious. *Church service?*" he said, with a look on his face like he had a mouthful of lemons.

Trick collapsed o'er her horse's neck, laughing and pointing at Oscar like she couldn't believe he'd fallen for it. Oscar narrowed his eyes.

"All right, all right. You have your fun. When we get back, I'm goin' upstairs with Jimmy, and you better not bother us."

My ears perked up, and I couldn't wipe the smile from my face. Trick's laughter increased.

"Oh, hell," she sputtered. "Jimmy looks like he plum won the lottery or somethin'."

"Hell, I feel like I did. My injury's healin' up, so maybe I can take care of my good boy proper now."

Oscar grinned, Miss June laughed and Trick nodded.

"Well, well, well. Maybe I got some tools in my bag of tricks you can use," she said, with a glint in her eye.

"Uh-uh," Oscar said. "We don't want company."

"I don't mean that," she said, making a face. "I mean, I got some things up in my room that you might find…useful and entertainin'."

"Oh yes," Miss June said. "Trick is a bit of a collector, you see. She has some very…interesting devices and tools you might find rather intriguing."

"Oh shit," Oscar said, his gaze flashing to mine. "I cannot even imagine. Though I'm sure I could if you give me some time…"

Trick grinned. "You ain't gotta imagine anythin'. You can come have a look at what all I got — then pick and choose what you want to try."

Miss June and Trick exchanged a knowing glance.

"Well," I said and cleared my throat. "I suppose we can have a gander."

* * * *

Once we'd given the horses into William's care, we followed Trick upstairs. I'd never been in Trick's room — or any of the other girls' rooms, neither — and I was surprised by the way 'twas decorated.

There were fancy red silk cloths everywhere — draped from the ceiling and on the walls — combined with black ones, to give the space a unique and a, frankly, sensual appearance. Her bed was covered with a red silk spread and piled with black cushions of all shapes and sizes. She had a wardrobe at one end of the room and a wood chest below the window, where the black drapes were pulled aside to let in the daylight.

Trick lifted the corner of her mattress and pulled a small key from under it. She used the key to unlock the iron padlock on the chest.

"If I don't keep the damn thing locked, things start to disappear," she said. "I don't mind the other girls borrowin' things now and then, but they need to ask me first and bring them back when they're done."

"Seems reasonable," Oscar said, licking his lips and chomping at the bit to see what might be in there. He elbowed me. "See, Jimmy? There's the treasure."

Trick took off the lock and lifted the top of the chest. It creaked as it opened, and I could see 'twas full of all sorts of things that I couldn't identify just yet.

Oscar lunged forward, reaching inside and pulling out a long piece of polished wood about three feet wide, with buckled leather straps at each end.

"Oooh. I don't know what this is for, but my mind is spinnin'!" He turned it o'er in his hands, touching the buckles and flashing me a mischievous glance.

"What on earth?" I said, completely flummoxed.

Trick sat on the edge of the mattress, folding her arms across her chest. "That there is a spreader bar."

"Hell," Oscar said, his cheeks flushed and his eyes sparkling. "What?"

"Uh," I said, "so what do you do with a spreader bar?"

I was almost scared to ask, except I was awful curious, and by the reaction the device had gotten from Oscar, well, I needed to know how to use it.

Trick held her hand out and Oscar passed her the device.

"Get on the bed," she said to him, and Oscar's eyes flew wide.

"You best do as she says," I muttered.

Trick shrugged. "I'm gonna show you. Don't worry. You can keep your clothes on."

"Gee, thanks," he said, sitting down on the side of Trick's bed. "Ooh, this is soft!" he said, gliding his fingertips o'er the bedspread.

"Now move your ass back so you're sitting in the middle of the bed with your knees bent."

"Fine," Oscar said, glancing at me slyly as he got into position.

Trick put the bar between his legs and fastened one cuff to Oscar's left ankle, and the other to his right one, as I watched with increasing interest.

"Hmm," Oscar said, gazing down at his legs. "Seems a bit strange. What on earth—?"

Trick smiled, reached down and grabbed the stick, then hauled it up so Oscar's splayed legs went in the air, and he slid down onto his back.

Desire rose in me as Oscar lay there, completely helpless, his eyes wide with shock and dawning understanding.

"Oh, I *see*."

Trick grinned and lowered the bar so that Oscar's legs lay flat on the bed, then wrapped both hands around it and, in one quick movement, flipped Oscar onto his belly.

Oscar made a sound that went right to my cock as he landed, his arms spread out on the sheets, completely vulnerable and overtaken, his back moving up and down with his surprised breaths.

Trick looked at me. "See? Now you got him at your mercy for whate'er fun you wanna get up to."

"Huh," was all I managed to get out.

Oscar gathered his elbows under him and swiveled his head around to look at me.

"I reckon we need to borrow this here spreader bar," he said, voice breathless and shaky.

Trick laughed as I nodded.

"I reckon so," I said, my voice unsteady.

"You'll need a special word for Oscar to say if it gets to be too much. That's standard practice when one partner's made so vulnerable," Trick pointed out.

Oscar grinned, using his elbows to rock himself into the mattress and sighing. "Oh, we already got a stop word."

Trick gave me a wicked smile.

"Oh, I see." She laughed. "You're already gettin' up to adventures. Well, maybe this here spreader bar will give you somethin' new to try."

"I reckon it will," I said.

All I wanted at that moment was to get Oscar upstairs so we could test it out.

"Wait," Oscar said, before I had a chance to speak. "I wanna see what else you got in that trunk."

"Sure," Trick said, unbuckling the bar and passing it to me.

I took it in hands that weren't exactly steady and examined it. The workmanship looked pretty good.

"Where on earth did you get this?" I asked, as Oscar slipped off the bed and went o'er to the trunk.

"Well, Jimmy," Trick said, quirking her lip. "You see, you meet all kinds of people in this line of work."

"I can quite imagine."

"Fella said he could get me one shipped all the way from London, England."

"Good Lord. What did that cost you?"

Trick gave me a slow smile as she drew her gaze down, then up, my body.

"Less than you might think," she admitted. "Some a these poor fellas are so darn lonely and aching for touch they'll do just about anything for a few quick spanks and a wank."

Oscar cackled. He was kneeling on the wood floor and peering into the trunk, like a child on Christmas morning.

"Oh, Jimmy, we're gonna take this here ridin' crop, too," he said, lifting out a black braided leather instrument. His gaze drifted o'er it like 'twas a holy relic. "I reckon it's got a nasty snap to't."

"Oh, you'll like that," Trick said. "If you like a spankin', that's the next best thing."

Chapter Twenty-Three

Playtime

"You got a paddle in here? I'd like to try a paddle," Oscar said, as I about fainted from the things I was imagining.

"Oscar, settle down. We can't take everything that Trick has in that trunk."

He held up some metal star-shaped items with screws aimed toward the center.

"I don't even know what these are."

I walked o'er to have a look.

"What do those do?" I asked Trick.

She took one out of Oscar's hand and held it in front of her chest.

"Nipple clamp. You screw it on and leave it there to drive a fella crazy — or a gal."

"Hold on a second," I said, scratching my chin. Something didn't make sense. "Do you use these things on the men you bring up here?"

Trick gave me a leer. "It might surprise you to learn how many men like to be taken in hand. And I ain't lettin' some stranger tie me up so's I'm helpless."

Oscar stared at Trick as if she were some kind of angel.

"Ho-ly," he said. "That's amazin'."

Trick actually blushed, but she looked pleased as punch. "Well, it's fun. If I can't have a regular kinda job in this man's world, at least I can get paid to whip 'em."

She walked to the trunk and fished around with her hand.

"I ain't got a paddle exactly, but a lot of 'em like it when I beat 'em with this old thing," Trick said, pulling out a device about three feet long, made of rattan or some such material, with a wide, flat end of criss-crossed strands.

"What?" I said, laughing. "A rug beater? You're jokin'."

I held out my hand for it, and Trick passed it o'er.

Trick watched me with a smirk as I played with the beater, slicing it through the air to make a swooshing sound and trying to imagine it as a spanking aid.

"Goodness. Look at your boy, Jimmy."

I glanced at Oscar, who was kneeling by the treasure trunk, his gaze locked on the beater in my hand like 'twas the holy grail, his eyes wide and his face flushed. I reckoned he wasn't embarrassed.

Desire coursed through me at the dazed look on his pretty face.

"Makes a nice slappy sound when it makes contact," Trick said, perching on the edge of her bed. "And I've been told it delivers a good sting."

Oscar shifted his gaze from the beater in my hand to my eyes. I realized I needed to get him upstairs to the privacy of our bedchamber.

"You got everythin' you want out of that chest?" I said to Oscar, hoping he'd understand why I'd asked him.

"Yes, sir," he said, pushing himself to stand, and clutching the riding crop and the nipple clamps to his chest.

"Then let's leave Trick be so she can rest. I got some things I wanna talk to you about upstairs."

"All right," he said, glancing at Trick, who seemed to be trying not to laugh.

"You fellas have yourselves a good night."

"Oh, we aim to," Oscar said in a breathless voice, as I took his elbow and nodded to Trick.

"Thanks. We'll see you sometime tomorrow."

"Not too early. I plan to do some sleepin' in," she said. "Bye now. Careful with them things. And remember your safeword," she said to Oscar with a wink.

Safeword. That was a good thing to call it, I supposed. I hoped he wouldn't ever need to use it, but 'twas good to have, in case. The last thing I wanted to do was hurt him.

Well, no more than he wanted me to.

* * * *

We were lucky not to run into anyone else on the way to our room, which was upstairs, along the hall a-ways from Trick's. When we got inside, and I'd latched the door, I told Oscar to put the things he was holding down on the bed and use the washbasin to clean up a little.

"You don't want me all dirty and sweaty, then?" he said, shifting his braces off his shoulders and starting to unbutton his shirt.

"Not today. I want you cleaned up and presentable."

Oscar drew in a breath that whistled through his teeth. "Ho-ly," he whispered, staring at the spreader bar that I'd tossed to the mattress. "You gonna take me in hand, then?"

"I reckon I am. You wanna try out all this stuff?"

"Sure. Well, maybe we can save the nipple clamps for another day," Oscar said, eyeing the offending jewelry.

I picked up one of the steel stars and examined it. "Hmm. They sure are pretty." I glanced at him. "Sure would look nice on you."

Oscar finished unbuttoning his shirt and drew it off, giving me a stern look as my gaze focused in on one of his pinkish-brown buds.

"Now, you look here, Jimmy Downing. I do want to try out the crop and the" — his breath hitched — "the rug beater and that fancy bar, but I don't want them nipple clamps yet."

"All right," I said, with a grin. "I'll give you some time to think on it. But I reckon you'd probably enjoy a little pain in that area."

"You do, do you?" Oscar said, turning to pour some water into the basin and swishing the soap around.

"Oh, I think so."

Oscar shook his head, as if I'd been the one with my eyes bugged out and my tongue practically hanging out of my mouth in Trick's room.

He didn't say anything else, and I sat down on the bed to watch him wash up, enjoying the sight of him swiping the wet cloth o'er his face and behind his ears, then under his arms and across his chest and belly. The cool water must have felt nice against his skin, sweaty from a day out in the summer heat and sun.

"I think you got a bit of a sunburn, Oscar," I said, getting up and walking o'er.

He glanced at me and shrugged, continuing on with his washing. I cupped my hand o'er his shoulder and placed a soft kiss on the red skin at the back of his neck.

"You ain't even washed your hands yet," Oscar grumbled. "Here I'm gettin' all cleaned up, and you're makin' me dirty again."

I grinned against his warm skin and pressed my covered erection against his clothed ass. "Oh, I'm aimin' to get you plenty dirty today, boy."

Oscar froze, and I heard his breaths get quick. Then he turned right around and lifted the hand holding the wet cloth to circle my neck, as he pressed his whole entire front half against me like a horny barnacle.

"Fuck," I said, the cold cloth on my neck and the warm man in my arms doing things to my body that made me crazy. "Need to get you naked and o'er my lap."

Oscar groaned and found my mouth with his, kissing me like his life depended on it. He tasted of whiskey and cheese with citrus afternotes, and my arms wrapped around him of their own accord and held him fast.

"Oh...God..." I panted, letting him feast on my mouth, and plunging my tongue into his when I could. The sounds of our harsh breaths filled the small bedchamber, and we almost knocked the washbowl onto the floor.

"Come on," Oscar said, "Get washed up so you can take me o'er your knee," he said, slipping out of my embrace and hastening to the bed, where he laid himself out and started playing with the riding crop, his suspenders hanging down and his hair all messed up and beautiful.

I took a deep breath and grabbed the cloth, wiping myself down as quick as I could manage after stripping off my shirt. When I turned around, Oscar was watching me with a hand down his trousers.

I gave him a stern glance as I strode forward. "That there nubby is mine, Oscar Yates, and you know it. Hands off till I tell you you can touch it."

Oscar smirked at me as he pulled his hand from his pants and leaned back on his elbows, the leather crop held lightly between the fingers of his right hand. He licked his lips as I moved onto the bed and hovered o'er him, pressing my front against his groin.

He lifted his chin and let me rut against him, bending my head down so I could kiss his neck and nuzzle into his shoulder.

"Oh, you smell like horses and sun-warmed grass," he said, as the fingers of his free hand came up to weave through my hair.

"So do you," I murmured. "'Twas a lovely afternoon."

He shifted beneath me, thrusting his standing nubby against mine. We still had our trousers on. If we hadn't, this whole thing would be close to being done already. We were both right on the edge.

I took a deep breath and extricated myself from his grasp, as I kneeled up and gazed down on him. He looked so wanton lying there, bare chested and aroused, his hair mussed, the riding crop in his hand.

"Give it me," I said, holding out my hand for it.

Oscar's eyes widened, but he passed the crop to me, and I took it, examining it. 'Twas a fine piece of equipment if you were riding a stubborn animal, but otherwise I'd never use it.

Except, of course, in this exact situation.

I backed off the bed and stood up, pointing at Oscar with the crop.

"Lean o'er the edge of the bed, now."

Oscar made a noise. His eyes went wide then half-lidded as he obeyed me, crawling off the bed and putting himself into the position I'd indicated. The bed was pretty high, so his legs stretched out behind him, and his bare toes found purchase against the floorboards.

"Like this?" he said, stretching his arms above his head and turning his face, so his cheek lay against the bedcovers. He blinked at me all innocent, like he didn't know the very sight of him was gonna be the end of me.

Chapter Twenty-Four

A Suitable Punishment

"That's fine," I said, taking a deep breath. "Now, push your trousers down. You've been such a naughty boy, Oscar."

I watched a shudder go through him as he closed his eyes. Then he crept his fingers to the fastenings of his pants. He pierced me with an incendiary gaze as he undid them, and lowered them to his thighs, revealing the perfect, pale globes of his ass.

I whistled. "Why, that's lovely."

Oscar blinked, his chest rising and falling with his breaths.

I stepped forward and tapped one pale cheek with the folded leather end of the riding crop.

Oscar started. Then his lips twitched as he settled in for what was coming.

"Be still," I said.

"Yes, sir."

He clutched the coverlet in his fists as he waited.

"Hmm. Let me get a feel for this thing before I start."

I wanted to make sure I could estimate the force of each blow, and I'd rarely even used a crop on a horse, so I turned away from Oscar and swept it through the air a few times. It made a lovely whooshing sound, and I was sure 'twould deal a nasty blow if I used enough force. But I only wanted to tease him with a little sting. I didn't want to leave a bruise or a cut.

When I turned back, Oscar was about humping the bed, he was so horny for that thing. I almost laughed, but 'twould have given the wrong impression. I didn't think he was silly at all. But the way he melted at the thought of a little discipline and pain from an ass whooping was amusing as hell.

"All right now. Settle down. I reckon this is gonna hurt. Remember your safeword, now."

"Yes, Jimmy, I will."

"Also, you can tell me to stop, and I will. I don't plan to have you beggin' for mercy until I've got my cock buried inside you."

"Oh fuck. Je-sus."

"Uh-huh. I reckon he won't be able to help you right now."

Oscar nodded frantically, and I went for it. I brought the crop down quick, so the tip snapped against the skin of his ass with a very satisfying *thwack*.

Oscar made a noise — something between a grunt and a groan — as he thrust against the bed.

"Don't you even think about spillin', boy. We just fucking started."

"I won't. I won't," he panted, sliding his cheek against the bedspread, his mouth open and his eyes wide.

"All right. Now I want you to count."

Silence. Then he pushed out a breath.

"What?"

"I want you to count each strike, after it hits you. That was a freebie. So start at one."

"Oh my — Okay."

"Okay?"

"Yes, sir, I mean."

Not sure where I'd got the counting idea, but it seemed right. I wanted Oscar to be mentally engaged in what was happening. Seemed like making him count would add to his debasement. And if I knew Oscar — and I *did* — debasement combined with a bit of pain was what he lived for.

Fortunately for him, I didn't mind providing it.

The next strike landed across both buttocks, and he squealed like an animal. If the sound hadn't become a low, throaty moan, I might have worried 'twas too much.

"One," Oscar said, gulping a breath and giving a soft grunt of pleasure.

"You all right?" I asked.

"Oh yeah. G-good."

I did chuckle then. He enjoyed this sort of thing so much, and I couldn't deny him anything he wanted, no matter how strange it might be. 'Twas his 'wanting' as he'd called it — something a person enjoyed that might not make sense to anyone but the person wanting it. I understood that because there were things I enjoyed, too, like having my boy bent o'er the bed like this, trousers around his ankles, ass in the air for me. I liked it an awful lot.

I gave him eight swats with the crop, 'till there were pink stripes laid out across him in a lovely pattern.

"Eight!" he yelled out after the last one and gave such a godawful groan I imagined I'd either killed him or he'd spent too early.

"Oh fuck, you okay?" I said, dropping the implement and flopping down beside him.

"Yes. Oh God. Jimmy, I'm...fine? I'm in such a good, floaty place right now."

"You are? Really?"

"Really."

"What do you want? You want more of the crop or somethin' else?"

He lay there breathing harshly, considering what I'd asked.

"Somethin' else," he said finally.

"Okay."

He turned his head to regard me, those soft brown eyes full of need. "I want you to spread me with that bar and fuck me. Please, Jimmy."

Those words from his sweet mouth about did me in.

"Fine," I panted. "All right. You wanna wait for your ass to calm down?"

He shook his head. "No. I wanna feel it and remember it while you're tuppin' me."

"All right then."

Part of me was glad, because I sure did want to do that. I only hoped he didn't regret it once we got going, though I supposed we could make adjustments if needed.

"Take your trousers down all the way then and fold them. Put them on that chair along with your other stuff. And don't you touch your little nubby. I don't care how desperate it feels. That nubby's mine, and I aim to take care of it when the time comes."

"Yes, sir."

I went and got the bar, while Oscar did as he'd been told. When he was naked, I had him get up onto the bed.

"Sit on your swatted ass and give me your ankles."

He shot me a saucy grin as he obeyed, flinching as the skin of his ass made contact.

"Oh, that smarts," he hissed.

"Good. Bad boys get whooped by their daddies."

"Fuck," he murmured, as I buckled one of the leather cuffs around his ankle.

I glanced at his cock. 'Twas bobbing there against his belly, wet at the tip and down the front, too, which was par for the course with Oscar when I took him in hand like this. I reckoned it had started leaking the first time the crop had touched him.

"You sure do like this," I said.

"You sure do know it."

I smiled. "Oh yes, I do. Now…"

I straightened and lifted the bar, like I'd seen Trick do when Oscar had been fully clothed.

He went down flat on his back and flinched again as his sore ass rubbed on the sheets.

"Goddamn," he grunted.

I stared at him for a long moment, savoring the control I had o'er him, before I flipped him quick onto his front.

Oscar groaned and reached for the bed covers, as I held the bar and eyed his rosy, cropped ass.

"Oh, my goodness," I murmured, licking my lips. My cock pushed against the front of my trousers at the debauched sight of him.

The way the bar kept him spread, I could see between the rosy cheeks of his ass, to that soft pink place I wanted so bad. I saw it contract and release as Oscar imagined what was about to happen.

"God, Jimmy. I'm trapped. You got me."

"I sure do. Now, what on earth am I gonna do with you?"

Chapter Twenty-Five

Earthly Delights

I had ideas. Boy, did I have ideas.

First thing I did was get naked. I made sure I was in Oscar's line of sight where he had his head resting on the bed, turned to the side, as I meticulously removed what was left of my clothing and folded everything up nice and neat. Making Oscar wait for his pleasure was a sure-fire way of inflaming him.

Sure enough, he groaned in anguish.

"God! Come on!"

"What?" I said, lazily pumping my cock as I regarded him.

"Jimmy!"

"What do you want?"

"You know what I want! Jesus!"

"You want Jesus? Pretty sure he wouldn't know what the fuck to do with you."

That got a frustrated laugh from him, but then he knitted his brows together.

"Jimmy, *please!*"

I sat down on the bed beside him and wove my fingers into his hair. 'Twas growing out from the severe trimming it had got at the hands of Irene this winter, and 'twas looking more like it had when we'd met. I liked it a lot, and it sure gave me more to grab.

I did grab it then, forcing his head back while I watched contemplatively.

"Open your mouth, boy."

Oscar gasped and did as he was told.

"Let me see that tongue."

He shuddered but did as I'd asked like the good boy he tended to be in the bedroom, and no place else.

"Very good. I'm gonna put it to use. But first, you're gonna lie there and take what I'm gonna give you."

"Yes, Jimmy."

"Good boy."

I relaxed my fingers and gave his head a tousle, then stood and moved behind him. Oscar gasped as I kneeled up onto the bed, with the bar under my calves, and grasped his ruddy ass in my palms, slipping my thumbs between them to slide along the sensitive crease.

"Oh fuck. Oh fuck," Oscar panted. "Ow."

"A bit tender?"

"Yeah. Feels good."

He couldn't bring his legs together, so he simply lay there and let me play with him. I took my time, too. We didn't have anywhere to go or anything else we needed to do. This was exactly what we both needed.

I was so much recovered that my injury didn't twinge or ache at all no more, and I figured 'twas time to take my boy in hand right proper — and believe me, I did.

Once I had him squirming and gasping, I bent to him and licked across his hungry hole, making him cry out.

"Jimmy!"

"Yeah?" I said, licking him again.

"Oh God, oh God, oh God."

"Ain't no use callin' out to Him, you godless, wanton thing. He ain't gonna help you."

"I know it. I don't want Him. I want you, Jimmy."

"You're gettin' me right now, the way I want you to have me. So be quiet and let me worship you."

He was quiet then, as much as he could be, as I used my tongue and fingers to drive him into a state of barely contained frenzy. By the time I had him about ready to explode, I stopped and moved up ahead of him on the mattress.

He watched me, his gaze dark and intense, as I settled with my back against the headboard and my legs spread to either side of him, stroking my cock in a lazy, anticipatory fashion.

"What are you doin'?" Oscar asked in a breathy, barely-there voice.

"Waitin'."

"For what?"

"This."

I let go of my cock and slid my hands under Oscar's arms, pulling him forward, so that he was in a good position to take my cock down his throat.

He didn't need any prompting. As soon as I'd placed him where I wanted him, he planted his hands on the bed either side of my hips and swallowed me up.

I cried out at the intense and sudden pleasure, shifting so Oscar could take as much of me as he could manage — and he could manage quite a bit. The choking noises he made as he hungrily went at me were the icing on the cake, as was the sight of his ankles bound to the stiff bar that kept his legs spread for me, for whenever I was ready.

Which was sooner rather than later.

"Stop, stop," I said, pushing at his shoulder to get him to back off. "I don't wanna spend in your mouth."

Oscar pulled off me with a slurp and a wink.

"Where you gonna spend, Jimmy?"

I gazed at the upstart who had stolen my heart all that time ago in Dawson City.

"You know where."

"Tell me."

I stroked the hair back from his forehead as we held each other's gazes. Then I cupped his face and said, "I'm gonna spend so deep inside you, you might well get with child — especially 'cause there's gonna be a quart of it."

His face took on a look of agony and he groaned. "Do it. Fuck me deep and hard. I'll be your good boy and take it all."

"I know you will," I said.

I kissed him hard and thrust my tongue in his willing mouth, then let him go and pulled away, moving out from under him and sliding off the bed. I walked around, admiring how he was placed, spread and waiting for me.

"I need to remember how this looks," I said. "This bar sure is a handy thing."

Oscar rubbed his forehead against the sheets as his hips swayed.

"I reckon I could probably make somethin' like this that we could use back home."

"Oh God," Oscar moaned.

I got up behind him kneeled on the mattress, with my calves o'er the bar to keep Oscar still.

"'Twouldn't be quite this nice, maybe, but 'twould work about the same."

I grabbed the bottle of oil that Trick had given us and dribbled some o'er Oscar's exposed hole, as he made the most delicious noises. Then I spread some on my cock and lined myself up.

Oscar grunted as I breached him, then keened as I pushed in. He felt so warm and tight, and my eyes rolled back in my head. I had to stop for a second to keep control of myself.

"You like that?"

"Oh. God. More."

"You need to wait. I gotta be ready."

"Jimmy!"

"So impatient. Such a needy boy," I said, pushing in a fraction of an inch at a time, eliciting whimpers and tortured cries.

"Please! I need it so bad. So, so bad."

"I know you do—and you'll get it. But only when I'm ready."

"Oh fuck. Oh God."

I gave a few shallow thrusts, to tease him, then I couldn't wait anymore. I pushed in all the way in one smooth glide, and Oscar about swallowed his tongue. There was a ragged gasp and a groan, and I thought he might have spent, but I quick found his cock with my hand and he hadn't...not yet.

"Oh," he moaned, panting and crying out as I plowed him.

I held his sweet ass, keeping his cheeks spread with my thumbs, and went at him slow and deep, as the sounds of our coupling echoed off the whitewashed walls of our cozy room.

"Fuck me. Hard," Oscar said through clenched teeth as I played with his cock.

"Who's in charge, Oscar?"

"Oh fuck. You, Jimmy. You're in charge."

"Then, you gonna ask me nice?"

"Please fuck me. I need it hard and quick. I wanna spend. Please."

"Hmm, I reckon you've been a good boy. I suppose you need a reward."

"Oh, please. *Please.*"

I quickened my pace and rammed him. I was close…so close.

"You want it? You want my spend inside you?" I panted.

"Give it me. I want it. *Please!*"

That last plea, in Oscar's choked and desperate voice, was what did it. I sank deep and stilled, emptying into him, my eyes squeezed shut and my mouth wide at the intensity of it. I tightened my fingers on his cock as it pulsed with the pinnacle of his pleasure, and hot spend gushed o'er my knuckles.

We stayed that way for several moments, stunned with the powerful cataclysm of our joining. As I came down from it, breathing hard like I'd run a mile, I became aware of a dull ache in my side — the echo of my injury. But I didn't give a good goddamn about that. I stayed where I was, enveloped in Oscar's body, till after what seemed a long time my cock shrank and slipped out of him, followed by a trickle of my spend.

I dipped my finger in it and pushed it back inside him.

"You keep it all, now," I whispered. "Clench that fine ass and keep my spend inside you."

Oscar whimpered. He'd collapsed onto the sheets when we'd spent. His ass was still pink from the cropping, and he looked so debauched and pretty I couldn't take it. I unbuckled the spreader bar and tossed it aside. Then I cozied in beside him on the bed.

"I love you, my good boy. I'm glad I can fuck you properly, now."

"Me, too. God, you treat me so good."

"You mean, so bad?" I joked. "I do like to tease you, so—then be rough with you. You sure you like that?"

He turned his head to throw me a dreamy, dazed look.

"You even gotta ask that?" he said, in a fucked-out voice. "You're my strict daddy, and I love you so much." He grinned. "You know I'm the one in charge, really. Don't ya?"

I smiled wider. "Oh, I do know that…ever since we met."

He grinned and kissed me sweetly, then pulled back so he could meet my gaze. "We're only playin' games. Because 'tis fun and naughty and I like it—and so do you."

"That's a fact," I said. "I only wonder sometimes why we like that…"

"Does it matter? Who the fuck cares? We ain't hurtin' nobody."

I nodded. "True. You're right."

"Yes, I am. And I don't want you frettin' about it, because 'tis only bedroom games, and it don't matter." He sounded so sure of himself, and I had to admit he was right. "And, anyway, I like it, and you know you'll give me anythin' I want. Right, Jimmy?"

I knew that was true.

"I can't help myself. You got me good. Right where you want me."

"And don't you ever forget it."

Chapter Twenty-Six

Ice Cream

The following week, Miss June, Trick, Oscar and I rode back to Cal's place. It made sense for us to go in a group, but we'd decided that Cal was most likely to confide in Miss June — and only if they had some privacy.

So, if it turned out that Cal's husband was still 'away', as we expected, Miss June would stay at the house with Cal, and Trick and Oscar and I would take the older children into the village, to see about some new clothes.

When we arrived at their place, the situation was the same as before. Caliope assured us again that Mr. Webster would return sometime soon, but we had our doubts. Trick asked if we could take the children into Agnes Hill and do some shopping, and Caliope gave us leave without any trouble. I reckoned she was glad to have a break, although we had to leave Sam, as he was too young to be taken on horseback, and anyway, none of us wanted to be in charge of such a young child.

Lizzie, of course, wanted to ride on 'Onis', so Oscar lifted her up in front of him, while Peter rode behind me on Dixie. Oscar and Lizzie made a pretty picture, and I exchanged warm glances with my husband as we rode to town on this mild summer day. In another strange universe, perhaps we could have had a little girl of our own to raise, but this was enough, and I enjoyed seeing him taking good care of the child.

Lizzie and Peter seemed thrilled to get away from the farm for a ride into town, and no doubt they looked forward to the acquisition of some better clothing. Miss June had provided enough money from the coffers of The Angel to get a new set of things for each of them, including shoes and boots. She said she was glad to do it and valued giving back some of her earnings to folks who needed help.

When we got to Agnes Hill, the first thing we did was stop for a bite to eat. I had no idea if the children had had any breakfast. From the way they scarfed down the milk and biscuits Trick bought at the roadside stand, I figured they hadn't.

Once they were done, we went shopping for clothes. Oscar and Trick went with Lizzie, and I took Peter to get some decent pants and shirts.

By the time we were finished, Peter had two new sets of trousers and shirts, a pair of boots and good shoes, and a nice hat that looked like mine and would keep the sun off. Lizzie had two new dresses — a fancy one and a plain one — new shoes, and a pretty straw hat. She'd also talked Oscar into getting her a soft cloth puppy dog that she'd seen in a shop window.

I swear, my young husband had the most generous heart this side of Saskatchewan. 'Twas probably a good thing we couldn't have a little one of our own, or we'd be plumb broke by the time it turned two. Between me indulging Oscar's wants and Oscar indulging the child, there wouldn't have been any money left!

But the way Lizzie held that little toy dog to her chest was enough to make me sigh with the tiniest bit of regret that there'd be no little 'uns runnin' through our house.

We decided to give the children one more treat before heading back and stopped at the general store for some ice cream.

"We ain't never had any before," Peter said, as we gazed at the small, framed chalkboard behind the counter, with the available flavors listed in large white printed letters.

"What flavor do you want, Lizzie?" Oscar asked, gazing up at the words on the board. "There's vanilla and chocolate. Why, there's even lemon," he said, with such a casual air that I blinked with surprise and couldn't help the smile that formed on my face. 'Twas because of me, and because of Oscar's hard work learning his letters and practicing, that he could read those words, and I was more'n proud. He turned to glance at me, and his smile matched mine. Then he looked down at Lizzie.

Her eyes had gone wide at the thought of the special treat. She looked at Oscar, her mouth open as if she wanted to choose but couldn't possibly. Peter seemed equally overwhelmed.

"Why, I think I'll have the chocolate," I said.

"You want chocolate, Lizzie? I was going to have vanilla, but I think I'll have what Jimmy's havin'," Oscar said.

"Okay," Lizzie said, in a very small voice. "Me, too, please."

"Peter?" Oscar said.

"I'll have vanilla, please."

Oscar ordered the sweet treats from the shopkeeper, and soon we were sitting around the corner on a bench, the children licking the cream from their cones with dazed and happy expressions on their sweet faces.

I couldn't keep my gaze off Oscar's tongue as he licked his chocolate ice cream, and then our gazes met, and I felt a jolt of arousal go through me. But now was not the time, so I averted my gaze as he smirked, and Lizzie uttered a startled cry.

I looked o'er to see little Lizzie staring down at her scoop of ice cream, which had fallen onto her brand-new dress that, of course, she'd insisted on wearing.

She started to cry before any of us had time to react.

"I'm sorry. I'm sorry," she sniffed. "I ruined my new dress! I should have been more careful."

Peter flashed me a panicked look, then put a hand on Lizzie's shoulder as we rushed to reassure her.

"But 'tis my *only* nice frock, the other one gots blood all over it and t'was my favorite. That'll *never* come out, so momma burned it up."

Oscar and Trick and I looked at each other, as Peter tried to shush the sobbing child.

"What do you mean it's got blood on it?" Oscar said, crouching down to be at eye level with the distraught youngster. "How did your dress get blood on it, Lizzie?"

Peter seemed uncomfortable and said, "She got too close when Pa chopped the rooster up, that's all."

"No, I didn't!" Lizzie whispered. "You know I didn't! You know what the blood's from. You *know*, Peter! You saw it, just like I did."

An icy shiver of dread sliced down my spine.

"Lizzie, shush! You know Momma wouldn't want us sayin'," Peter said, in the same hushed voice, as if what they were referring to was something secret and private.

Lizzie's next words, uttered in that same low whisper of shame and despair, made everything clear in one, fell swoop, like an axe cutting through a sheep's skull.

"She chopped him up. 'Twasn't the rooster and Pa, 'twas *Momma* and Pa…in the barn." Lizzie hiccupped and took in a shuddering breath. "And I'm *glad* she did it, Peter, 'cept it stained my best frock, and now I've ruined this one, too!"

Peter looked like he wanted to grab Lizzie and run, but he realized 'twould be futile. Instead, he stood stock still, staring at the ground for a moment before raising his gaze to mine.

"I'm sorry," he whispered. "Momma didn't want us to tell."

I looked at our surroundings. We were fortunate that there weren't any townsfolk near enough to overhear the alarming conversation. Then I met Oscar's gaze. He looked the way I felt, like everything had become clear, but 'twas nothing we'd ever expected or knew how to handle.

"It's all right, Lizzie," I said. "You ain't done nothing wrong by telling us."

Lizzie's sobs increased.

"Is Momma gonna be locked up?" she said, in the smallest voice. And Oscar jumped into action.

He crouched down and clasped her slim arms, so he could get her to look at him. "No. No, Lizzie, your momma ain't goin' nowhere. We ain't gonna tell no-one, so you can stop cryin'. And now you've got *two* new dresses, and we can get the ice cream mark off this one easy. Don't you worry. It ain't ruined at all."

I could have kissed him as Lizzie nodded and tried to smile through her tears.

"Peter, can I talk to you for a minute?" I asked, gesturing for him to follow me down the sidewalk a ways. Trick eyed me but she didn't comment and stayed with Oscar and Lizzie.

Peter followed me to a spot in the shadows of a sycamore tree, where we could speak in some measure of privacy.

"Now I need you to tell me the truth. Did your momma kill your pa, like Lizzie said?"

Peter nodded, his face pale and his eyes wild. "Yes, sir."

I put a steadying hand on his shoulder. He'd gone all pale, and I reckoned this conversation was bringing it all back to him, but we needed to know.

"Why do you suppose she did it?"

"Because—" Peter said, but he only got that word out before tears started to fall from his brown eyes. He was silent at first, then his lips trembled as his face contorted, and he started to sob in earnest.

Chapter Twenty-Seven

The Truth

I moved forward and pulled him against me. His arms went around me, and he clutched at my jacket, like 'twas the only thing he had in his life that was sure.

"It's okay. You don't have to say," I reassured him, wondering what had driven Cal to an act of such aggression, but knowing the ways of the world well enough to have an idea. I didn't want to think about it, and neither did Peter, it seemed.

"Come on. Let's go back to the others," I said, holding out my hand. Peter let me walk him back to where Oscar was cleaning Lizzie's dress with a wet handkerchief.

"See? 'Tis coming right out. Once this dries, nobody'll be able to tell."

"You're right," Lizzie said, tucking her chin to her chest in order to see the front of her dress. She gazed up at Oscar with adoring eyes. "Thank you."

He straightened and flashed me a look. "'Tis nothin'," he said, as Peter and I joined them.

Trick stood there watching with concern etched on her features. I left Peter with Lizzie and took Oscar and Trick aside.

"He ain't ready to say why, but he said what Lizzie said was true. That Cal—that she...murdered her husband—their pa."

"I knew Cal was hidin' somethin'," Trick said, as Peter brought Lizzie o'er. Seemed they didn't want to be far from us, and I couldn't blame them. "Never thought 'twas murder, though."

I glanced at Peter and gave him a reassuring smile.

"I reckon she had a good reason for it," Oscar murmured. "Seems the children think so."

"Sure," I said, keeping my voice low.

The children could hear, but I reckoned none of what we said would hurt them any more than they already had been.

"It explains why her husband ain't around, and why her situation's so desperate... She's all alone with these children," I said. "She ain't got no help but us."

"My pa was a terrible man," Peter said.

We all turned to face him.

"Did he...did he beat you? You and Lizzie?" Oscar asked.

Peter's face was red, and he'd curled his hands into fists. "No, sir."

His answer was a surprise to all of us. Oscar was about to say something else, but I held up my hand to stay him as Peter continued speaking.

"Not with fists or his belt. But what he did was worse."

Oscar leaned against the side of the building we were standing next to. "Worse?"

"He...our pa..." Peter looked to Lizzie, who was staring at him with wide eyes. "He said terrible things to us...all the time. And to Momma. And at night, he'd pray out loud and ask God to save him from us because we were evil, Momma was leading him astray and he didn't know what to do about us. He said we were... He said we were all full of sin—even the baby—and that God would punish us."

Lizzie covered her ears as she snugged up against Peter.

"But Momma? She told us that wasn't true, that our pa was troubled and we weren't to believe the things he said. Only 'twas hard, because he was always sayin' it, and lookin' at us and at Momma like we had the devil in us."

"You call Caliope your momma. Did your pa make you?"

"Yes, sir, he did. He said she was our momma now. That's the only good thing our pa ever did was bring Momma to us."

"What happened to the momma who birthed you?" I was afraid to ask. If their pa had been so cruel, what had happened to her?

"She died of typhus, two years ago," Peter said. "I was eight and Lizzie was five, and Sam had barely been birthed. I know 'twas hard for Pa, and I tried to help. And he'd always been holy and talkin' about God and the devil, but after our first momma died, it got so much worse. He said God took our other momma because we were so bad, and God would punish us— or that pa would, one day. He said he'd kill us if he thought God would want it."

"Now, Peter, you know that ain't true, those things he said."

"'Course I know it. We's just kids. Look at Lizzie. Why, how could she be evil?" Peter said, with scorn and contempt for the very idea. "And Sam's a baby!"

As if to emphasize this, Lizzie snuggled into Peter and cuddled her toy dog with the most beguiling innocence. I put a hand on Peter's back, so proud of his good sense and the fact that he hadn't let his pa's misguided ideas poison him or his siblings.

"That's right. There ain't nothin' evil 'bout any of you. I reckon the evil was all in him, only he couldn't admit it to himself, so he struck out at you all."

"Yes, sir. Momma got the worst of it. He'd yell, throw curses at her and tell her she should go throw herself in the river. He said she was a demon, and she didn't deserve to live. That she was nasty and vile, and he only put up with her because she looked after us." Peter's face screwed up with puzzlement. "But Momma is the kindest person, and I don't know how he could e'en think that about her."

I glanced at Oscar, who'd gone as pale as a ghost at the thought of that man treating his own children, and Cal — *our* Cal — that way.

"He said almost every day that he'd murder her when she was sleepin' and us in our beds, too, but that was only to control us and keep us scared. We were scared. We never knew what he might do...or when. I reckon 'twas only a matter of time until he did what he kept sayin' he'd do." Peter wrapped his arm around Lizzie and met my gaze. "I wasn't upset when Momma took the axe to him. 'Cept 'twas gruesome to watch, and I tried to hide the others from it."

I couldn't speak for a moment, imagining living with those threats, day in and day out.

"I know you did your best, Peter. I'm so sorry you had to see that."

Peter nodded. "I don't blame Momma one bit."

"I don't blame her either, if 'twas as you say." My voice was soft and careful.

"'Twas because of *us* — me and Lizzie and Sam — that Momma stayed with him and put up with him for so long. She wouldn't leave us."

We were sober as we mounted the horses to head back to the homestead. The children were quiet and so were we, thinking about everything we'd learned. Peter laid his head against my back as we rode back to Telegraph Creek, and I hoped my warmth and my steady heartbeat was a comfort. But as we got closer to where Miss June and Cal were, I felt him stiffen and sit straighter, his arms clasping me tight.

"Are you gonna tell Momma that you know what happened?"

"I reckon we won't tell her that right away. But we're gonna have to let her know soon enough."

"I hope she won't be mad at us. 'Twasn't Lizzie's fault. She's only seven."

"Of course not. We knew somethin' wasn't right. You all were livin' in such a state, and there weren't no sign of your pa, even though Cal said he was travelin' to find work. We didn't really believe her."

Peter nodded.

"And when Sam wouldn't go in the barn, 'twas even more obvious that something had happened in there."

"Uh-huh. We ain't been in there since."

I wanted to ask Peter what Cal had done with the body, but I didn't have the heart to. And, anyhow, at that moment Trick pulled her horse up and said my name.

"Yeah?"

"Look."

The view of Cal's home was still blocked by the trees, but we could see the old barn in the distance.

"Is that Cal?" I said, squinting.

"And Miss June, I think."

I could make out a hunched figure that must be Cal, sagging against the barn door, her hands planted flat on it and her forehead pressed against the wood. Miss June stood beside her, her lips moving and head bobbing, and she was holding Sam, who was crying and trying to escape her hold. Cal was rocking back and forth and shaking her head. A heart-wrenching sob rose from Cal's crouched form.

"You keep the kids here. I'll go," Trick said.

"All right."

We stayed behind, while Trick dismounted and approached them.

Cal didn't seem to take any notice of her, and Miss June said a few things to Trick then took the baby back to the house, glancing to us and gesturing for us to come to the house with her.

"Looks like Miss June wants to speak to us at the house," I said to the children.

Lizzie was peering at her momma crouched by the barn.

"Is Momma all right?"

"Trick'll make sure she is," I said. "Trick and Cal — your momma — have known each other a long time."

We left the horses with Trick's mount and walked to the house, the children glancing at their momma but obediently following us.

When we went inside the house, Miss June had Sam in his highchair with a wedge of seed cake in his small fists that he was taking bites off with the utmost concentration. The tears had made streaks through the dirt on his face, but he seemed content now that he had cake to eat.

"Hello," I said.

"Well! I can see that your trip to town was a smashing success!" Miss June said. Her face was flushed as if she'd been crying, but she smiled and put on a pleased expression. "My, what a beautiful green dress, Lizzie!"

"'Tis my favorite color. Only, I got some ice cream on't."

"Never mind, we can look after that. Did you get some new clothes, too, Peter?"

"Yes'm. A pair of boots and some shoes — and a hat, too!" he took off the cowboy hat he was wearing and showed her.

"Well, that's fine, isn't it? You look the proper country gentleman now." Miss June glanced at Sam, then looked at Peter. "Would you mind watching Lizzie and Sam for me while I speak with Jimmy and Oscar?"

"No, ma'am. I mean, yes, I'll watch 'em."

"Thank you. There's fresh lemonade with ice on the counter for all of you."

Peter's eyes bugged. "Thank you, ma'am!"

She motioned to me and Oscar.

"Let's go outside for a moment."

We stepped out of the door and into the yard. Of course, the first thing I did was to check on Trick and Cal from a distance. They were sitting together on the grass by the barn. Trick had her arm around Cal, and she was talking to her, which was an improvement from before.

"We know what happened to Cal's husband," Oscar said, in grave tones. "When Lizzie got some ice cream on her dress, she let it slip that her other good dress got ruined with all the blood."

Miss June glanced back at the closed door of the house, her hand o'er her mouth. "Those poor children."

"I reckon they're better off now, though," I said.

"Yes," Miss June said. "Did they tell you anything else? Cal told me she killed Albert, but not how or…"

Oscar looked to me for assistance.

I took Miss June's arm to keep her steady. "They said she…chopped him up with the axe."

Miss June's face went from shock to grim determination.

She glanced to where Cal was huddled with Trick. Then she turned back to us and crossed her arms.

"Caliope wouldn't have done something like that unless there was no other option."

I nodded. "I know it."

"Peter said something else," Oscar added.

Miss June gazed at us, her eyes wide.

I frowned. "He said that their pa was cruel and hurtful, but he didn't use physical force. Seemed like their pa believed in all the wrong things and tried to convince the children and Cal that they were evil and vile."

"In some ways, that's worse."

"Yeah. That can mess a person up. But those children, they're strong. And Cal protected them as well as she could," I said.

Miss June put a trembling hand to her head but stayed silent.

"Sounds like he only wanted Cal so she could look after the little ones and satisfy him in the bedroom," I said. "E'en though he told her she was vile."

Miss June nodded. "I suppose that's how he felt about himself. Shame can do terrible things to a person."

I snorted. "I can't find it in me to feel one bit sorry for that man."

"I didn't mean that. I'm just trying to make sense of it."

Oscar cursed. "Goddammit. 'Tain't fair."

"No, it ain't," I muttered. "Life ain't fair, Oscar. Why, you'd know that better'n any of us."

He gazed at me out of grateful brown eyes. "Except now I got you. And I only wish Cal could have been lucky enough to find a man like you to love her."

I stared at him, feeling how lucky we both were. And the truth of it was, if I hadn't already given my heart to Oscar, I might have found a place for Cal in my life. I'd been fascinated and enthralled by her, back in the fall, but I was already taken. And she'd been different to what she was now. I only hoped she could find her way back.

Miss June found the will to smile.

"Well, there aren't a lot of men like Jimmy in the world, I'm afraid."

"Come on, now," I said. "I ain't anythin' special." A lot of the time I felt I was barely above contempt, what with my history and all. But I tried to be a good person, to make up for it.

Miss June and Oscar smiled at each other, and Oscar snugged into my side, placing a soft kiss on my cheek.

"Now look," Miss June said. "We need to help Cal get past this, if there's even a chance that she can. 'Twas a violent, horrible thing she had to do, but I reckon that was the easiest part. Now she has to live with what she's done, and so do those children. I have a feeling Cal's been wrestling with the guilt of it, and that's what's dimming the light inside her. And God knows she's been struggling to look after the little ones all by herself."

"What do you propose we do?" I said, glancing at Cal and Trick, then looking at Miss June. "Oscar and I can stay for another few weeks, I reckon, but then we'll have to go back to Port Essington and see about getting some work."

"I know," Miss June said, placing her hand on my arm. "I'm so grateful to you for being here. If we can only keep you a little longer, I'm sure we can sort this out somehow."

I nodded and glanced at Oscar, who had straightened up and now stood beside me.

"We ain't goin' nowhere until Cal's doin' okay. Right, Jimmy?" Oscar said.

"Of course. We did come to Telegraph Creek to help her, after all. Turns out findin' her was only the start of it."

"Yes, it seems that's the case," Miss June stated.

The door creaked, and Peter stuck his head out.

"Miss June, I changed Sam's cloth 'cause he shat himself. Where should I put the dirty stuff? Momma usually takes it somewhere."

"Oh, Peter, bless you. Thank you. You are such a great help to your momma and me. Here... Let me show you what to do."

Miss June went inside with Peter, while Oscar and I stood together, watching Trick and Cal.

"Those children are so lucky Cal came to 'em, e'en if 'twas through trickery," Oscar said. "Cal may have done something horrible, but I reckon 'twas deserved."

"I reckon so," I said, gazing into the distance, where Trick and Cal sat by the old barn. "I wonder where the pieces are."

Oscar paled and looked at the barn.

"I suppose we'll have to ask her...but not yet."

"No, not yet," Oscar agreed.

We stood under the trees near the homestead as the sun climbed higher and the breeze picked up, giving us some relief from the sticky summer heat.

Chapter Twenty-Eight

A Puzzling Dilemma

Eventually, Trick brought Cal back to the house and left her in the care of Miss June, while the three of us strolled back to the barn.

"Do you suppose Albert's—bits—are buried here somewhere?" Oscar said with distaste, as he gazed at the barn and its surroundings.

I glanced his way. "I did think it strange that there was fresh straw o'er the floors in there, when Cal had said they didn't use the barn and that nobody had been in there for so long."

Trick murmured something.

"Huh?" Oscar said.

"She threw him in the river. Well, she threw what was left of him in the river," Trick said, kicking at a stone with her boot. "Anyway, 'twould stink if she'd put him under the floorboards in the barn. Cal's not that stupid."

"But how—?" I couldn't picture it, what with the children around.

Trick stopped walking and stood there, giving us a steady look as she related what Cal had told her.

"She took the children to the well and cleaned everyone up, put them to bed and told them everything was fine, that she had to do what she did and that their lives would be much better for it."

Our somber gazes flitted between each other, as we thought about that.

Trick continued after a minute.

"I doubt those children were all that upset about Albert's death, only the glimpse they got of their kind and loving momma bein' so...efficient."

I stared at the ground. "Did she tell you how he was? How he threatened and maligned them at every opportunity?"

"Uh-huh."

My heart wept at the cruelty of it all. That Cal had been forced to do something so awful for the sake of her own survival...and the children's.

"Once the children were in bed, Cal snuck back out to take care of it. She must have been exhausted, but she got rid of all the evidence of her husband's demise, cleaned up the barn and spread the fresh straw on the floor to hide any stains that were left."

Trick gazed into the distance, toward where the Stikine River cut through the valley. "Nasty business, but from what Cal and the children say, 'twasn't much else they could do."

The three of us were silent for a long while, as we stood in the grass by the old barn.

"Well," I said, finally, "if there ain't nobody's bits buried in the barn, I reckon we should think about makin' it weatherproof and gettin' Cal a milk cow and, maybe a horse and small cart — and some chickens."

Trick grinned and pulled her hat down on her forehead.

"I reckon that's a good idea. We don't gotta say nothin' more about what happened to Cal's husband. Nobody's come lookin' for him. I bet he ain't got no friends around here. Sounds like a right nasty piece of work."

"Trick, I gotta ask you somethin'. Were you suspicious at all, when he came to see Cal at The Angel? What I mean is, did he seem like he was a good man who might make all of Cal's dreams come true?"

Trick frowned. "He put on a pretty good show of caring for her — though, in retrospect, all the showy stuff might have been a giveaway that he was tryin' to hide something. 'Tis easy to bring flowers and pretty words for someone, and make them care about you, 'specially if that person ain't got much in their life already. Anybody can do that. Takes a real good man to fulfill his promises, I reckon."

Trick kicked at the ground and shoved her hands into the pockets of her trousers. "I could murder the bastard myself for turning Cal into this — *husk* of a person. She ain't the same as she was."

"No, she ain't," Oscar said.

"She's got the children now. They seem to mean a lot to her," I said.

"That's true," Trick said.

She looked at the house, then at me and Oscar. "Well, now that the truth has come out, she and the children can put it behind them and get on with their lives."

I nodded. But I wondered what kind of lives they could have, without a working man to bring money in.

All they had was the small house, the old barn and the land, with no means to farm it.

We were all thinking that, I figured, as we stood by the barn and waited for Miss June to join us.

Eventually she did, striding across the grass in her long skirts and pretty blouse. She was carrying the broad-brimmed hat she wore by its strings, and the expression on her face was sober and sad.

"Everything all right?" I asked as she approached, which seemed like a silly thing to say, what with everything we'd recently learned.

Miss June shrugged.

"I suppose. As much as it can be," she said. "Although I reckon it'll be good for all of them for the truth to be known amongst us. We can give them more support, now that we know the full extent of the situation."

I nodded, but Oscar seemed unconvinced.

"How we gonna do that?" he said. "Cal can't go back to work at The Angel. There ain't no room for the children, and it ain't a proper place for 'em to be," he said, glancing at Miss June and Trick. "No offense."

"None taken. You're right. 'Twouldn't work," Miss June said.

"And she can't turn tricks outta the house, here."

"Well, she could," Trick said slowly. "But, no, 'twouldn't be ideal."

Miss June nodded. "Those poor children have been through enough without worrying about strange men coming over to sleep with their momma. No. That's no solution, either. Plus, word would get around, and folks wouldn't like it. 'Tis one thing for me to set up The Angel and have all that going on. But for women who do it on their own? Well, it's a complicated business."

"What are we gonna do?" I asked.

"I don't know, Jimmy. My head's spinning with everything that's come out today." Miss June turned to Trick. "Did Cal tell you what she did with what was left of her husband? I couldn't get that out of her."

"The river," Trick said. "I reckon he's been eaten up by the fish by now." She shrugged, as it none of it mattered. "Me and Jimmy and Oscar reckon we can fix up the barn enough that they could keep some animals there, but we'll need money for supplies, and money to buy a cow and some chickens."

Miss June nodded. "Don't worry about the money. We've got enough funds at The Angel to provide all of that. I reckon Cal can count on me helping out financially over the long term, but it won't be enough to keep them all out of rags. Let me think on it for a few days. You all think on it, too, and we'll see what we can come up with."

"All right," I said, glancing at Oscar.

I toyed with the idea of the two of us staying here and trying to provide for Cal and the children, but we were gonna be hard pressed to provide for ourselves, and we had a house and a home in Port Essington that we wanted to go back to. I knew Oscar wouldn't be keen on staying in Telegraph Creek and, honestly, I wasn't either. I was glad we could help Cal and the little ones in the short term, but Miss June, Trick and the girls would have to think of something else to make Cal's life easier.

We rode back to The Angel with sober thoughts and a clearer understanding of what had happened to Cal. My heart broke o'er the turn her life had taken, for only dreaming of having a husband to care for her and love her. She'd been such a carefree and happy soul when we'd first met her. I'd no doubt she'd had her share of troubles by then, being the person she was, but nothing compared to thinking she'd found love and finding cruelty and maltreatment instead. And Trick was right. Cal was a husk of herself. It seemed the only thing keeping her going was those three kids.

But maybe, if we could let her know we didn't hold what she did to Albert against her, and if we could help her make a life for herself and those children, Cal would come back to us.

'Twas all we could hope for, I reckoned.

* * * *

As we got ready for bed, Oscar seemed sad and forlorn, and I felt a weight in my chest, as well.

"I don't know why people gotta be so mean," Oscar muttered.

"What?"

"This Albert Webster, what tricked Cal into trusting him then led her into such a — a vicious act." He gazed at me. "You knew Cal, like I did. She didn't have a nasty bone in her body! I never even thought she'd have been capable of something like that."

"I reckon she didn't think so, either. But when a person gets beaten down like that, on a daily, unrelenting basis, and they don't know how else to escape it, they do desperate things," I said, thinking back to our encounter with Spook and Whitlaw, and how I'd not hesitated to kill them in cold blood in order to save Oscar.

Oscar must have realized where my mind was turning.

"Yeah, that's true," he said, in a soft voice, as the angry look on his face dissipated. "They make murderers outta good, innocent folk."

I shrugged, not enjoying where this conversation was leading.

"That's true in Cal's case. But I ain't innocent. I was never innocent."

Oscar walked o'er to where I'd sat on the edge of the bed, in my shirtsleeves and nothing else. He stood before me, pressing against my knees until I moved them apart to let him slide himself between them. He was still in his trousers, but he'd taken his shirt off. The pale lines of his shoulders and chest shone in the moonlight.

"I reckon you was, Jimmy. You musta been pretty innocent before the gang got hold of you." He reached out and ran his fingers through my hair. It needed a trim, but Oscar didn't seem to mind it on the longer side.

I closed my eyes, enjoying his gentle, loving touch.

"Maybe. Sure, I guess," I admitted. "But that was a long, long time ago."

Oscar nodded. He was quiet for a moment, then his mouth quirked at the corner.

"Well, I reckon you were pretty innocent before I gotta hold of you," he said, in lustful, low tones.

The sick feeling in the pit of my stomach lifted like fog blown away on a crisp breeze, and I gazed at him with gratitude for changing the subject.

"Oh, I know that's true," I said, reaching forward and pulling him against me. "You and your wicked wiles... You done turned me into a wild, ravenous beast."

Oscar laughed and took my head between his hands, guiding my mouth to his. He kissed me — soft and sensuous — to show me what good care he would take of me, like he always did.

Oscar could be a lewd and adventurous fella in the sack, 'twas true, but when he was in this kind of a mood, things ran more to the soft and romantic. We were married, after all. I supposed we had a right to be sweet and gentle together.

Sure enough, Oscar pulled back and gazed down at me, still holding my face between his hands.

"I ain't in the mood for anythin' rough or rude tonight, Jimmy. But I wanna lie with you, with no clothes on, and just see where that leads. All right?"

I blinked, my heart bursting for this man.

"All right. Of course."

We finished getting undressed then slipped under the blankets and cuddled up together. Oscar was still so slight compared to me. I liked it, and he did, too. He said it made him feel protected and cherished, to be close to a big fella like me. And I felt good to be able to shield him from things.

Cuddling with no clothes on led to other things, but 'twas languid and lazy, and only involved moving together and taking each other in hand, until we were spent and able to sleep.

But as I drifted off, the difficulty and cruelty of Cal's situation lingered, and I truly wondered what would happen to her and the children, if we couldn't think of something.

Chapter Twenty-Nine

Comfort and Fresh Milk

Miss June said we needed to go back and see Cal and the young 'uns right away, so they'd know for sure we weren't gonna abandon them because of what we'd discovered. They needed to know we were on their side, and that we wouldn't leave them to their own devices as of yet, even though we didn't quite know how to help them.

She wanted us to tell Cal about the plan to fix up the barn and get some livestock, and see what Cal thought about that. If she didn't have a problem with it, we should get that started. And while going about it, we needed to keep thinking about a long-term solution.

I had supposed that Trick would go back to her work at The Angel, now that Cal had been found, but Miss June hadn't said anything, and Trick seemed to be a whole other person out here in the world, in the buckskin trousers she'd bartered for in Agnes Hill and the men's shirts and jackets she'd gotten to wearing. 'Twas fascinating to see her blossom, and she didn't seem in any haste to go back to pleasing men for money.

I recalled that Trick and Cal had had a close friendship when they'd worked under Miss June at The Angel, and now Trick was invested in and concerned with Cal and the children's well-being.

"Now, look here. We want to help you," she said to Cal, when Cal hesitated o'er the plan for the barn.

Cal gazed at Trick with a great deal of vulnerability in her eyes. "I know. And that's...that's mighty kind of you all."

"We ain't tryin' to be kind!" Trick said, losing her composure. She reined it in, though. "Well now, of course we are, but more'n that, we're tryin' to help you to make somethin' of this place. You can't go on as you have been, Cal. You gotta see that."

Cal gazed around her at the small home she shared with the three children, whom Miss June had taken outside.

"I suppose. I know, I..."

"You did what you had to do, Cal," Oscar said. "And you've done your best to look after the wee ones. But you can't go on like this...none of you."

A look of melancholy came o'er Cal.

"I know. But what else can I do?"

Trick kneeled on the wood floor in front of where Cal was sitting. She gazed at Cal with an adoring expression and placed a hand on Cal's knee where it sat under her rough skirt.

"You can let us do what we have to, to give you and these children a chance at a happier life. Don't you want that?"

Oscar and I watched in silence as Cal's fingers crept forward o'er her skirts to clutch Trick's. She nodded as tears cascaded down her cheeks.

"Oh, Cal," Trick murmured, as she moved forward to take Cal into a gentle embrace. "I know you're in there, the Cal that I knew."

I blinked back emotion as Cal held on to Trick, and the sound of Trick's broken sobs ripped through the small space. Oscar and I stood sentinel as Trick and Cal clasped each other in a cathartic embrace.

After a time, Miss June poked her head in the door and saw what had happened.

"Good. She needs to get it out. What happened to Cal and these children will take time to recover from, but the first step is grief for what was lost, not particularly the husband — good riddance to him — but the rest of it. The children will be fine. They're resilient. But I don't mind saying that I'm awfully worried for Cal. But maybe this" — Miss June nodded at the two friends — "this will help."

"I'm sure 'twill," I said.

I motioned to Oscar and Miss June, and we left Cal and Trick to their sorrow and their comfort.

* * * *

O'er the next few weeks, Cal began to come back to herself. She wanted Trick near her, though, and Trick didn't seem to mind so much.

Oscar and I bought supplies in Agnes Hill and fixed up the barn. We had experience now, and I reckoned we did a good job, even without Tim and Carson to help. We got a nice little spotted cow for a good price from an old man in the neighboring district, and the children lit up when we brought her to the homestead.

"Oh, she's so pretty! What's her name?" Lizzie exclaimed, wringing her hands with excitement.

I glanced at Oscar, who shrugged.

"We forgot to ask," I admitted.

"Why don't you name her?" Oscar suggested.

"What about Spot?" Peter said.

I could see that he was as excited about the cow as Lizzie was, but he was trying to act as though he wasn't.

Lizzie frowned. "No, that's too plain for a cow as pretty as she is. What about...Gwendolyn?"

Peter laughed, gazing at Oscar and me, as if waiting for us to protest such a grandiose moniker for a simple milch cow.

I glanced at Oscar and raised my eyes.

"I think that's a mighty fine name for her. Don't you, Jimmy?"

"I suppose it's all right. Bit long, though."

"Seems a bit fancy," Peter said, "for a cow."

"'Tisn't! 'Tis a fine name for such a lovely cow. And we can call her Gwen for short," Lizzie said.

Peter rolled his eyes. "All right. I suppose."

"Let's get Gwen settled into the barn, then. We've got a nice little stall built for her," Oscar said, holding out his hand to Lizzie. "Come on."

None of the children had gone in there yet, and I held my breath as Oscar waited patiently for Lizzie to decide if she would do it.

She glanced at Peter, who nodded, as if to let her know he thought 'twas all right. Then she took Oscar's hand, and he led her and the cow into the barn, with Peter and me following behind.

The children seemed wary as they entered the space, but I hoped it looked different enough from what it had been like before that 'twouldn't be too hard to see it in anew. We'd installed a glass window near the roof to let in more natural light, and that made a world of difference.

Peter and Lizzie gazed about them — at first, with trepidation, then with more relaxed expressions.

"Here… Help me get her into the stall." Oscar fished a small carrot out of his pocket. "Can you lead her in?"

Lizzie nodded and took the carrot.

"Here, Gwendolyn," she said, showing the cow the treat.

Gwendolyn's ears flapped forward, and she bellowed, making Lizzie and Peter laugh.

"Come on. It's all right," Lizzie said, backing into the stall as Gwendolyn followed her. In a moment, the sweet cow was munching on the carrot, and Lizzie was standing beside her, petting her and saying kind things in her big brown ear.

Peter rested his crossed arms on the stall door and gazed at them, appearing relaxed and content — more so than I'd ever seen him.

"I reckon she likes you, Lizzie," he said.

Lizzie beamed at him. Then she turned to me.

"I need to learn how to milk her, don't I?"

I nodded. "Sure. And Peter, too, so you'll both know how."

'Twas beginning to feel like the children and Cal might be all right. But we still needed to come up with a long-term plan.

Chapter Thirty

Maggie Corrigan

'Twas a few days later, at The Angel, when Miss June came to see us.

We answered the knock on our bedroom door, and there she was, standing with Trick, who was still dressed in men's clothes. I wondered if Trick would ever go back to working at The Angel, and if Miss June would care if she didn't.

Miss June's eyes were shining with excitement, and she seemed to have some news.

"Can we come in, please?"

I nodded, grinning. "Of course. You own the place, don't you?"

Miss June rolled her eyes. "That's true enough. But I respect people's privacy, unless I have reason to interfere."

She gestured to Trick, who followed her into our small room and went to stand by the window. Trick looked — different. She looked…satisfied, and like she had something to say.

Oscar's gaze shifted between them, then locked onto Trick. "You look like you wanna say somethin'."

Trick turned to face him and actually blushed. I don't know as I'd ever seen her blush before.

I turned to Miss June.

"What's goin' on?"

Miss June sat on the edge of our bed.

Oscar, who'd propped himself on one elbow as he leaned against the pillows, sat up.

"Well, it seems as though we may have a solution to our problem," she said, glancing at Trick.

"Go on. Tell 'em," Trick said.

"Well" — Miss June spread her hands on the coverlet — "it seems that Trick — I mean, Maggie Corrigan, because that's her real name — has quite enjoyed the life she's been living the past few weeks."

"Maggie Corrigan!" Oscar said. "Why, that's such a nice name, though I don't know if I can imagine you as anyone but Trick. But I'll try to call you Maggie from now on."

Trick — *Maggie* — shrugged. "Don't matter. I'll answer to either of 'em. But I'm gonna need a regular name if I'm to live on the farm with Cal and the children."

"Live on the — " I said, my gaze going from Maggie's to Miss June's and back again. "You're gonna...you're gonna help Cal raise those wee ones?"

Maggie laughed. "Oh, I reckon Cal will be doin' most of the child raisin'. But I'm gonna live there with her, and we're gonna make a go of the place."

Oscar stared at Maggie like she was shooting stars out of the top of her head.

"Truly? Are you and Cal...?"

I knew what Oscar wanted to ask, but he was having trouble figuring out how to ask it.

Maggie laughed, but the blush on her cheeks deepened. "We ain't lovers," Maggie said. "Not yet, anyway. Only friends. But I reckon we're the best of friends, and all's we need is each other."

My vision blurred, and I blinked the moisture away, then cleared my throat.

"Well, I think that's a wonderful idea. I think you and Cal can be wonderful parents to those children, and if you're workin' together, I'm sure the two of you can make something of that place."

"Thank you, Jimmy. We surely mean to."

"Does Cal know what you're proposin'?" Oscar asked.

"I told her about my idea a few days ago. She told me I was misguided, but if I wanted to help her and the children out, she'd be mighty thankful," Trick said. "I still need to convince her how much she'd be helpin' *me* out. I don't wanna go back to my life at The Angel. Not that t'was all that bad, but I feel like I can finally be the person I've always wanted to be if I go live with Cal and help her with the farm and the animals. I'm smart, I'm strong and I can learn how to till a field. I already know about animal husbandry. I simply never had a place to...husband any." Trick grinned.

I turned to Miss June.

"You'll miss her here, won't you?" I said, wondering what she thought of the plan.

"Oh, I'll have lots of men asking where she's gone, I'm sure. But I've got a lot of girls here who don't have many options and would rather do this work than be scullery maids, so that won't be a problem. Maggie's been a good draw, but she's got this opportunity now, and Cal sure could use her. So, I've given her my blessing."

"Thank you, Miss June. I surely do appreciate it."

Oscar jumped off the bed and ran to Maggie, grabbing her into a fierce embrace that took all of us by surprise.

"What the hell?" Maggie said, laughing and hugging him back. "Jimmy, you oughta keep this boy on a leash."

"Believe me, I've thought about it."

"'Tis so poetic!" Oscar said. "Why, the two of you will be the most interestin' couple in the county."

Miss June shook her head. "I suppose tongues'll wag at the fact Maggie wears men's things, but I reckon that's not so unusual."

"Are you—?" Oscar said, letting Maggie go and stepping back, his forehead creased with thought. "Are you gonna live as a man, like Cal lives as a woman?"

Maggie shook her head. "No, I ain't gonna do that. I reckon I don't look manly enough, and anyway, I don't *feel* like a man. But I don't feel fully a woman, neither. Don't see why I can't be somethin' in between. I reckon most folks won't ask questions, as long as I'm polite and conduct my business fairly."

"You'll have some men who won't take you serious at first," Miss June said. "But I have no doubt you'll set them straight."

"Yes, ma'am, I will."

It seemed like the perfect solution.

"God, I can hear you thinkin', Jimmy," Oscar said.

"I'm sorry. I'm still processin'. But I think 'tis a good idea."

Maggie inclined her chin and pulled up a chair, sitting astride it as she gazed at us.

"At first, Cal didn't want me to give up my life at The Angel, but I managed to convince her 'twas what I wanted. Anyway, those kids need a father figure, and I aim to give 'em one as best I can. I aim to teach 'em all the things their pa would've taught them if he'd been a good man, and the things we've already started teachin' 'em, like how to milk a cow and how to ride."

"Sure," Oscar said. "I reckon you can be as good a Pa as any man — sure better'n the one they had."

"Amen," Miss June said.

"You gonna get them to call you 'Papa Maggie'?" I asked. 'Twas a joke, but Maggie straightened up and nodded.

"I do like the sound of that. Why not?"

I grinned. Truth of it was that Cal and those children were goddamned lucky to have our Maggie on their side. She was a force to be reckoned with, and if anyone could keep them safe and thriving, 'twas her.

"All right," I said. "Well then, I suppose this calls for a celebration."

Miss June stood. "I've got some lovely bourbon in the cupboard, waiting for an opportunity like this," she said. "I'll go get it, and we can have a nice little tot in here with you boys. Then we'll leave you be, so you can do some private celebrating," Miss June said. "I figure if you can stick around another week to help us get Cal and Maggie set up, I can let you boys go home."

Chapter Thirty-One

A Private Gathering

I'd rarely seen Oscar so addled with the drink. I supposed the thought of being able to return to our home and friends in Port Essington had made him carefree, and he'd overdone it. At least I was here to make sure he didn't trip and smash his head into the mantel.

"Oscar, be careful. You ain't too steady right now," I said, grabbing his arm as he careened toward the wall.

"I'm fine, Jimmy," he slurred. "Stop babyin' me."

"Oh, I ain't babyin' you, I reckon. I'm only watchin' out for you."

"Oh, you are, are you? Watch this, then," Oscar said, tugging his shirt from his trousers and lifting it to bare his chest as he wiggled in a deliberately alluring way.

Miss June threw back her head and laughed, while Maggie whooped and stomped her feet, raising her glass. We'd brought in a couple of straight chairs for them to sit on, and both of them had a look of relaxation and pleasure on their rosy faces as they enjoyed the fine bourbon.

"Settle down," I said. "Can't you see we got company?"

Oscar let his shirt drop and grinned with a devilish air.

"I guess you're lucky, then, else I would have stripped myself completely and laid on that bed there," he pointed to it. "Then I would've taken my—"

"All right, all right, now." I glanced at Miss June and Maggie.

Maggie had leaned forward, and now she was shaking her head.

"What would you have done, Oscar? Don't be shy on our account."

I put my head in my hands as Miss June grinned. I should have known 'twas no use trying to stop him.

"Well, I..." Oscar said, hesitating.

I glanced between my fingers to see him watching me with a fond, sympathetic look.

"I suppose I would have taken my—pillow—and turned in for the night. That's all."

"Uh-huh," Maggie said. "Sure."

"Well, I am feelin' mighty tired all the sudden."

I lowered my hands, and watched as Oscar gave a great, and probably fabricated, yawn. I reckoned he only wanted to be alone with me, and I couldn't say I objected to that idea.

"Maggie, would you like to continue our celebration?" Miss June asked, as she forced herself upright. "I have some of that very good cannabis in my room—or we can share a cigar?"

"Well, that sounds like a mighty fine idea, Miss June. I ain't ready for bed, yet, though I can see that these boys are. Although I don't expect they're gonna do any sleepin'."

"Come on now. Let's leave them be. Jimmy looks like he's going to melt away with embarrassment."

I sat on the edge of the bed, a half-drank glass of bourbon in my hand, while Miss June and Maggie picked up their chairs and took them along, closing the door on us. I stared at the brown liquid in my glass, enjoying the silence and the fact that we were alone.

Oscar came and stood before me, his arms crossed as he gazed down at my drink.

"You gonna finish that?" he asked.

I blinked up at him. I'd be damned if I was gonna contribute to his drunkenness. I held his gaze as I lifted it and drank the rest of the bourbon down in one gulp, then put the empty glass on the nearby dresser. The disappointment on Oscar's face was comical.

"Well, that ain't very nice," he said, lowering his arms and preparing to step away.

"C'mere," I said, reaching out and taking his wrist, so I could turn him and face him toward the hearth, where a low fire burned steadily. The patter of the evening rain and the crackle of the flames were the only sounds but for Oscar's hitched breath.

I pushed the braces off his shoulders and let them fall, then with one hand I undid the front of his trousers and pulled them down.

"Jimmy. God. What're you doin'?"

"You were awfully rude to me in front of our friends. You think that's gonna go unpunished?"

I gave his bare ass a slap with the flat of my hand, holding him still, and Oscar yelped, then tried to break free. But I only tugged him around and pulled him o'er my lap.

He landed with a grunt and wriggled in protest, but I had a good hold of him. I didn't think he was trying to get away. He pretended he didn't want what I was giving him, when, in truth, 'twas exactly what he was craving.

"Be still, son," I murmured, feeling my cock plump up underneath his writhing body. "And take what you got comin'."

Then I remembered he'd had a lot to drink and loosened my hold. "Ah shit. I shouldn't do this when you're drunk."

Oscar snorted a laugh. "I ain't drunk. Not really."

"But you were slurrin' and swayin' a minute ago."

He turned his head to stare at me from beneath the flop of his bangs. "I may have been playin' it up a bit, since I knew 'twould vex you."

Yeah, he did that a lot, it seemed. *Instigating little brat.*

"Oscar Yates," I said, "why, you are even naughtier than I'd imagined. 'Tis a good thing you're across my lap."

He huffed a laugh and gave another half-hearted wriggle. "I reckon so."

Then I swatted his bare ass so hard that he jerked and uttered a surprised yelp.

"Jimmy!" he said, the yelp turning into a soft moan. "Gawd."

'Twas like the first time I'd ever spanked him, in the hotel the day after we'd met, after he'd woken me with his mouth on my privates and I'd realized I'd got more than I'd bargained for when I'd offered a helping hand.

Turned out he'd known exactly what to do to get me to forget all my principles and give in to my baser instincts. At the time, I'd been confused and startled by my feelings. By now, I was used to them, and I savored how joyful it felt to have Oscar safe and contained o'er my lap, taking a spanking that symbolized my love and care for him and knew he had wantings that matched mine. I'd long gotten o'er the guilt and shame of it, and Oscar had never struggled with any of that.

"You are a very naughty boy, Oscar Yates," I said in the gravelly tones he liked so much. "And I aim to teach you how to behave."

"I am," he muttered, grinding his hard cock against my thigh. "I am so goddamned naughty. I might have drank a bit too much of that nice bourbon. That's not very responsible of me, is it?"

"No, it ain't," I agreed, glad he was fully on board with pretending. "I reckon 'tis only because you ain't had any proper rearin'," I said, spanking him again. "And I aim to fix that right now."

He made a choked sound as I started to go at him in earnest—not as serious as a punishment, but hard enough to inflame him, let him know I meant business and that I was priming his ass for what I wanted even more than this. If I wasn't careful, I'd have him making a mess on my trousers, which had happened on occasion.

Since we were in an actual cathouse, we didn't have to worry about the noises of our strange pastime, even though it did make me a tad self-conscious to know other folks could hear us. Nobody would pay it any mind, though, and 'twasn't gonna stop me from taking him the way I wanted.

"Are you sorry? Are you sorry for your bad behavior?"

Oscar grunted as I spanked him, and I wondered if he was gonna answer me. Finally, he said, "I'm sorry, mister. I'm so sorry. I'm a terrible tease and a rude fella.

Is there any way I can make it up to you? I'll do whatever you want!"

Well, this was interesting. Oscar had altered the rules of this game all of a sudden, and I liked where he was going with it.

"Oh, you'll make it up to me, I reckon. Don't you worry about that," I said, smoothing a hand o'er his plump behind where I'd spanked it and feeling warmth on my thigh from his leaking cock. "I ain't stoppin' yet, though. You're gonna take a few more swats so's I know you've learned your lesson. I saw you take that woman's pocketbook, and that ain't the way a gentleman behaves."

"No," Oscar moaned, as I rained more slaps on his poor behind. "Stop. Stop! I'm sorry. I only needed money. I'll behave!"

"You will. And you better not spend on me, because I got plans for that little dick of yours."

"Oh fuck, oh fuck," Oscar panted. "I'm gonna spend for real if you keep talkin' that way."

I stopped, and brought both of us to our feet, holding him firm with a hand on his arm, as I wrapped strong fingers around the base of his cock and squeezed.

"*Don't. You. Dare,*" I whispered, the pressure around the base of his cock preventing him from going o'er and driving him mad in the process.

"Fuck, fuck, fuck," he cursed. "I won't. I won't. Oh goddammit." He hissed in the pain of holding back when there was nothing else he could do but suffer it — and curse.

I had him right where I wanted him. When his body had backtracked from the edge and his breathing calmed a bit, I released my hold on his cock and his arm and stepped back. I grabbed one of the straight chairs and pulled it o'er, sitting on it and leaning back as if I were ready for a show. I crossed one leg across the other and folded my arms.

"Go on," I said. "You wanna keep playing this game?"

Oscar stood there, swaying, and gazing at me out of dazed and confused eyes. "Huh?"

"You wanted to strip for me earlier, when our guests were here. I reckon you can do it for me now, so's I can enjoy it in private."

"Well shit, mister," Oscar whined. "You sure got a strange way of punishin' me for stealin'. I reckon I'll think twice about it in future."

I grinned. "See that you do. Anyway, I'll make sure you don't want for nothin', if you stay with me. I'll keep you safe and fed, and I'll look out for you."

Oscar lifted his chin. "Does that include spankin' me like you just done?"

I winked. "Oh, it surely does...when you've been bad." I uncrossed my arms and leaned forward. "Do you like to be bad, Oscar Yates?"

His lips parted, and his breaths came quicker as he nodded.

"I thought so. Well, I aim to teach you to be good. And if you're good, you'll get a reward. You want that?"

He nodded, his gaze burning into mine.

"All right, then. Take the rest of them clothes off...*now*."

In a flurry of motion, Oscar stepped out of his crumpled trousers and stripped the rest of his things off, leaving them in a pile. 'Twasn't exactly a tease like

I'd hoped for, but more of a surrender, which pleased me as much.

"*Good. Boy.*"

"Oh fuck," Oscar said. "I am your good boy, mister. I'll be your good boy, if you'll keep me and fuck me and spank me."

I raised my brows. "My, my... Seems we may have a deal, then. Git o'er here, on the bed on your hands and knees. And spread them knees so's I can see your sweet hole."

Oscar almost choked on his own spittle.

"I swear, you're gonna kill me, Jimmy."

I grinned. "Oh, I hope not. On the bed, *now*. And how did you know my name was Jimmy? Maybe you oughta keep calling me 'mister'."

Oscar scrambled himself onto the bed and got into position, his hand going to his little nubby for some relief.

"Uh-uh. Hands off your cock. That there nubby is *mine* from now on, not yours."

Chapter Thirty-Two

A Tasty Tumble

"Okay, mister. All right."

Oscar put his hand back on the bed and knelt on all fours—naked, his legs spread, his thigh muscles trembling as he waited for whatever I might do.

"Now, that's more like it. You stay there, in that position, and you wait for your reward."

Oscar sighed and stared down at the mattress. "Yes, mister."

His voice was barely above a whisper, and I thrilled to have him at my command. This was what we liked and how we liked to do it, and we didn't care if it made no sense. We were only playing, the way children play at make believe. Only we were both grown, and because of that, our play had a sexual side to it. And what was wrong with that?

When I sat down in the straight chair again, it made a loud creaking noise and caused Oscar to start. He craned his neck so he could see me.

"Now I want you to leave your little nubby—what's my property—alone. But I want you to play with yourself in other ways, so's I can sit back and watch you."

Oscar looked confused for all of a moment, then understanding dawned. "You dirty fucking bastard."

I grinned, pleased as punch to have shocked *Oscar*, who always seemed to be a step ahead of me in the dirty department.

"Play with your hole, boy. Show me how much you like it."

The sound that came out of Oscar's throat then was halfway between a moan and a whimper. His cheeks went even redder than they had been — ruddier than his freshly spanked ass — as he blinked twice and swallowed.

"F-fine," he murmured. "Okay."

I settled into a comfortable position as Oscar gazed down at the sheets again and reached behind him with one hand. He hesitated, as though this thing I'd asked him to do was gonna destroy him, when I knew he'd think about this for days afterward. Some shame and mild humiliation took Oscar's desire to the next level, and I gloated with satisfaction as I watched, knowing I'd thought of the perfect thing to exploit that. He took his time, as if he needed to work himself up to it. As I watched, he splayed his fingers across his lower back, then slid them between his cheeks, so that his middle finger pressed against that lewd, luscious spot.

"Now rub it," I said, my breaths harsh and shallow. "Slow and steady. Tease yourself, boy."

Oscar made a vulnerable noise, widening his thighs as he teased his fingertips o'er the wrinkled skin of his taint and up to his pink, exposed, hole.

I stood, slow and easy, because I didn't want him to stop what he was doing and went to the chest of drawers to get the saddle grease. I brought it with me to the foot of the bed and screwed it open as Oscar played with himself.

"Don't stop now. You keep doin' that."

Oscar shuddered and moaned, and my gaze fixated on the tips of his long fingers as he obeyed me.

"Looks like you're gettin' yourself plenty worked up, ain't you?"

"I can't—You're gonna make me talk? While I'm doin' this?" he whispered.

"Yes, I am. You're gonna answer my questions, and you're gonna keep playing with that soft hole of yours or it's gonna stay empty and unused."

"Oh. Gawd."

I laid a hand on his bottom, pushing that cheek so it spread him, and I could see better. I knew 'twas awkward for him to reach back like that, but to make it work, he'd had to arch his back and brace his shoulders on the mattress, and the sight of him about killed me...in a good way.

"Who do you belong to?"

"You, Jimmy. I belong to you."

"And who's nubby is this?" I said, touching it with a finger and making Oscar gasp.

"Yours. 'Tis yours."

I sighed and leaned in, kissing his buttock where my hand was resting to anchor him and soothe him in his embarrassment.

"And whose fine ass is this?"

He giggled, but then made a soft sound, like a gasp and a moan combined, as he continued to tease himself.

"Oh. Yours. Oh, *fuck*..."

I leaned down and licked across his fingers and o'er his hole, as Oscar made a desperate, surprised sound.

"That's very good, Oscar. Now I want you to stop playin' with yourself and hold yourself open for me. You understand?"

He nodded against the mattress and did as I'd asked, arching his body even more, and pulling his cheeks apart to present his pink hole to me.

The entire tableau was so profane and exquisite that I couldn't contain myself any longer. I shoved my trousers and my drawers down and gave my cock a couple of vicious pulls with my dry hand, before I scooped some grease from the jar and slapped it on the delicate skin of Oscar's cleft and around his hole, till 'twas shiny and slippery and beckoning me like a slice of hot apple pie.

If we hadn't been at The Angel, among whores and other lustful men, I might have been worried about the reach of the sounds Oscar made. Someone might have mistaken them for sounds of distress and pain, when they were the opposite, and he was only dying of pleasure.

"Easy there," I said, as I slicked my cock up and positioned myself.

"Please! I need you. I need you so much."

"Shush. Put both your hands on the bed now. You're gonna need to brace yourself."

I waited for him to do so before I pushed forward and breeched him, causing a yelp and a cry from him — and a stuttered groan from myself.

"Oh God, Oscar. Jesus." I said, as my cock slipped into his warmth, and my brain melted.

Oscar grunted as he lifted up and pushed back, his body swallowing me in one long swoop.

"Fuck!" I yelled as a raw sound came from Oscar's throat. But I recovered myself and whimpered as he fucked me from below. "I swear, Oscar," I said, panting "you're like a wild fucking bronco, sometimes."

Oscar made stuttering noises as he moved against me, until I grabbed his hips in my hands and kept him still, so's I could control things. He didn't like that one bit, I reckoned, except that he did, because nothing pleased him as much as when I took him in hand.

"Be still and let me take my pleasure. Then you can have yours."

"God. Oh God."

"You hear that?" I said, plowing him now, and making sure to drag my cock across that sweet spot inside him with every goddamn thrust. "I'm gonna fuck you till I spend and fill you up with my seed, you hear me? Then I might let you come—or I might not. Mayhap, I'll simply keep playing with your hole, letting my seed dribble out and pushing it back in, until you're right mad with it." My words were broken and split with my panting breaths and little grunts and groans. I was working myself up as much as he was.

"Jimmy! Oh, Jesus. *Jimmy!*"

I knew what those choked words meant, and I quick grabbed Oscar's cock and started stroking it, just in time for him to spend, as he screamed my name to the rafters.

'Twas a good long time before either of us e'en tried to speak. Oscar lay, supine and spent, his face turned away. When I was able to move, I stroked his back until he turned toward me, his fucked-out expression satisfying to see.

"Howdy."

"Howdy?"

"Ain't that what the cowboys say?"

"After they been fucked into the bed by their bunkmate?"

Oscar shrugged. "Maybe."

I smiled and pushed the stray hair from his forehead.

"Did you like that?"

"What do you think, cowboy?"

"I think you loved that...all of it."

"I did. I'm growin' your little babies right now. Can't promise the delivery'll be very entertainin', considerin' where they'll have to make their exit."

I chuckled. "Well, the regular place ain't all that excitin' neither. Ain't that much of a difference, I don't think."

He rose up on his elbow and gave me an incredulous look.

"Jimmy Downing, are you saying you think women basically shit their babies out?"

I grinned. "Maybe."

"I suppose 'tis a good thing you ain't a doctor, then."

"I suppose so," I said, grinning at his amusement and content in a way I'd not been for a while, what with all the stress of finding Cal and sorting all that out.

"Well, anyway, I reckon I love the way you fuck me."

"I reckon I love the way you take it. And I know you'd make a fine momma to my babies."

The astonished look he gave me only made me laugh and kiss him sweetly on the mouth.

Chapter Thirty-Three

A Surprise for Cal

I was excited to think about returning to Port Essington, but I was dreading saying goodbye to Miss June, Maggie, Cal, the children and everyone else that we'd gotten to know, or know better, on our visit. We still had most of a week before we were gonna head out, and we spent it helping Maggie and Caliope get set up.

Miss June had managed to locate a three-month-old sheepdog pup, and she'd given it to the children as a pet. Only Oscar, Maggie and I knew that 'twas intended as a measure of protection for them. Being two women on a farm without a man could be a vulnerable situation, and Miss June figured a dog on the property would dissuade quite a few folks who might consider mischief. 'Twas a beguiling little beast, and the children had been overjoyed with the furry brown-and-white animal that they'd promptly named Teddy. Peter had promised to take responsibility for the feeding and care of the creature, since Cal was busy with his young brother. I reckoned the love of that dog might help the whole family recover from the trauma they'd all been through, and I commended Miss June on her thoughtfulness.

One pleasant afternoon, while the others were busy introducing the new hens and the rooster to the freshly built chicken coop, I was able to take a walk with Cal, across the fields near her and Maggie's place. 'Twas nigh August, and the days were shortening. The grass had grown real long, and it waved in the breeze. The mountains all around the small valley loomed green and lush. In another month, the leaves would burst out orange and red and yellow as the dark days of winter approached. I only hoped that Cal and Maggie – and their little family – would be warm and cozy within the repaired and shored up walls of their small home.

Cal had on a pretty blue bonnet that Miss June had insisted on getting her, and truly, she looked beautiful. The color in her cheeks from the makeup Maggie had provided only emphasized the natural tint there. Gus had gifted her a new razor and soap brush, so 'twouldn't take much effort to keep her looking girlish and feminine. To be honest, she looked fetching in the new things Miss June and Maggie had provided her. 'Twas plenty obvious that she felt good in her own skin these days, and I delighted in it.

Her eyes flashed toward me from under the bonnet's raffia-trimmed rim.

"Jimmy, I already spoke to Oscar, but I wanted to thank you for coming all that long way to help Miss June find me. I'm so sorry to cause all that trouble, and I feel awful that you had to leave your new home and all your new friends – "

I clicked my tongue. "Now, stop it. 'Twas worth the trip, and our new home and our new friends are waiting for us. Never you mind."

We walked on, Cal lifting her skirts so she could make her way unhindered o'er the rough, uneven ground. She was wearing new brown leather boots, too, and I reckoned they'd last her a long while.

'Twas real good to see her thriving, now that she had enough food on the regular and wasn't so worried about how to manage. I'd seen the same change in Oscar after I'd brought him with me on my journey, when I'd made sure he got three meals a day and felt secure and cared for. Having someone looking out for you made a world of difference. It pleased me to know that I'd had a hand in it, and I felt some of the darkness of my past lift a bit. 'Twas my duty to try to put good things into the world, after all that foulness, and I planned to keep doing it. It healed me as much as it healed Cal. And I reckoned it healed Oscar as well, to see a soul in such dire straits get the help they needed.

"Miss Caliope, you look awful nice in them new clothes, if you don't mind my sayin'."

Cal giggled and flashed me a look I remembered from almost a year ago—a look of mischief and flirtation that I'd sorely missed.

"Jimmy Downing, you got a silver tongue, and you know it. Thank you." She stopped walking and raised her face to the sky. "I'm feelin' more and more myself these days."

"You're lookin' so much better, Cal. I'm so sorry you had to go through all that. But now you're on the other side of it, and I can't help but feel grateful that those children have you as their momma—and grateful that you got them."

Cal turned to me with a sober intensity. "I know what you mean. They mayn't have been mine to begin with, but they *are* mine now, and I mean to do right by them. You know, I" — her voice hitched and she put a hand to her forehead — "I love 'em like they were my own, like I birthed them."

"That's plain to see. And they love you the same."

She nodded but stayed silent. I could see the emotion swelling in her eyes as the muscles in her throat tensed. Since she didn't trust herself to speak, I carried on.

"You're gonna be all right, Cal. And those children are gonna grow up and do incredible things, I know it. With you and Trick as their mommas? I mean, *Maggie*." I laughed. "Hard to think of her as anyone but Trick, but I'm tryin' to use the right name. All I'm sayin' is that you and Maggie are the best thing that's ever happened to those wee ones, and they are gonna grow up feeling loved and secure and cared for. I know that for a fact."

"Thank you, Jimmy," Cal said, her voice soft and her eyebrows knit together. "We'll surely do our best."

"Now I'm hopin' that in a couple of years, Oscar and I can see our way to come back and check up on you all. What do you think about that?"

Cal nodded, blinking quick and reaching for my hand, which I gave her. She didn't look at me.

"Oh, yes. Those children will be furious if you don't. And Miss June and Maggie, too. And I'd be heartbroken."

"You'd be all right. You're a strong, capable, resilient woman, and I'm proud to know you. And God willin', we *will* be back, and we can all go on another fine picnic again."

She laughed, and untied the strings of her bonnet, slipping it off and swinging it from her fingers. Caliope's chestnut hair, which Miss June had trimmed and shaped, fell to her shoulders in soft, natural waves in such a charming way that a good many others would be envious. 'Twas nice to see her with it down, for normally she put it into braids to keep it out of the way.

We kept walking as the sun lowered in the sky and the birds changed their songs to reflect the lengthening day.

* * * *

"Come here. You gotta see this!" Oscar said as we got back to Cal's house. "Come on. Come on!"

Part of the reason I'd taken Cal on a walk was to get her out of the house for an hour, so the others could work their magic while we were gone. We'd been secretly installing a pump from the existing well to the sink in the house. We'd passed off the digging it had entailed as foundation work, and Cal had been so busy looking after Samuel that she hadn't been able to keep track of exactly what was being done. They'd delivered the new stove that morning, and we'd had them put it behind the house, while Miss June had distracted Cal. I hoped they'd been able to install the stove and attach the pump by the kitchen sink while we were gone.

"What on earth?" Cal said, as we strode inside.

Sure enough, the brand-new, shiny black iron stove was sitting where the old one had been, and I reckoned Cal was so entranced by that that she hadn't e'en noticed the pump yet.

"What on earth?" she repeated, staring at the much bigger and fancier piece of cookware that would keep their little house heated much more efficiently in the cold of the winter and had four burners and a sizable oven. "How?" Cal gazed at us, completely flummoxed and surprised, in the best of ways.

Miss June, who was holding little Teddy, the sheepdog pup, laughed. "We got the stove for you, Cal, to make yours and Maggie's and the children's lives easier."

"Oh my goodness," Cal said, her hand o'er her mouth. She gave a little laugh. "I ain't really much of a cook." Her expression darkened. "Albert used to complain," she said, her gaze flitting around the room, as if Albert's ghost might appear. But then Cal looked at the new stove and smiled. "But I reckon I'll learn a lot better on this one."

Oscar walked over and gave Cal a kiss on the cheek.

"I'm sure you'll be a right good cook in no time. Why, I can even make a few things on our stove."

"That's a fact. If Oscar can cook, I'm sure you can learn to. It only takes practice."

"That's true," Miss June affirmed. "If you like, I can send Cook over to give you some lessons."

Cal blinked, clearly overwhelmed. "Thank you. I'd appreciate that. And 'twould be nice to see Mrs. Hansen again."

"She's been asking about you. I'm sure she'll be delighted to help."

Sam pulled at Cal's skirts. He was dressed in a fresh smock, and his face was clean and bright.

"Tirsty, Momma. Tirsty!"

Cal glanced at the young child with a fondness that warmed my heart, but before she could respond, Peter said, "Look, Momma. Watch this!"

He grabbed a tin cup and placed it under the spout of the hand pump, as Teddy yapped at the sudden activity and wiggled in Miss June's arms. Peter pushed the handle up and down until clear water splashed into the cup. When 'twas almost full, Peter took the cup to Sam and gave it to him.

Cal watched all this with wide eyes and a dazed smile.

"That should make your life much easier," Miss June said, "as well as having Maggie here to help you. Where is that girl, anyway?"

"She took Lizzie to see if our hens have laid eggs yet," Peter said.

"Well, now, they're pretty new," I said. "You might not get any eggs for another week or so."

But, even as I said that, Maggie and Lizzie came in. Lizzie was holding a small basket.

"We got four eggs!" she said, lifting it, her face bright with a gap-toothed grin. She'd lost one of her baby teeth t'other day.

We gathered around to look in the basket. Sure enough, there were four large, brown eggs, nestled there in the checkered cloth.

"Well, my goodness!" Oscar exclaimed, tousling Lizzie's brown hair. "That's enough for an omelet. Do you like omelets, Lizzie?"

Lizzie scrunched up her nose. "I don't know. I ain't never had one."

Oscar stepped back and put a hand to his chest, his expression one of surprise.

"Never had an omelet? Why, that's shocking." He turned to me. "Jimmy, Lizzie's never had an omelet."

"Neither have I," Peter said, not wanting to miss out. He was at the sink, filling and refilling the tin cup, and drinking the fresh water from the pump. He placed the cup on the counter and came o'er to us.

"Well, now, is that a fact?" I said, glancing between them.

"Yes, sir," they answered.

"I suppose I'll have to make one, then. I can use this brand-new stove, if your momma don't mind not bein' the first to try it."

Cal laughed, sitting on the old settee that Miss June had provided and cuddling with Sam. "Be my guest — and thank you, kindly."

"Did someone milk pretty Gwendolyn this mornin'? I'm gonna need some fresh milk to mix with the eggs, and salt and pepper, if you've got it," I said.

Miss June indicated a small stone pitcher with a folded cloth o'er the top, that was sitting on a lower shelf of the counter.

"Peter milked Gwen this morning," Miss June said, "with Lizzie's help."

"I petted her and made sure she wasn't mad about it," Lizzie said.

Maggie, who had taken the pup from Miss June and was leaning up against the counter, said, "Most cows don't mind bein' milked. Takes the pressure off their teats. Why, they need to be milked every morning and evening."

"All right," Peter said, echoed by Lizzie. "We'll do that."

"Why, you can even milk her three times a day if you want, and if you can use the fresh milk," I said. "You could milk her in the morning, then late afternoon, and again in the late evening. That might be a wise thing to do, since you got five mouths to feed — and since three of you are still growin'."

I wasn't sure where this knowledge came from, except that I'd grown up on a farm, way back when, before the gang, before the killin' — and way before Oscar.

"I expect we can manage that," Maggie said. "Then we won't need to worry 'bout keeping the morning milk fresh all the day, since we'll get more at suppertime."

"True."

"I'd like to learn how to milk the cow," Cal said. "Then, if we all know how, there won't be a lack of hands available to do it. I reckon 'tis gonna take a lot of work to get this place up and runnin'. And we'll all have to get along together. You ready to do that, Peter? Lizzie?"

"Yes, Momma. We want to help," Lizzie said, grabbing Cal's skirts and cuddling up to her. The absolute adoration in that child's gaze was heartwarming to see.

"Yes, Momma," Peter said, with a smile. "I'm strong, and I can help Miss Maggie build and fix stuff, I reckon."

"Yes, I'm sure you can, Peter," Cal said. "You've already been the biggest help to me, and I do thank you for it."

Peter stood straighter. "Well, ain't I the man of the house? I gotta be strong and protect the rest of you."

He seemed puffed up with himself, which on the one hand was pleasing to see, but on the other hand, 'twasn't fair that he thought he was better'n Cal or Lizzie, because he was a boy.

I was about to say something when Oscar beat me to it. He was leaning against the counter beside Maggie, petting wee Teddy, who rested happily in her arms, and he eyed the youngster with a serious air.

"You don't gotta be the man of the house, Peter. You're ten years old. I think, between Maggie and your momma, you got enough strength around this place." He put a hand on Peter's shoulder. "Now, you're strong, I know that, and you're capable — 'course you are. You been helpin' your momma manage for a long time, and that's mighty fine of you. But now Maggie's here to help out, and you need to enjoy bein' young and carefree for a time yet." He glanced at Cal and Maggie, who seemed to appreciate what he was saying to Peter. "I reckon if you can keep Lizzie and Samuel safe and entertained, that would help your momma out the most. And they'll ask for your help when they need it, I'm sure. But you ain't the man of this house yet, and even when you become that, you need to know that Maggie and your momma are quite capable of runnin' things."

Peter looked sober, and he nodded. "Yes, sir."

"You understand me? Don't put your childhood behind you just yet, and don't look at men as stronger'n women, cause they ain't. Women are plenty strong, and menfolk shouldn't beat them down they way they often do."

I cleared my throat, and I had to look away. 'Twas touching to see Oscar protect for Peter what he'd never had — that precious childhood that he'd had to leave behind awful early. My gaze met Miss June's, and she seemed to be thinking the same.

"I won't, Oscar. I promise."

"That's good," Oscar said. He stood and gave Peter's shoulder a pat, then made a grand gesture with a bow, to invite me to the stove.

"Well, Jimmy, you better start cookin', else these here children are gonna get mighty upset. Can you imagine? They ain't never had an omelet before! The injustice of it!"

I shook my head with amusement at my husband's theatrics and made my way to the basket of eggs that was sitting on the counter. I happened to glance at Trick, and I noticed that she was watchin' Cal in a way that made me wonder if there was more to their friendship than she was admitting to – or p'raps would be very soon.

Chapter Thirty-Four

Goodbye

There were few dry eyes at The Angel when we had to bid our farewells three days later. We'd made so many friends among the girls who worked there. There was always some sort of drama going on between them, although any major disputes were settled by Miss June. 'Twas an entertaining environment for the most part. And 'twas refreshing to be among folks who didn't hold any moralizing principles o'er the pleasures of sex and the right to enjoy one's body, even if these girls were forced by society to prioritize getting paid. I knew 'twas a job like anything else. Aspects of it were enjoyable, and other parts were a drudgery. At least, at Miss June's well-run establishment, these women were spared the harsher aspects of their profession.

Even Trick seemed sad to be leaving in some ways, although she was excited to venture forth on a new path as Maggie, in a place that was hers and Cal's to manage the way they liked, and where they didn't have to be at the whim of strange men all the time.

Miss June thanked us again for coming all the way from Port Essington to help her and told us we'd always have a place at The Angel if we ever needed it — and that she'd miss us greatly.

"We'll miss you, too," I said, giving her a hug and a kiss. "Thanks for lookin' after me — and after Oscar last fall. We might not have survived without your kindness."

"I'm happy to put my skills to use, Jimmy," she said, smiling. "I hope you're able to make your journey home unscathed."

"God willin'."

Oscar made a sound. "You ain't even a religious fella. Why you lookin' to God to protect us?"

I gave him a look. "I ain't never said I didn't believe in God. I just don't believe most pastors speak for him."

"Hmph. I suppose that's true. And I reckon we could use any protection that's available."

We said our goodbyes and set about loading up the mule with our supplies. We'd thought about leaving Poke with Cal and the children, but Miss June assured us she would get a horse for them as soon as she could manage it. They'd need a horse if they meant to farm the land, and the children wanted to keep riding.

We stopped by Cal and Maggie's place on our way out.

The children, who were playing with the puppy in the field when we arrived, saw us and shouted cheerful greetings, before they noticed the packed mule behind me and Dixie. Their expressions sobered, and they took their time walking to meet us by the house, Teddy running back and forth and yapping with excitement.

We dismounted and hitched the horses and the mule to a shrub, then turned to the children.

The only one of them with a smile on their face was Samuel, whom Peter was leading by the hand. When they got close, the little boy reached his arms out.

"Up!"

Oscar glanced my way and smiled. "Go on."

I gave Oscar a rueful look then turned to the child. "You want up?"

He smiled even wider. "Up!"

I shrugged and reached down, and the child threw himself into me. I lifted him and held him in the crook of my arm, as he reached out to my chin, blinking his soft eyes contemplatively.

Oscar met my gaze, and he watched me and Samuel, his hands on his hips. "Well, ain't that one of the sweetest things I ever did see," he said in a soft voice, nodding. "Suits you."

The child's weight was practically nothing, and his fingers on my chin were gentle. I tried to think of something to say in response, but then Peter spoke.

"You're goin' then? Truly?"

Lizzie started crying, and Oscar knelt down to her level. "It'll be all right, Lizzie darlin'."

"But I won't ever see you and Onis again," she sniffed, throwing her arms around his neck. He shot me a desperate glance as he held her close and tried to soothe her.

"Well, that might not be true. Why, I'd love to come back and see you all, see how the farm's goin', how tall you and Peter and Sam have got."

Peter blinked back his tears, although I could tell 'twas a struggle. He was still so young.

"We'll miss you," he said, looking at me out of eyes that knew more than they should at his age — more about cruelty and violence and death. Then again, he also knew love and caring and kindness, so there was that.

I put Samuel down and stepped toward him. "I'll miss you as well, Peter Webster."

Cal and Maggie had discussed giving the children Cal's last name, or Maggie's, but they'd decided 'twould be best to avoid any kind of suspicion regarding Albert's disappearance by continuing to use his last name. Besides, the children were used to it, and 'twas probably best to avoid further disruption to their young lives.

I held out my hand, and Peter took it to shake, giving me a shy smile. But I pulled him to me for a hug, because boys needed comfort as much as girls, no matter how old they were. He wrapped his arms around my neck and hugged me back.

"I promise we'll do our best to come back and visit you. Port Essington ain't that far. Why, Oscar and I've traveled more'n twice that distance."

Peter nodded against my chest.

"Maybe you'd even be able to come to Port Essington someday, when you're older. We'd always have a spot for you to stay, I reckon."

"Can I come to Port Essington, too?" Lizzie said, sniffling back her tears and petting Onyx's broad black neck while the horse tore fresh grass and chewed it, snorting at the flies.

"Of course, you can," I said, "when you're bigger and can ride well. You keep practicin', now, once Miss June gets you a horse."

"I will. I promise." She stepped even closer to Oscar's black mare and pressed her forehead against Onyx's neck. Now she was missing a tooth, she had a bit of a lisp, which made her version of Onyx's name sound even sweeter. "Onis, I'm gonna miss you...so much."

I glanced at Oscar. He frowned and shrugged, the tension in his face showing his reaction to Lizzie's sorrow at losing her sweet friend. 'Twas useless to try to keep an emotional distance from these children. I reckoned we'd stopped trying.

"We ain't leavin' yet," Oscar said, his voice rough. "We gotta go say goodbye to Cal and Maggie."

"Can I please stay here with Onis until you need to go?" Lizzie asked in a quiet voice.

"Sure," Oscar said, looking anywhere but at them. "I know she'll appreciate the company."

"Come on," I said, nudging him toward the house.

Peter followed, with Samuel. "Momma, Jimmy and Oscar are here to say good–goodbye."

Cal was crouched before the open hatch of the stove, stirring the wood so the flames kept their heat. She was wearing a dark blue skirt and a linen blouse with tiny yellow flowers all o'er it, her hair up in the braids again. She stood and placed the poker in its stand, before turning toward us. She wrung her hands together and opened her mouth a couple of times, as if she didn't know quite what to say.

Then we all started talking at once.

"It's all right, Cal–" I said, as Oscar said, "Now, don't worry about–" and Cal herself said, "I can't possibly thank you enough."

Oscar frowned and put his hands on his hips. "Oh, yeah, you can." He almost sounded angry, and I reckoned the emotion of this moment was getting to him.

Cal blinked, waiting for him to continue.

"You can thank us by lookin' after these young 'uns, and yourself, so when we come back to visit, we find you in a much better situation than we did a month ago."

Cal nodded, swallowing hard, and smiled at Oscar. "I will. And you look after that fetchin' fella of yours." She glanced my way. "Jimmy acts tough, but he needs coddling and sweet handlin' as much as you and I do."

"I know it. And you don't gotta worry about that." We exchanged a glance and, though I was embarrassed, I saw such love and care in Oscar's gaze that it didn't matter.

Oscar and I had told Miss June we could be reached through the General Store in Port Essington if she ever needed us again and to not hesitate to write to us. Hell, e'en if she didn't need us, we wanted to hear from her. We'd want reassurance that our friends at The Angel were all right, and that Cal and the children and Maggie were getting on well.

After lots of hugs and kisses and promises to keep in touch, I glanced at Oscar.

"Well, we'd best be gettin' on," I said. "Maggie, you'd best come out with us. Lizzie's gonna need someone to help her let go of that horse — or hold her back from comin' with us."

There was a tug on my sleeve, and when I turned, Oscar pointed out of the window, where Lizzie stood close to Onyx. The little girl, in her pink frock, black stockings and black leather boots, had her hands cupped to the horse's ear as if she was saying a private goodbye. Then she threw her arms around Onyx's neck and shook with sobs, as the brown-and-white sheepdog pup wandered nearby.

"Jimmy," Oscar said, in a strange voice, "I don't know if I can bear it."

Chapter Thirty-Five

A Very Special Gift

"Oscar."

"That little girl ain't had anyone to protect her and love her the way Onyx would. They've already formed a bond. See?"

I gazed at him with wide eyes. "But you love that horse."

Oscar looked pained.

"I do. 'Course, I do." He squared his shoulders and nodded, as if he'd made a decision. "But I feel like...like Lizzie needs her more'n I do."

I stared at him, my heart swelling at his generosity and his courage, to be willing to give up an animal he loved for the happiness of a little girl that he'd only ever met a month ago.

"Oscar," I said, my voice thick.

He held up his hand, and I noticed 'twasn't exactly steady.

"Now, Jimmy, I know we paid a lot for her, and I surely do appreciate you buyin' her for me. I will miss her very, very much. But" — he nodded again at Lizzie and the mare—"I can't bear it. If you can bear it, go ahead, and I'll meet you down the street." He met my gaze with a pleading one. "But I can't do it."

I didn't say anything. The others were quiet, too.

"You sure you want to do this, Oscar?" I asked, my voice low. "We won't be able to come back for her or that girl's heart'll break twice as much than it would if we take Onyx now."

"I know."

"Oscar," Maggie said, "it's mighty kind of you to gift Lizzie that horse, but I'm sure we can get another one somehow. Miss June promised that she'd handle it."

"Yes, but horses can be finicky, and at least this way, I'd know the children had a good, kind horse to ride. And I'd know that Onyx was loved and cherished, even if 'tweren't by me."

His voice broke, and I reached out, tucking him against my chest. I wanted to tell him he was the kindest, most generous person I'd ever met, but I couldn't speak because I was so overcome, and there were so many people around. So I simply held him tight and kissed him on the cheek.

"You're gonna have to ride behind me on Dixie, then."

Oscar pulled away and brushed at his face, grinning, though his lips trembled.

"Now, you know, that ain't never been a hardship, Jimmy," he said. "That way I can keep an eye on you, make sure you don't fall and injure yourself again. And if I get tired of it, maybe we can load some of the smaller packages onto Dixie, and I can ride Poke."

"We ain't got no saddle for Poke. And we gotta leave Onyx's fancy saddle for Lizzie and the others."

His eyes flew wide. "Hey! Remember how Mr. Morris said he'd got Onyx for his granddaughter, and that was why the saddle was so fancy?"

"Yeah, I remember."

"Well, maybe this horse and this saddle were meant for Lizzie all along."

I smiled at his sweet, excited face. "Maybe."

Cal came up to Oscar and, without saying a word, she wrapped him in her arms and held him for a long time. She whispered something in his ear, and Oscar nodded.

Finally, she pulled away and took Peter's hand… and Samuel's. "Well, let's all go and tell Lizzie the good news."

Teddy gave a loud bark when he saw us and romped o'er to dance about, his tail wagging. Lizzie held on to Onyx e'en harder and hid her face in the mare's mane.

"Lizzie," Maggie said, as she stepped forward, putting a hand on Oscar's shoulder to stay him. "Get off that horse. Oscar and Jimmy need to leave now."

We were all a bit impressed when, instead of clutching tighter, Lizzie forced herself away from the grazing horse with an incredible amount of will for a seven-year-old.

"Yes'm," she said in a tight voice. "I already said goodbye."

"Lizzie, Oscar has something to tell you," Maggie said, gesturing for him to approach.

Lizzie gazed at Oscar, her face a paroxysm of stifled grief, as Oscar came forward and knelt in front of her.

"Now, Lizzie," Oscar said, in his kindest voice, "if I'm gonna leave you this horse, you gotta promise me to take real good care of her."

She blinked and nodded, though I reckoned she didn't e'en understand what Oscar was saying. Sure enough, she gave him and Maggie and Cal a confused look.

"Wh — at?"

Oscar smiled at the child, and I could hardly believe what this man was about to do. I could hardly believe that he was my husband and loved me with the same heart that must be breaking right about now.

"I want you to have this horse, Lizzie. I want you to have Onyx as your own."

Lizzie still seemed in shock, for she only nodded, her mouth open and her eyes wide in her dear, tearstained face.

"But you gotta share her with Peter and with Sam. She's for all of you, really, and she's for Maggie, too, so she can help out on the farm. So you gotta share her, all right?"

Lizzie was nodding now, as fresh tears coursed down her cheeks. Then she smiled so wide I thought her face might split apart.

"I'll look after her, Oscar, I promise! And I'll share her — a'course, I will."

She launched herself into Oscar's arms. She hugged him with a ferocity that came from a desperate, lonely place. Then she ran to Onyx and threw herself around the horse's neck. The mare snorted in surprise and sniffed Lizzie's head, nosing at the strands of hair as if she were trying to figure out if she could eat them.

"Oh, Onis! I get to keep you! I get to keep you! I love you so much!"

Oscar walked over to them. He stared at the mare for a moment, then rubbed her whiskered chin and placed his lips against the white stripe on her broad face, as Onyx huffed a breath and pushed her head against him. Then Oscar stepped back and took a deep breath.

He went and untied the holster that held his revolver from the fancy saddle. He ran one hand reverently o'er the tooled seat of Onyx's saddle, then brought the holster o'er to tie onto Dixie's saddle, near where the rifle was affixed in its leather holder.

"All right, Jimmy. Let's go." His voice broke on those last words.

I tousled little Lizzie's hair and kissed the top of her head, before mounting Dixie and holding my hand out for Oscar. I hauled him up behind me. He encircled me with his arms right away, and I reckoned he was doing his best to be strong.

'Twas nice to have him so close, and I squeezed his hand with mine to give him solace. The day was cool enough that riding together wouldn't be uncomfortable, and Dixie could handle the extra load, especially since Oscar was a wisp of a fella.

"Bye, then," I said, giving a wave to all the folks we'd come to love and respect o'er the past several weeks, then turned Dixie quick to get out of there before I lost my own composure.

"Bye!" Peter shouted, after we'd gone a few paces. "Don't wait too long to come back, now!" he said, as Teddy yapped and growled.

Neither of us turned to look, but I raised my hand and gave Peter a backward wave as Oscar tightened his hold around my waist.

I didn't know when or how, but we surely would be back one day.

* * * *

By the time we'd got away, the sun was well past its midpoint, and I figured we only had about six hours of travel left in the day. We were awful quiet for the first little while. I'd never ever needed or wanted to have children in my life, but I couldn't deny that these three had burrowed their way into my heart, and I knew Oscar felt the same.

"Jimmy," he said after a little while, "do you think 'twas a good thing I did, giving Onyx to Lizzie?"

I guided Dixie around an outcrop of rock as Oscar clutched my waist to keep steady.

"Oscar," I said in a chiding tone, "I think 'twas the most generous and unselfish thing I ever saw anybody do. And I think that little girl will love you forever, and she'll take mighty good care of that horse for you. I reckon you just changed her life."

"Really?"

"I do. Truly. And I" — I cleared my throat and dropped a hand from the reins to cover Oscar's — "I'm mighty proud of the man you've become, Oscar Yates."

Oscar gave a sigh that sounded half like a sob, and I reckoned 'twas hitting him that he wouldn't see Onyx again for a very long time, if ever. I continued speaking so he didn't have to reply.

"I'd like to think I had a hand in it, but I reckon you've always been the kindest man I've ever been lucky enough to be with. This proves it."

"Thank you," he whispered. "I feel like — I'm gonna miss that horse, but I feel real good knowin' I was able to do somethin' big for someone."

"Oh, Oscar," I said, stopping Dixie and turning in the saddle to look at him. "You already did somethin' big for lots of people, including me. But I know how much you love that horse and givin' her away was the most amazing thing I seen anybody ever do."

Oscar nodded against my back, rubbing his forehead against the leather of my jacket, and I got Dixie moving again. I figured Oscar needed to have a good cry, and sure enough, he shuddered and started to let those powerful emotions out in quiet, sniffly sobs.

I kept my hand o'er his and rubbed it, giving him the comfort that I could. And I kept talking, because I knew he was probably embarrassed about giving way to his intense feelings.

"Don't you forget that I spent a lot of years surrounded by the most selfish, awful men, who did terrible things to people for the amusement of it. To see what I did — why, you've given me back the faith that people can be good, and generous, and kind, and that means a lot to me. You'll never know how much."

Oscar nodded against my back, gave a louder sob and tightened his hold, as if he needed to anchor himself in a world that seemed unsteady again.

And we rode out of Telegraph Creek under the intensity of the afternoon sun, making our way for home.

Chapter Thirty-Six

Port Essington

The weather turned out mostly fair for traveling, and we didn't encounter any untoward incidents on our way back to Port Essington. The mosquitoes weren't as bad, either, but we slathered ourselves with the marigold ointment anyway, to keep off the bugs that were around.

Oscar's mood remained morose for the first days of our journey. I don't think he regretted what he'd done, but he missed that horse, and I reckoned he missed those children, too, like I did. There was something joyful about the innocence of wee ones, who were full of life and optimistic promise.

The second night of our journey, Oscar woke me from a deep sleep.

"Jimmy."

"Hmm? What's wrong?"

"Nothin'. But I can't sleep."

I turned on my bedroll to wrap my arm around him and snug him close.

"You want me to sing to you?"

He didn't say anything for a moment.

"Maybe you could read to me, instead?"

I squinted in the darkness, trying to see his expression, but 'twas too dark.

"All right. I'll light the lantern."

'Twas a warm night, so I was only on top of my bedroll. I found the lantern and lit it, then got the book that Sally had gifted me the day before we'd left.

"You're almost done with that book," Oscar said, as I sat down near him, with my back against a convenient rock. "Is it good?"

"Yeah, 'tis real good," I said, smiling at him. "C'mere then."

Oscar scooched o'er so that he could lean against the rock and snuggle against me, while the campfire crackled and the lantern hissed.

"Now this here story is told from Buck's point of view — that's the dog who's half St. Bernard and half Scotch Shepard — about his life up in the Yukon, after a slew of owners that mistreated him and some who only looked on him as a useful servant."

"Okay."

"Only now he's with a man who's caring and loving of him, and he talks about how that feels after a life of toil and cruelty."

I flattened the page and held it so 'twas bathed in light from the lantern, then began to read.

"This man had saved his life, which was something; but, further, he was the ideal master. Other men saw to the welfare of their dogs from a sense of duty and business expediency; he saw to the welfare of his as if they were his own children, because he could not help it. And he saw further. He never forgot a kindly greeting or a cheering word, and to sit down for a long talk with them — 'gas' he called it —

294

was as much his delight as theirs. He had a way of taking Buck's head roughly between his hands, and resting his own head upon Buck's, of shaking him back and forth, the while calling him ill names that to Buck were love names. Buck knew no greater joy than that rough embrace and the sound of murmured oaths, and at each jerk back and forth it seemed that his heart would be shaken out of his body so great was its ecstasy. And when, released, he sprang to his feet, his mouth laughing, his eyes eloquent, his throat vibrant with unuttered sound, and in that fashion remained without movement, John Thornton would reverently exclaim, 'God! You can all but speak!'

"*Buck had a trick of love expression that was akin to hurt. He would often seize Thornton's hand in his mouth and close so fiercely that the flesh bore the impress of his teeth for some time afterward. And as Buck understood the oaths to be love words, so the man understood this feigned bite for a caress.*"

I stopped reading then, a heat spreading through my body that warmed me through, and I felt like we were both thinking how these words expressed some of what we felt for each other.

Sure enough, Oscar stirred against me.

"Jimmy, that's...why, that's us! That's you and me, for sure. How is that possible?"

I shrugged, so glad that he saw in those words what I did—a connection based on love, respect and adoration, that didn't find its strength in flowery words and romantic promises but in rough gestures and sharp jibes that meant much, much more when you looked beneath the surface.

"Well, I suppose the writer maybe had feelings like that, possibly for another man, and the only way he could express it was through the eyes of a male dog for his master, in this here story."

I watched Oscar blink at this hypothesis then he nodded. "I reckon you might be right."

He snuggled into me, and I kept reading, as the stars shone in the sky above and the promise of Port Essington and our home lay just out of reach.

* * * *

We rode into town late on the Thursday. The smell of the fish canneries greeted us before we got there, now that they'd gone full bore again, and there were lots more people walking the streets, even in the rain. We got some queer looks, but nobody would directly question two men sharing a horse in these times.

Seemed fitting to arrive in a downpour once again, and we were right soaked by the time we rode up to Jensen's Saloon. I pulled Dixie to a stop and helped Oscar slide off before getting down myself.

We stepped inside the door and right away, Carson Moore looked up from behind the bar. His face broke into a grin, and he whooped real loud, lifting his bar towel into the air.

"Oscar! Jimmy! You're back!"

"Yeah, we're back," I said, glancing around the place. "I see nothin' much has changed while we were gone."

There were a few people at the tables, drinking and playing cards in the late afternoon, before the dinner rush.

Carson came around and strode o'er to us, holding out his hand.

"Welcome home, gentlemen."

I greeted him as his gaze shifted between the two of us, and I remembered what he'd said to me before we'd left, about understanding the true nature of the relationship between Oscar and me. But he seemed genuinely glad to see us, as if it didn't make a difference to him and that he wouldn't let on to anyone else what he'd figured out. I only hoped the whole entire town wouldn't be able to tell we were more'n real good friends.

"Good to see you, Jimmy!" he said. "And, Oscar, how're you?"

Oscar took off his hat, droopy with water, and swiped the wet hair out of his face. "Soggy."

Carson chuckled and clasped Oscar in a hearty hug that seemed to take him by surprise.

"Well, pull up a stool, and I'll get you a towel and something to drink. You hungry?"

"I could use a drink and something to eat," Oscar said. "Sorry to drip all over your saloon."

"Don't mind it one bit! Come on."

We sat on stools at the bar while Carson went to get towels. When he came back, Tim Jensen was with him.

"Well, well, well, our fair travelers have returned," he said, with a broad smile. "Welcome home."

"Thank you," I said. "'Tis real good to be back."

'Twas good to have a place to call home, and I didn't think I'd ever remembered feeling so welcome, except for back at The Angel.

"Did you have a successful trip?"

"We did," I said, as Carson passed us each a towel and we dried our hair and our necks and hands. 'Twas not pleasant to be wearin' our wet clothes, but the rain was still sheeting, and I'd rather wait for it to lighten up before we headed out to the homestead. We needed something to drink and eat, anyway.

"Were you able to help where you were needed?"

"Yep," Oscar said. "We came in all hero-like and we found the person that was missing. She's all sorted now and in a better situation."

Tim frowned. "I hope she wasn't too badly off."

Oscar glanced at me and shrugged. "Well, she's better off now, that's certain. So 'tis real good we went." 'Twas probably better not to go into the details with Tim.

"I'm glad to hear it."

"Anythin' major happen while we were gone?" I asked.

Carson laughed as he put a pint of dark ale in front of each of us.

"Nope. Nothing of note, I don't think. The same boring old cannery town that you left in the spring."

I cocked my head. "You know, that makes me glad to hear. I've had enough goddamn excitement in my life. I reckon I'm ready for some long, dull days, personally."

"Amen to that," Oscar said, lifting his glass so we could toast to it.

Carson's ale tasted like ambrosia on our tongues, which had been the only dry part of us. After I'd taken some long draws, I asked the question that had been on my mind since we'd left Telegraph Creek.

"The house all right?"

Some part of me worried he'd say it had got knocked down in a windstorm or the land had flooded, but he only smiled.

"It's exactly the way you left it. I've been out to the place every week, and Irene and Clarence have checked it more often, I reckon." Carson said.

The relief was like a wave passing o'er me, and I hadn't realized how scared I'd been that the first real home I'd ever had as an adult would be taken from me, somehow. Like how, every once in a while, I still felt like I'd lose Oscar. The trouble with having good things in your life was knowing how bad 'twould be if or when they were gone.

"And that blasted cat won't leave your front porch. Every time I go out there, she's layin' in front of the door, waiting for you two."

"Sprite?" Oscar said, perking up from the drink and the mention of his beloved cat. "God, I'd almost forgotten about her. At least I've still got Sprite."

Carson looked concerned, so I told him about Oscar giving Onyx away.

"That was a very selfless thing to do, Oscar," Carson said. "I don't know that I could have given away an animal that meant so much to me.

"Yeah." Oscar cleared his throat. "'Twas hard, but I'm mostly glad I did it."

I put my hand on Oscar's back, then thought better of that and took it away. We needed to get used to being in public again.

Carson saw the gesture and smiled as I spoke to Oscar.

"Cal and the kids needed a good, kind horse. Giving them Onyx was the best thing you could have done, and I'm so proud of you."

My voice was quiet, but Oscar and Carson heard what I'd said.

Oscar nodded and took another sip of his ale. He'd already eaten the slices of cheese and tear of bread that Tim had brought out.

"I suppose we'd better get home and out of these wet clothes," I said, finally, after we'd chatted more and finished our drinks. "What do I owe you?"

"On the house. Consider it a welcome party."

"Thank you," I said. "I expect you'll be seeing us around pretty often, now we're back. You got any leads on work in town?"

"Well, there's always the cannery. But let me ask around, and I'll let you know."

"Sounds good."

"Bye," Oscar said.

I knew he was plumb beat and probably sore. 'Twasn't all that comfortable to ride double on a horse if you were the fellow in the back. I'd offered to trade off with him, but he'd said he preferred having me in front. Our clothes were damp and clammy, and I reckoned we only wanted to get home.

Chapter Thirty-Seven

Where the Heart Is

The ride to our homestead seemed shorter than ever, after the distance we'd traveled the past week. In no time at all, we came upon it, my heart pounding as if I was seeing a long-lost friend for the first time in years.

Our pretty house rose up from the land like a benediction. The sky had cleared, and the droplets of rain sparkled on the shingles of the roof. Her pale-yellow board walls shone out o'er the surrounding grasses with a newness that hadn't diminished in the couple of months we'd been gone. I found myself blinking back strong emotions again.

What the hell was happening to me? Now I was a married man with a home, I was turning into some kind of sensitive fella that got teary o'er everything. 'Twas probably Oscar's influence, and the fact I actually had a life to get emotional about.

Sure enough, there was Sprite, curled up sleeping under the bench by the door, guarding the place for us.

I helped Oscar to swing down, then I dismounted, and that woke her up. She made a bleating sound and ran for us, rubbing all in and around our legs while making that strange noise, her tail up in the air as it quivered with happiness.

"Aww, Sprite, 'tis so nice to see you," Oscar said, scooping her into his arms and cuddling her against him. She wouldn't stop wriggling and stretching, and she butted his chin then smoothed her cheek alongside his. The sound of her purring was a challenge to the cicadas that had broken into song now that the rain had stopped.

"As much as I want to go right inside, we need to stable this horse and mule. We might as well unload Poke and pile everything on the porch."

Oscar nodded and put the cat down. We took all our things off the mule then led him and Dixie to the barn. The cat followed and seemed happy to join us in the clean, bright space while we dried off the animals and put them up with some fresh hay and grain.

We stood there and watched them for a time, while they settled themselves in their familiar surroundings. I glanced at Oscar. His expression seemed conflicted.

"I know you miss her."

"Seems strange to not have her here. I don't—I don't regret givin' her to Lizzie, but it's gonna take some gettin' used to."

I moved close and put my arm around him, pulling him into my side.

"We'll get a new horse for you, Oscar, as soon as we can manage it. I know there ain't a horse out there who'll match Onyx, but you'll have the chance to make a new friend and get to know a new horse soon—and that'll help take your mind off of her."

He clutched my arm then tucked his forehead into my neck and exhaled a raspy sob. He sucked in more air and let out those horrible feelings of grief and loss, while I held him still and safe in the quiet of the barn. And I realized again what a brave and selfless thing it was that he'd done and fought my own emotions as I held him.

"You're a good, kind man, Oscar Yates. You're the best thing ever happened to me. You saved me, I reckon, from a life of loneliness, bitterness and barely even livin'. My life is full and good because of you."

We clutched each other and mourned the loss of his horse, with Sprite winding around our legs as if to remind us that we still had her. When Oscar's sobs died down, he rubbed gruffly at his face and pulled away from me. He took a deep breath.

"Let's go in, Jimmy. I wanna see our beautiful house and all our things again."

"Me, too," I said, taking his hand and leading him out of the barn. "Me, too."

We left our mucky boots on the porch, with all the wrapped parcels we'd unloaded that could wait until morning. Inside, the house was clean and quiet, as if she'd been waiting for us to come home. We gazed about us at our familiar things that we'd barely arranged the way we wanted them before we'd had to leave.

We headed upstairs, the friendly creaking of the steps a reminder of all the work that had gone into building this place. 'Twas silent, tranquil and looked welcoming with the sunlight coming in the windows. The sunbeams broke through the remnant clouds, dancing through the dust and spreading on the floorboards of our bedroom.

We didn't spend long appreciating the space but got out of our wet clothes and found some towels to dry off with. We dressed in clean, dry clothes from the wardrobe, and I went down and started a fire in the stove so we could make something to eat.

By the time night fell, we were fed, dry and content to sit on the back porch and gaze out at our land. The mountains rose around us as they always did and had even on our journey and in Telegraph Creek. 'Twas a feature of the landscape in British Columbia, and those great hills seemed like giants watching o'er us. They were strong and big and sure.

Oscar and I sat in silence. We listened to the crickets and cicadas chirping, the frogs bellowing and the birds making their evening calls as the sun went down.

When I next looked at Oscar, before darkness had enveloped us, he was sound asleep, his head laying back against the wood of the chair, his mouth open, as he snored like an eighty-year-old fella. But the sight of him made my heart melt in my chest, and the knowledge that he was safe, sound and comfortable in my care made me happy.

* * * *

In the early morning, I woke to the birds singing and the brightness of a sunny day beginning. The comfort of our own bed and the softness of the sheets Irene had gifted us what seemed like a lifetime ago made my heart sing.

We'd made it. We'd done what we'd needed to do for Miss June and Cal, and we were back here in our dear home, with all our limbs attached and none the worse for wear, except for a pale scar on the side of my belly that would mostly disappear in time.

AE Lister

I glanced at Oscar, who slept soundly beside me, with his lips parted and his nose making soft huffing noises. I turned on my side to watch him sleep, as if I had all the time in the world to appreciate him. The ticking of the clock, and the calls of the summer birds outside the open windows were an agreeable backdrop.

After a little while, Oscar snuffled the bedclothes like a piglet rooting for a teat, and his eyes flew open.

"Was I snorin'?" he asked, in a sleep-roughened voice.

I'm sure I had a foolish smile on my face, because he looked so innocent lying there and younger than ever. I pushed a lock of hair from in front of one eye.

"Mm-hmm. 'Twas sweet."

"'Twas?"

"Mm-hmm." I kissed him on the nose. "*You're* sweet."

Oscar pushed himself up on one elbow and rubbed his nose. "I ain't. I'm rough and brave and strong and fierce," he said, flashing me a goofy smile.

"You're all those things, too. But you're sleep-soft and delicate right now, and I'm appreciatin' it."

He blushed and pushed me away, then threw off the sheets and sat up.

"We got stuff to do. We need to get all our packs in, then we gotta go tell Irene and Clarence we're back."

I sighed. "You're right. What was I thinkin'?"

"Come on!"

We got dressed and washed at the basin that I'd filled before we went to bed. Then I made some coffee on the stove, and we ate some of the bread and cheese we still had left, neither of us wanting to waste time on a big breakfast.

"You know, we can get a dog, if you want—and name him Buck like the dog in *The Call of the Wild*. I reckon it'd be a good idea to have a dog about the place."

Oscar's eyes lit up, and he nodded with enthusiasm. "Okay. Sure."

I fed and watered the animals, while Oscar made a start on unpacking and bringing in our supplies. We didn't have that much, but for the tent and the food we'd brought along. Trick had given Oscar the red silk robe with the dragon on it, and the corset and bloomers that she didn't need, now that she was wearin' men's things, and I reckoned I was gonna be treated to some kind of a burlesque show one night very soon. I smiled to myself, and my cock plumped a bit with the anticipation of *that*.

After getting everything sorted at the house, we saddled Dixie, I helped Oscar up behind and we headed out on the familiar path to our neighbors' place.

It seemed Sprite didn't wanna let us out of her sight, so she followed at Dixie's heels the whole way, as we rode through the familiar trees and past the landmarks we knew so well, until we came out into the little clearing near their place.

There were two familiar figures in the distance. It looked like they were working in the small vegetable garden Irene kept in the summers. Oscar saw them a little bit after I did, and I could sense his excitement as he straightened up behind me.

"Look! It's them," Oscar said.

I laughed. "A'course it's them. Who else would it be?"

But even before I'd finished speaking, Oscar slid from Dixie's saddle, landed in the grass and moved with haste toward them.

Clarence turned and leaned on his hoe, shading his eyes from the morning sun. Irene followed his gaze and grabbed Clarence's arm, then let go, gathered her skirts and started running, waving her hand with excitement.

I watched Oscar race toward her, as I thanked God again for putting Irene and Clarence in our path. I didn't quite know what the future held for us in this place, but I knew we were surrounded by love and friendship — and I had high hopes for it.

Want to see more from this author?
Here's a taster for you to enjoy!

Hot Bite: Bloodlines
AE Lister

Excerpt

I noticed him on the first day of summer session classes at the University of Toronto.

The season had arrived with its stifling, sticky heat, endless hours of sun beating down upon the pavement and high-rises that crowded this self-important city. There were still people who imagined this northern country covered in ice and slush all year round, but summers in Toronto were brutal. Due to the lack of significant green space, the concrete city reflected and amplified the intense heat so that if you didn't have climate-control capabilities in your dwelling, you were doomed to days and nights of sweltering discomfort.

He wasn't human. Sitting in the midst of those forty-eight souls brave enough to sign up for my *Pyramids of Giza — Ancient Egyptian Art and Archeology* class, he glowed like a radioactive leak...but only to others of his kind, like me.

Vampire. Undead. Eternal.

He must have seen me.

I could tell from the vibrancy of his electric ambience that he had only recently been made, perhaps a handful of years ago. He was young, both in human years at the time of his change and in vampire years. But for all the luminosity, he didn't look out of place among the other twenty- and twenty-one-year-old students in my third-year course.

In comparison, my radiance would appear faded and composed of varying underlying colors, rather than the bright white aura of a brand-new supernatural being. But he would see me, that was certain.

He was blinding—and not simply due to his supernatural youth. Whoever he had been before he'd become one of us, his physical appeal could not be debated. I was mesmerized by the way he moved as he strode into the auditorium and took his seat, apart from the rest of the crowd. Trying to manage his blood lust, I supposed.

It must have been raging. I recalled the first few years of my vampiric initiation, and the burning hunger that had lit my veins and made me look for food everywhere I had gone. It had made me reckless and careless—and had caused me no end of trouble, because older vampires did not like the younger ones, who threatened our practiced existence by calling attention to themselves in dangerous ways. If a new vampire was out of control and behaving in ways that made all vampires a target of attention, they would be dealt with...and swiftly. It wasn't the mortal policing institutions that would bring them down, but their blood-lustful brothers who were able to manage their needs and desires with finesse and discretion.

In my own case, I'd managed to draw the attention of an older supernatural who'd taken me under his wing, taught me the skills to live among humans and the ways to manage the hunger. He was long gone, now—a victim of the despondence and despair that many of our kind succumb to after untold centuries, when existence itself becomes a burden and they simply want out.

Immortality was a dubious gift.

Only after four hundred years spent in this non-life was I able to be in a room full of young, vibrant humans and not want to murder and drink from each and every one of them. The hunger was there. It simmered below the surface like a gas-fired furnace, keeping me warm and aware of everything, but it didn't control me, and I no longer found it painful to resist those urges.

This was not completely a process of maturation and practice. It was, in large part, because of Sage.

I had kept a host of human acolytes—I hated the word 'slave', and it didn't fit what they were to me or I to them over the years—and Sage was the latest. They had been pets more than anything, and Sage had begun as such. But in the mere decade that I'd known them, they'd managed to exert a hold over me that none of the others had managed. I didn't know what I was going to do with Sage when they became too old to serve me and wanted the easy final exit that most of their precursor's had asked for—namely, a swift, intimate, peaceful death at my hands, in my bed or wherever they chose.

It was undeniably difficult to watch a human age out of existence.

But it was fascinating. The mental transformation was as captivating as the physical.

In their ten years at my side and under my teeth, Sage had eclipsed all others.

They were light and beauty and devotion. If a vampire could love—well, I loved them already. Our time together was not even a blink of an eye in my long immortal life and yet Sage had made such a huge imprint on me in that brief time.

I had begun to contemplate turning them into someone like me, but I couldn't quite give up what we had just yet. They'd not lost their youthful glow and were gaining that bit of an edge that came when humans were approaching thirty.

Sage worked as my Executive Assistant, which was only a cover for us to be consistently together. And they supposedly 'rented' a room in my home. I knew there were rumors about us...but only concerning our sexual relationship. Nobody would guess the truth.

I was lucky enough that Sage, knowing who and what I was, permitted me the honor of feeding from them so that I could satisfy my blood lust in a manner that was measured and controlled and gave both of us a feeling of euphoria and pleasure similar to how humans felt when they copulated. And also, Sage let me fuck them, which gave us two times the pleasure when it was accompanied by a quick snack.

Let you fuck them? Let you feed from them? How could they have had free choice when you are so much more powerful?

Perhaps this argument had merit, and Sage was more my slave than I ever realized or intended. But I had gone to the point of pushing them away to let them know I wouldn't keep them under my thumb. They were free to leave me, and they were always free to deny me food or sex—or both. They could withdraw their consent at any time. I told them this almost every day. And yet, they never did.

If there was anything inside me that resembled the human capacity to love, I felt it for Sage. In only ten years, they had made me more of their prisoner than the other way around. I didn't know how long they'd deign to put up with me. At some point in the future, the question of Sage's chance at immortality would be a force to be reckoned with. But I wouldn't do it until they asked for it explicitly—maybe not until they begged.

Because immortal life was not a gift if it was given by force and circumstance. I had learned that lesson well.

* * * *

My students began to disappear.

Although not unusual for people to drop out of a class in university, I suspected the reason for their absence had less to do with not enjoying the subject matter and more to do with Clove Noble. But I couldn't be sure until I spoke with him.

At the end of my regular lecture in the third week, I directed him to come and see me in my office after class. I didn't normally have available hours on Mondays, and I didn't want us to be disturbed.

I walked to my small office on the second floor, hoping that Clove would show up. I could sense him in the building. I could feel his effervescent glow as he moved through the halls and approached my office door.

Three concise knocks.

"Enter."

The door creaked open, and his luminosity blinded me.

"You wanted to see me, Professor Wilde?" he said.

"Shut the door, please."

He did, the click of the latch sounding louder than it should have.

"Have I...done something wrong?" Clove asked, as he folded himself gracefully into the seat by my desk.

I examined him, my vision acclimating to his vibrancy.

He looked the same age as his classmates — twenty or so — and he was dressed in the modern style of this age group. Ripped jeans and Doc Martens — did they ever go out of style? — a Greta Van Fleet concert T-shirt and a black vinyl leather-look jacket that fell to mid-thigh, with pockets and zippers all over the place. The latter was excessive in the summer heat, but not for one of us. I imagined he wanted to keep his skin covered where he could, so that its unusual paleness wouldn't be questioned, but the intense heat didn't touch us, and the sun's rays weren't the threat the myths pretended.

His hair was died purple and green, and in a modern shag cut, so that he looked like an angsty little pixie-boy — when I knew he was anything but.

He gazed at me with curiosity, then sat straighter as a slow smile formed on his face.

"What is it?" he asked, the tone of his voice different.

"I know what you are," I stated.

He blinked. The smile widened.

"No. You don't." A pink tongue came out to glide along his bottom lip.

We stared at each other.

The smile got bigger, and Clove leaned back in the chair, folding his arms over his chest. "What am I, professor?"

The tone of his voice hit me right in the groin, and my cock stiffened as if to a siren's call. I narrowed my eyes.

"Vampire. Like me."

"*Bzzz*. Wrong." He laughed, looking only a little uncomfortable. "Don't be ridiculous."

Except, if I truly were wrong, he'd be calling the police or the Royal Ottawa and not laughing. And anyway, I knew I was right.

"I'm not wrong," I said. "That's what you are. It's what I am."

The smile vanished. He looked me over from the top of my head to the bottom of my dress shoes. We were at an angle, so he could see me where I sat, half behind the small desk.

"Maybe. But that's where the similarity ends, I bet."

"Hmm."

My irrepressible cock hardened more, and I mentally chastised it. I hadn't called him to my office for *that*. I cleared my throat.

"I've lost seven students in my class so far this semester."

He raised his eyebrows and parted his cherry lips to speak, but I beat him to it.

"Four have officially dropped the course."

He closed his mouth, but a hint of the smile returned. He cleared his throat and looked everywhere but at me.

"Three are simply gone. Missing."

He rubbed his bottom lip and shook his head. The smile returned in full.

"Clove?"

He raised his gaze to mine. Something ignited within me—something violent and ravenous. I saw the same thing spark in him. The smile disappeared, and he shifted in his seat.

"Jeeze, don't look at me like that," he said.

"Like what?"

"Like you want to fuck me over this desk."

"Like I want—" I stared at him, legitimately shocked. True, I was a creature of the night who

survived off human blood and killed at will—
discretely—but I was not the type to throw around
vulgar language…or generally receive it.

"Oh, surely you know what fucking is." He waved
at the desk between us. "You want to *fuck me. Over that.
Desk.*" Clove said, enunciating perfectly so there was no
misunderstanding. How could there have been, when
the language he used was so blunt, and when he ran his
slim fingers along the crease in his jeans where a
sizeable bulge was obvious.

Good Lord. I hadn't prepared for this. And he was
right. But it wouldn't be over this desk. And it wouldn't
be now. Maybe it wouldn't be ever.

"Are you hunting my students?"

He blinked again, settled himself comfortably in the
chair again, rubbed at his lap then shrugged.

"Clove," I said.

His gaze met mine. He seemed amused more than
anything.

"Professor Wilde."

I shook my head. He was infuriating—self-assured
and unapologetic. I wanted to slap him…or spank him,
something to wipe that insouciant smile off his pretty
face. And yes, I did want to fuck him, which only
irritated me more.

I leaned forward, using the force of centuries to glare
him down and show him my power.

"You cannot feed with so little regard for our
circumstances."

"*Our* circumstances?"

"Yes."

He scowled. "Why not?"

"Because I'm certainly not the only one who has
noticed them dropping like flies. You'll draw too much
attention to us."

To us.

"Ah. I see," he said, leaning forward and matching my intensity with his own youthful flare. "You're scared."

I blinked.

He continued. "Worried I'll blow your cover."

He quirked his lip as his gaze locked on the bulge in my chinos. He licked it again, and I knew exactly what he was thinking.

I stood languidly from my chair, looming over him. We were similar in height, but he was shorter, even when he wasn't sitting down.

He didn't flinch, even though a human in the same situation would have been shitting themselves.

"You need to stop," I said.

He laughed. "I need to feed," he said, licking his top teeth. "Don't you, Professor?"

"To feed?" I repeated.

"Or are you so old you can't stomach the rich taste of fresh human?"

I let the insult go. I knew I was old, but it was a strength, not a weakness. I wasn't mortal, and I looked the age I had been when I was made — which, of course, was a couple of decades older than Clove was now. But a twenty-year age difference was a joke from my ancient perspective.

"I handle my needs with discretion and sense."

He laughed again. "Wow. Sounds awesome."

I narrowed my eyes, wondering how we were going to come to an agreement on this. And that was when Sage chose to interrupt us.

"Benjamin, I have your—"

They stopped dead just inside the door.

"Oh. Sorry. I didn't know you were—"

My androgynous assistant scanned young, bright, vibrant Clove from top to bottom, and I knew we were going to have a problem when Sage dropped the papers and made a noise I recognized.

Oh Gods.

Clove finally seemed to find a care and bent to help my Sage to collect the papers that had fallen, giving me a sidelined glance as he did so.

"Here... Let me help you," he said.

"Oh, yes, thank you so...much. Yes. Please. Thank you."

They stared at each other, and I could almost feel the hunger and desire rise in Clove.

"Don't you dare," I said, as he eyed my lovely Sage with the intensity of a ravenous predator. "Clove. No."

But he'd already grabbed Sage's arm and pulled them close. So I lunged forward and grabbed Clove's chin as he opened his mouth and bared his fangs. I wrenched his face away from Sage and threw him against the wall.

Clove hissed as he fell to the floor, but he was already gathering for another attack. I held up my hand.

"Stop!"

"Why the fuck should I?" he snarled, saliva dripping from his lips.

"Because Sage is mine, and you haven't asked if I'll *share*."

This confused him enough that he stilled and looked between the two of us.

Sage trembled but also stared wide-eyed at Clove, as if they *wanted* him to feed. Knowing Sage as I did, that was probably accurate, but they didn't yet realize that Clove would kill them if he went ahead, whereas I had the control to hold back and keep Sage with me. Then again, perhaps Clove could do it if I helped him. Perhaps he should learn some restraint. But did I want to risk my dearest Sage on a youngster's appetite? Did I want to share them, even briefly?

"Sage, please go."

Sage gave Clove a lingering look but nodded — *my obedient darling*. "Yes, Professor."

And they were gone and closing the door behind them.

I was ready to restrain Clove if he tried to follow, but he didn't. He braced himself against the wall where he seemed crouched to spring on…something. But as I watched, he regrouped and calmed himself, and his body relaxed. He slid down the wall and sat on the carpeted floor, his long legs extended in front of him.

"What is the human to you?" he asked. He seemed dazed and exhausted, as if it had taken all his strength to resist.

Hearing my beautiful Sage referred to as 'the human' by this upstart newborn caused my anger to flare, but I tamped it down. I stepped forward and locked the door, then sat down in my desk chair, keeping my eyes on Clove all the while. He was so very new, and I had to be prepared for anything, although he truly didn't stand a chance against me, and he must have known it.

"Sage is —" I tried to think of a suitable descriptor for Sage and waved a hand in the air instead. "Never mind. They're mine. That's all you need to know."

"Human."

"Yes."

"Blood slave?" he licked his lips as if he could already taste it.

"In a manner of speaking." Except Sage was free to refuse me if they chose to do so. I didn't say that. Better for Clove to think they were my captive and that I'd protect them like a prized possession.

"How do they identify?"

"Pardon?"

"You're using they/them pronouns. Are they trans...or something else?"

"That's something they may choose to divulge to you. It's not my place to say."

"Hmm." He looked at the closed door, then back at me. "Pretty."

It was such a tame descriptor of Sage that I couldn't help but give a short laugh. "More than you'll ever know."

"Professor Wilde." He said my name like he was tasting how it felt in his mouth.

"Mr. Noble."

Now he laughed—a bubbly, happy-sounding noise that shocked me in its purity. He didn't seem like a vampire when he laughed. He came across like a young, carefree human. And it warmed me more than I wanted it to.

"So formal. I like it when you call me Clove."

Hmm.

"Clove, then. Will you stop feeding from my students? And anywhere else on this campus?"

Clove smiled and opened his mouth. He bared his fangs and swiped his tongue over them in an obvious display.

"Well, that depends."

Upstart.

"On what, may I ask?"

"I want to make a deal with you, Professor Wilde," he said, looking me over with a different kind of hunger.

I couldn't truthfully say I was unaffected. In fact, I felt an answering need—not for blood, because Clove didn't have any to spare. But a hankering for something else he could give me, perhaps wanted to give me.

I cleared my throat. I didn't feel flustered very often.

"What kind of a deal?"

He grinned. "A fair one."

"Hmm."

He brought one knee up and flicked a piece of lint off his jeans. "I'll stop hunting your students, Professor Wilde, on one condition."

"Which is?"

He gazed hard at me with something like impatience. "That you show me what you do with Sage."

"*Show* you!"

"Oooh! By your outrage, I assume it's lit. And that there's some...sucking involved." He clapped his hands together like a delighted child.

I frowned. He knew how to get what he wanted. I'd give him that...but not yet.

"No. Not that."

Clove shrugged. He laced his fingers over his knee and swung it gently from side to side. He leaned his head back against the wall, like he had all the time in the world to lounge in my office.

"Oh, come on. You're not so stodgy you won't show me how to feed properly, are you?"

Stodgy? That hit right where he'd wanted it to.

"I'm *not* stodgy."

"Prove it. Let me *see*."

Gods, he was fucking infuriating. And part of me did want to show him—the part of me that liked games in the bedroom and teaching. But...what about Sage and what *they* wanted?

Who was I kidding? Sage would be fully on board. Was probably fully on board already, after one glimpse of this compelling youngster.

And I had to give Clove points for asking for help, even if it was in a self-serving sort of way.

"*If*—" I said, and at that, the alluring bugger smiled wide, knowing he had me. I held up one finger. "*If* I do as you ask…"

I stood again and walked around the desk and over to him. He craned his neck to gaze at me from where he was sitting.

"If I introduce you properly to Sage and see where we go from there…"

He narrowed his eyes. "You're talking like Sage has a say in what happens."

"They do. Always."

He eyed me. "Interesting."

"If I do this, I want you to promise to keep your hands off my students."

We held each other's gazes for a long moment. Finally, Clove gathered his legs under him and stood. He stepped forward so that we were barely a foot apart. He smelled of laundry detergent and aftershave. And something else…

"I promise to keep my hands off your students."

"And your teeth."

"And my teeth."

"Prove it."

He blinked. Then laughed at the throwback of his own words. Perhaps he hadn't expected it of me.

"What?"

"No students missing from my class for one week, and you can come home with me and Sage for one night."

He narrowed his eyes. "But...how am I going to feed?"

"You're going to do it off campus. I don't care where, but I'd better not hear of any mysterious deaths. You choose your victims with consideration, and don't leave a trail of corpses for the police."

"You're pretty big on discretion for a guy with a blood slave who probably serves him in other ways as well."

"No comment," I said, stepping aside and showing Clove the door. "One week. Prove you can be sensible, and I'll help you."

He crossed his arms over his chest and didn't move.

"I'll do it, but I want something from you, too."

"That's not the way this deal is going to work."

"A kiss."

"Oh, for God's sake."

He grinned. And shrugged. And waited.

"I don't even like you," I said, with steely resolve.

Clove looked me up and down again, hesitated deliberately on the bulge in my trousers. "Oh, I think you like me a little."

I cleared my throat and shifted my gaze. He moved closer and took the lapel of my jacket in his fingers, leaning into me.

"Just one kiss. I've never been kissed by another vampire. Or...anything like that, really."

"What do you mean?" I said, my breath hitching. "Of course you have." I pulled back and met his open gaze. "Haven't you?"

"No. I was made then abandoned. I only got the kiss of this undead life, nothing more interesting than that...ever."

Good gods. So his patron had fed on him, created him then left. It was a harsh way to enter our existence, but not all vampires were kind and considerate. Perhaps few were. Most would have tried to keep him, at least to have a loyal follower and desperate servant. This explained some of his behavior—*perhaps all of it*. Nobody was looking out for him. Nobody was guiding him and teaching him the skills he needed.

"Well, then. That's a shame."

"I've had offers, believe me."

"Oh, I'm certain of that," I said, unable to keep my gaze from wandering over his sleek form.

"But not from anything I'd trust within an inch of me."

I inhaled the heady scent of him. "Until now," I whispered, my gaze focused on his sweet lips that were only inches from my own.

"Until now. Until you."

"All right," I said. "You can have your kiss. Take it."

I heard Clove's sharp intake of breath, heard the sound of his undead heart quicken, its mimicry of a human's exquisite in its perfection.

Then his lips touched mine with the softest pressure.

It wasn't what I'd expected. I'd anticipated the roughness of desperate hunger and raging lust. Our kind were ravenous in all sorts of ways, especially at the beginning of the immortal journey.

But Clove's kiss was remarkably restrained. Perhaps he had some control, some sweetness even, under his external bravado.

I made a sound that must have encouraged him and parted my lips. I put a hand to his waist, both to steady myself and to protect me if he tried anything. It could all be an act, although he'd be astoundingly stupid to match himself against me.

Clove put his hands to my chest and slid his lips from mine, baring his neck to me in the most beautiful supplication. I licked down his throat, unable to stop myself, and placed my teeth against him in a benevolent show of dominance.

Clove sighed and remained motionless. I sucked gently on his neck and swiped my tongue over the spot where his pulse would be if he were alive.

"Fuck..." he said. "Oh *fuck*."

I wanted to do more — so much more. But this wasn't the time. And the intense desire I felt for this upstart of a fledgling vampire made me wary...and vulnerable.

I let him go and pulled away.

"One week. If all goes well, you can meet Sage."

We stared at each other, our lips parted and our breaths harsh with the need we both felt.

"Fine," Clove said. "If it makes you happy."

"Trust me... It's not me you have to worry about."